Readers love AUGUST LI

Iron and Ether

"I have to recommend this story if you love high fantasy, epic storylines, fantastic characters, love and loss, hard times and lives lost, glimpses of happiness and hope and an ending that lets you know there is still more to come."

—MM Good Book Reviews

"This is a powerful, almost overwhelming portrayal of the character of the men and women involved. It's written in a lyrical style which challenges the imagination as well as the emotions. To say it is well-written is an understatement."

—Rainbow Book Reviews

On Tinsel Wings

"I felt truly immersed into the story, every word drawing me in."

—Top 2 Bottom Reviews

"This novel is well-written and captures your attention from the very first page."

—Joyfully Jay

By AUGUST LI

Coal to Diamonds
Neskaya
On Tinsel Wings • This Same Flower
Steamed Up (DSP Anthology)

BLESSED EPOCH
A Lesson and a Favor
Ash and Echoes
Ice and Embers
Iron and Ether

Wine and Roses

With Eon De Beaumont
STEAMCRAFT AND SORCERY
Boots for the Gentleman
A Grimoire for the Baron
Snowdrop

Published by DREAMSPINNER PRESS
http://www.dreamspinnerpress.com

Wine
AND
Roses

AUGUST LI

Dreamspinner Press

Published by
DREAMSPINNER PRESS

5032 Capital Circle SW, Suite 2, PMB# 279, Tallahassee, FL 32305-7886 USA
http://www.dreamspinnerpress.com/

Wine and Roses
© 2014 August Li.

Cover Art
© 2014 Anne Cain.
annecain.art@gmail.com
Cover content is for illustrative purposes only and any person depicted on the cover is a model.

ISBN: 978-1-62798-953-4
Digital ISBN: 978-1-62798-954-1
Library of Congress Control Number: 2014943216
First Edition August 2014

Printed in the United States of America
∞
This paper meets the requirements of
ANSI/NISO Z39.48-1992 (Permanence of Paper).

Glossary

Abode of Shades—The realm of the Cast-Down, the unworthy dead, and all those rejected by the goddesses. Also known as the Shades' Abode.

Bairn—The second highest title of nobility in Selindria, after valen.

Cast-Down—A term used to refer to those gods and goddesses disowned by The Thirteen because of their wickedness. Most pious Selindrians will not speak of them. In some rare cases, a person can be referred to as Cast-Down.

Emiri—An ethnic group, or possibly a completely different race of people, who arrived in Selindria about a hundred and fifty years ago. Their name is derived from "*Emir*" the word for the sea in their language. Emiri have no formal homeland and are expert mariners. Their culture and values are quite different from that of Selindrians, and this leads to many misunderstandings.

Eru—The Emiri word for wind.

Espero—A large and wealthy island nation to the southeast of Selindria, best known for the high population of mages and the arcane university there.

Estrella Lake—A huge freshwater lake in the northernmost corner of Selindria. Aside from providing most of the nation's water, it has a religious significance, is surrounded by shrines and temples, and is often visited by those on spiritual pilgrimages.

Everdale—A fertile valenny near the center of Selindria, which provides most of the kingdom's food, sister-province to Merryvale.

Eyrle—The third highest title of nobility in Selindria, after bairn.

Fane—A legendary mage-emperor who ruled over a period of unimaginable peace and prosperity aeons ago. He demanded his people worship him instead of the goddesses, and the ensuing war destroyed the known world. No one knows if Fane ever actually existed, but his story is told as a cautionary tale and given as the reason mages are forbidden to rule.

Gaeltheon—A powerful nation to the east of Selindria, across the Kanda River, almost equal in size and wealth.

Hai Mira—An Emiri greeting: "Good sailing to you."

Kanda River—An enormous river separating Gaeltheon and Selindria. The Kanda is fed by Estrella Lake and considered holy by association.

Lapir Mountains—A huge, impassable mountain range marking the eastern border of Gaeltheon. No one has crossed them in centuries, and what lies on the other side is a subject of much speculation.

Lockhaven—An ancient valenny, ruled by the L'Estrella family for as long as anyone can remember. Because it houses the sacred Estrella Lake, Lockhaven is highly respected throughout Selindria.

Meritage—The oldest and largest city in Selindria. Meritage is a port along the Kanda River, and while it is held by the Selindrian monarch, the territory around it is unstable and ruled by barbarians and warlords.

Merryvale—A fertile plain, sister province to Everdale.

Mir—An Emiri ship's captain.

Muri-ku—A very potent Emiri beverage made from fermented sea plants.

Narxium—A tree that produces a fatally poisonous sap. It grows only in the Forest of Elwyd.

Order of the Crimson Scythe—A legendary and unstoppable cult of assassins. Thalil is their patron. While many people doubt the existence of the Crimson Scythe, their symbol, the red crescent, is still the most feared icon in the land. The Crimson Scythe is considered almost supernatural. When they have marked someone for death, that person has no chance of escape.

Selindria—The most powerful kingdom in the known world.

Shagiri—The Emiri word for death.

Starmont—The highest peak in Selindria, marking the northern edge of Estrella Lake. In the past, many Selindrians believed the goddesses resided atop Starmont, but that belief has been abandoned by all but the most superstitious.

Syrai—The Emiri word for friend, used to express a wide variety of relationships from casual acquaintance to intimate partner.

Tam—The lowest title of nobility in Selindria as well as a common expression of respect, similar to "sir."

Thalil—A very powerful Cast-Down god associated with seduction, subterfuge, murder, and deceit. He is the patron god of assassins, particularly the Order of the Crimson Scythe. Thalil, usually portrayed as a beautiful youth, is also associated with male beauty and homoerotic love. The Thirteen Goddesses forbid his name from being spoken, and his worship is punishable by death. Thalil is known by many epithets, some of which are: He Who Stands Just Out of Sight, The One You See at the Last, The Whisper Heard Too Late, and The Invisible Blade, and most often, The Dark and Beautiful One.

The Thirteen, or The Thirteen Goddesses—The main and most important deities of Selindria and Gaeltheon. They have many sons and daughters, both benevolent and Cast-Down. They are sometimes referred to as the sisters. Each goddess presides over a month, or moon, of the year.

Valen—The highest title of nobility in Selindria, second only to the royal family. Valens rule large holds of land known as valennies.

THE GODDESSES AND MONTHS

Both Selindria and Gaeltheon observe a thirteen-month lunar calendar. Each month, or moon, is presided over by one of The Thirteen Goddesses.

Berris—The goddess of farming, plenty, and the harvest. She presides over the ninth month.

Diarana—The goddess of travel and transition. She is the patron of children coming of age, and rules the fifth month. Certain worshippers of Diarana maintain the goddess favors men and women who favor the clothing of the opposite gender. This belief is not widely accepted.

Fayelle—The goddess of purity. She is a virgin goddess and presides over the first month. Fayelle, while compassionate, is a very demanding goddess who expects perfection from her devotees.

Illira—The goddess of music, poetry, history, and communication. She is the patron of all storytellers and presides over the twelfth month.

Ix—The goddess of the wilds and protector of forests and animals. Ix is well-known to favor those who follow instinct over reason. Ix is also associated with the moon. She presides over the tenth month.

Jelsyn—The goddess of artisans and merchants. She presides over the eighth month and adores handmade items. Jelsyn is also said to protect the poor.

Laud—A mysterious goddess associated with fate, the passage of time, and abstract concepts. Her devotees live hermetic lives of deprivation and contemplation, and she rules the seventh month.

Mother Goddess—The only goddess without a name, she is the matron of all living things. She rules the third month, a time of devotion and celebration. The Mother Goddess is said to love all her creations, even the Cast-Down.

Myint—The goddess of warfare, battle, weaponsmiths, armorers, and martial arts. She is the patron goddess of all knights and presides over the fourth month.

Pherara—The goddess of magic, scholarship, and patron goddess of Espero. Most people feel Pherara values only her mages, and turns her back on those without the gift. She presides over the thirteenth month.

Sarmine—The goddess of romantic love and marriage. She presides over the second month.

Strella—The goddess of the sun, stars, and weather, Strella is also a liaison between humans and the goddesses. She carries prayers to the goddesses and guides the worthy dead to their rest. She presides over the eleventh month.

Vestrafori—The goddess of truth and justice, protector of the blind and mute. Vestrafori's priestesses conduct all legal proceedings in Selindria and Gaeltheon, and the goddess presides over the sixth month.

LESSER GODS AND GODDESSES

Ilverus—A deity (usually depicted as male) associated with the knowledge of healing elixirs and potions.

Keltha—A daughter of the Mother Goddess, patroness of pregnancy, childbirth, and nursing.

Tyrinna and Tyrinnius—Twin children of the goddess Berris and patrons of vineyards and wineries.

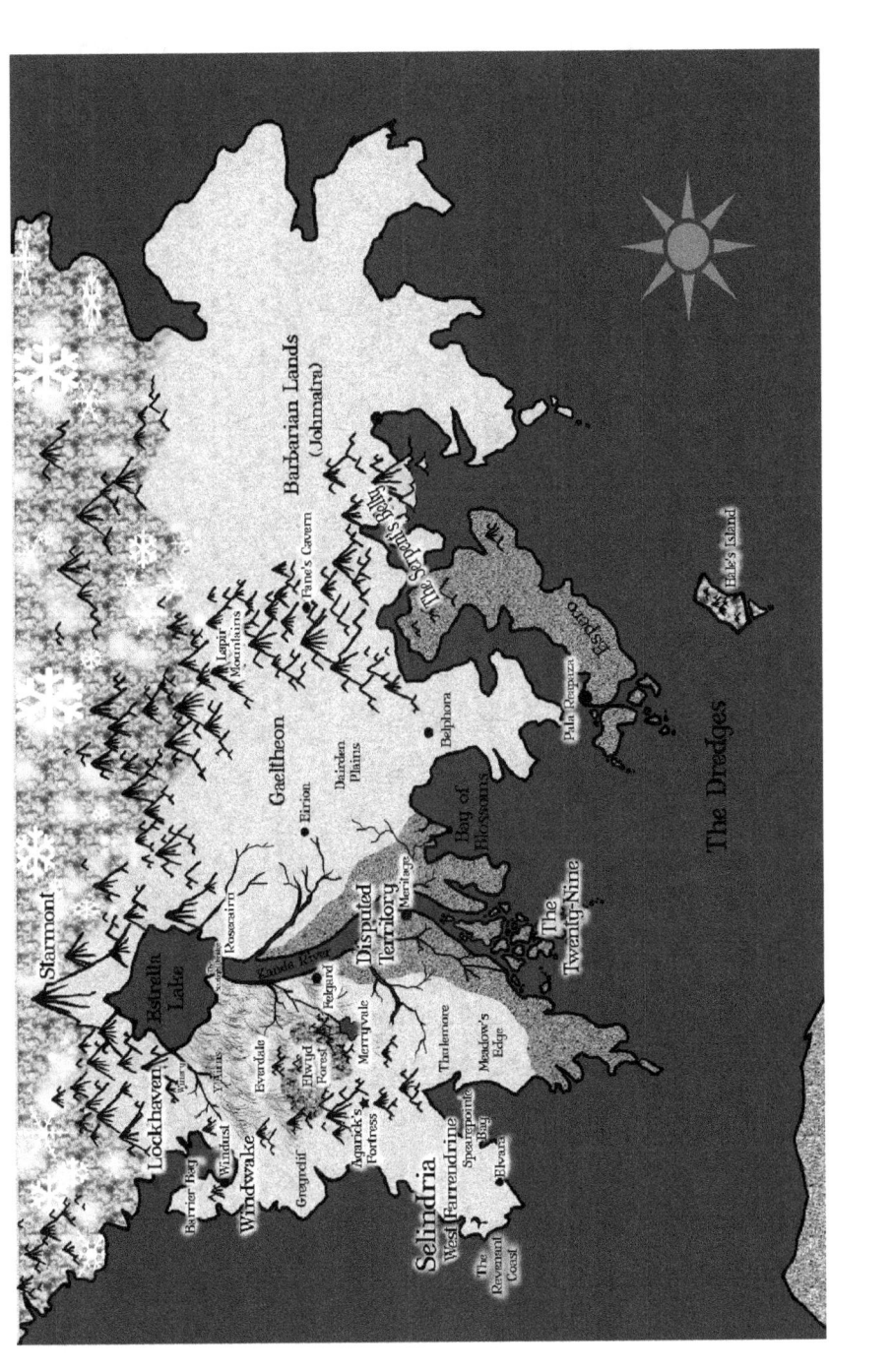

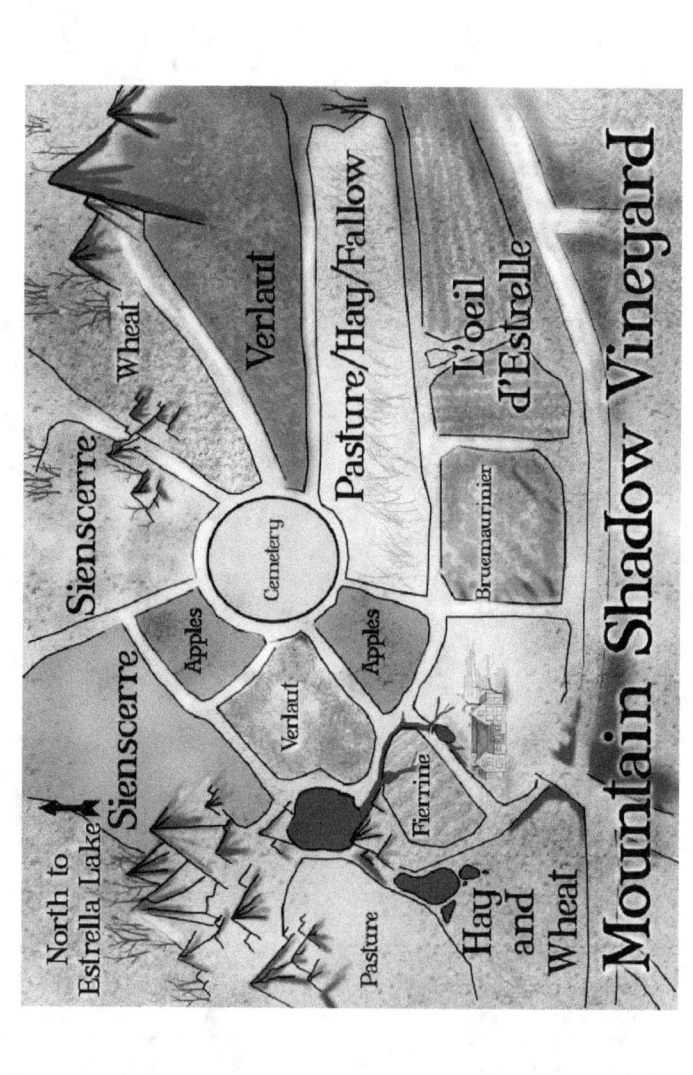

Chapter
One

SOLDIERS HAD been marching past the vineyard for a week and a half, some bearing livery from a nearby valenny or bairny, others in mismatched armor that marked them as swords for hire. Their passing had left the frozen ground muddy and rutted, the high, brittle grass on its edges trampled to pale gold scraps. Everything pristine and pure about winter had been fouled with horse dung and the heavy boots of men unconcerned with the beauty and health of the land—men who felt their endeavors took precedence. Alain Lamont paid them little attention aside from offering water from the deep wells on the property to those who requested it. Boyce, Alain's brother-in-law, kept Alain's niece and nephew far from the armed men, and the ancient stone wall protected their lands from being ravaged. Alain didn't know who fought against whom, or for what reason, and he didn't care. He just hoped whatever folly the wealthy and powerful struggled over would end quickly, so the rest of the people could return to the routine of their simple lives. He hoped the movement of so many men wouldn't harm the countryside irreparably, but he had no way to prevent it.

Alain stood near the iron gate, facing the road, as the sun diluted the darkness of the night, washing the blackness to mottled gray. He leaned against the shovel he'd been using to clear the snow and rime from the footpath as he watched another group of warriors plodding through the muddied snow on the road as they passed. Noting their armor and weapons, he knew them for mercenaries. Mercenaries could be dangerous to a prosperous landhold like theirs; they owed the king no explanation for helping themselves to the food stores and whatever else they felt entitled to take. They weren't subject to the monarchy's laws—or rather, they ignored them. Fortunately this group barely glanced sideways at Mountain Shadow Winery and all its fruitful fields and pastures as they trudged past. Alain leaned the handle of the shovel against his shoulder as he turned to make his way up the long gravel path to the main house. Before he went inside, he shielded his eyes from the increasing sun and looked out over his miles of land. The gnarled old vines stood dark against the snow, and curls of smoke rose from the cottages of the many families who lived among and farmed the rolling hills.

Inside, Alain hung his heavy wool cloak on a hook near the door. He made his way through the warm and quiet house, the old floorboards creaking beneath his steps as he passed through the sitting room and dining room the family rarely used. A savory smell wafted up from the kitchen, and Alain's stomach rumbled in response. He hurried down ironstone steps, the edges rounded by generations of his family's feet, and into the large kitchen. The underground room, along with the pillars supporting it and the many ovens, had been built from the rock cleared to make way for the vines. Alain's grandfather had often told him the house had bones as strong as the L'Estrella family's castle to the north. Alain had believed him… and still did.

Every few years, they put a fresh coat of whitewash over the stone walls. They'd done it that spring, and the cavernous space looked crisp and clean, while the fires at either end burned brightly and made it warm and inviting. Boyce sat on a wooden stool by the inglenook, stirring something that smelled like bacon in an iron pan. He looked over his shoulder, met Alain's gaze, and smiled before returning to his cooking. The children, Courtenay and Fenn, sat on a long wooden bench. A loaf of fresh bread, a crock of butter, fresh cream, and dried apples waited on the rough-hewn table.

Alain sat down across from them. "Good morning, my loves."

"Good morning, Uncle Alain," Courtenay said. At ten, she had a reserved dignity and soft-spoken cheerfulness that reminded Alain of his sister even more than the girl's golden hair, cornflower blue eyes, and round, rosy cheeks. "Do you think you can find me another book after breakfast? I finished the *Tale of Lady Thetis and the Seven Songbirds*."

"Well, that was fast," Alain remarked. "If you aren't careful, you'll have read every book in our library by this time next year. We'll find you something after you see to the chickens."

His niece smiled and turned a little pinker while her little brother bounced on the bench beside her. Fenn never seemed able to keep still. With his coppery hair and greener eyes, he looked more like his father than Alain's deceased twin. The boy reached across the table and almost knocked the milk pitcher over in his haste to tug Alain's sleeve. "I want a story too, Uncle Alain!"

"And what kind of story would you like, my fine young man?"

"One about knights fighting wyrms and harrow-wolves and marlcats and mages!" The dishes wiggled on the table as the boy fidgeted and squirmed.

"Why would knights fight mages?" Courtenay asked with a superior look that reminded Alain so much of his sister Sabine when they'd been young his eyes burned. "Mages aren't monsters like wyrms and marlcats."

Fenn picked up the wooden spoon and brandished it like a sword. He leaped from his seat and swung the utensil wildly, rattling the garlands of dried herbs hanging from the low ceiling above him. "They are if they're bad mages! I'll show them like this and this! Ha!"

"That'll be enough, lad," Boyce said as he came to the table and placed the hot pan of bacon strips and scrambled eggs well away from the children. After he filled their plates, he sat down next to Alain and gave Alain's knee a squeeze beneath the table. They shared another shy, private smile as Alain poured wine and the children attacked their breakfasts. "Your cheeks are nipped bright red. Been at work already?"

Alain dipped a slab of bread in his wine, lifted it, and watched the rich red liquid drip from the crust into his clay cup. He'd been anxious since the soldiers had started moving past the vineyard, and he'd had trouble sleeping, but he didn't want to worry Boyce or, worse yet, frighten the children. "It was windy last night. I thought I'd clear the snow that drifted onto the paths."

"It could have waited," Boyce said.

"And now it's done," Alain replied. "No sense in putting off work."

"I suppose. Did you see anything out there? More soldiers?"

Alain looked at the children and found them watching intently, Fenn practically lying across the table as if he could learn more about the warriors by getting closer. He considered his words. "A small company. Sell-swords."

Fenn's eyes widened. "Did they say where they're going? Off to kill the traitors up at L'Estrella Castle? Did they have crossbows and spears and swords and daggers? Did they say if they're fighting for the king or the turncoats?"

"No," Alain answered. "I didn't speak with them. They're nothing to do with us, Fenn. We're better off minding our business and looking after our grapes and our land."

"But I want to hear about them fighting the traitors!" the boy said, sticking out his lower lip.

"That's enough, lad," Boyce told his son. "Finish your breakfast."

Grumbling, Fenn turned his attention back to his eggs, slurping and chewing noisily until his face was smeared with grease.

"Queen Denna Corinna's at L'Estrella Castle," Courtenay said. "I would like to see her someday. She's a mage and a queen!"

"She is," Boyce said. "But I'd wager she isn't as beautiful as you."

Though she colored, Courtenay shrugged. "I'll never be a queen or a mage."

"No, you'll be part of this wonderful winery," Alain said. "A fine and beautiful lady with a wonderful, strong husband and many healthy children. And when you marry and start a family, we'll all work together to build you a lovely house. How does that sound?"

The girl shrugged. "Can I have a balcony and a rose garden?"

"I think you've read too many stories about princesses, my girl. And Lockhaven's too cold for roses," Boyce said.

Alain nudged his ribs with his elbow. "Nonsense. When our ancestors founded this vineyard, everyone said they couldn't grow grapes on ironstone, that it was too cold. They said the land was too unforgiving to bring anything forth and it would never yield anything. We proved that wrong. So if you want roses, you'll have roses."

Courtenay's eyes sparkled as she looked up at him through her lashes. "Thank you, Uncle Alain. You'll make them grow, won't you?"

"I'll make them bloom until the ladies up at the castle envy their perfume," he promised. "Now eat your eggs."

"If anyone can do it, it will be you," Boyce said, his eyes telling Alain all the things he didn't dare say aloud.

The children finished their food, and Fenn filled his pockets with dried apple slices before Boyce ordered them to see to their chores. Courtenay kissed Alain and her father on their cheeks, gathered up her skirts, and hurried off to feed the chickens and collect the eggs. Fenn promised to make his bed and gather his holey socks so Alain could darn them. Boyce barely managed to catch and restrain the boy long enough to wipe his face. Moments later, his footsteps thundered above them as he ran through the house. Finally, only the popping and crackling of the fires accompanied the scrape of silverware against ceramic as Alain and Boyce finished their meals. Alain drained his wine and poured a little more as he leaned his shoulder against Boyce's.

Boyce reached for Alain's hand and braided their fingers together. "You're troubled. What is it?"

"I'll be glad when all this nonsense with the soldiers is over, that's all." Alain lifted Boyce's hand and kissed the back.

Boyce raked Alain's unruly waves of blond hair back to press his lips to Alain's temple. His lips and whiskers tickled Alain's skin as he spoke. "You worry too much about this place. It isn't all on your shoulders, Alain. I'm here. Plenty of people are here, and asking for help doesn't mean you're weak."

Alain closed his eyes and pinched the bridge of his nose. "I know. But none of us are warriors. If those men decide they want what we have, what will we do? Goddesses, the women. Courtenay—"

"Shh. We're no knights, but we won't let that happen. Besides, if it hasn't yet, it isn't likely to. Don't upset yourself. As you said, it's nothing to do with us. It will pass, and we'll go on as we always have. Come now, it's winter, and we have no work today. Let's sit by the fire, read to the children, and just enjoy our peace. The goddesses have been good to us. We have a wonderful family, Alain."

"We do. Do you plan to marry again? Sabine's been with the goddesses six years now. Will you look for a wife?"

Boyce wrapped both arms around Alain and pulled Alain's back against his slightly broader chest. When he spoke, his breath warmed

Alain's cheek and fluttered his eyelashes. "I wish you would not say such things. I have everything I need or want. I wish you knew that."

Letting his eyes close, Alain leaned back against his brother-in-law, guilty over how content he felt. How blessed. "Your children deserve a mother, and you deserve a wife. Maybe more children. A family."

"You're my family. *Our* children have everything they need. They're cared for, provided for, and loved. *You* are loved."

Alain smiled and ran his fingertips over Boyce's forearm. He could think of nothing to say but "Thank you."

Boyce pressed a kiss to the top of Alain's head. "I don't want anyone else. You, you're the end of it for me, all I need and then some. Come on. Let's enjoy the quiet. I love the winter in a way. Before we know it, we'll be tending the vines from dawn till dusk. And then making the wine! Come sit by the fire with me while we have a chance."

"Go on without me, and I'll clean up the dishes. Then we'll enjoy today. I promise. Boyce, I… I'm happy. Thank you."

ALAIN, BOYCE, Courtenay, and Fenn were in the sitting room, with Boyce reading from a book of prayers to the goddess Berris, when they heard the screaming outside.

"Is that crows in the field again?" Courtenay asked, looking up from her embroidery. "Filthy blighters."

"Courtenay!" Boyce scolded.

Alain listened to the screeching in the distance. "Awfully loud for crows," he muttered. "I'll just go have a look."

"Not on your own," Boyce said, setting his book aside and standing.

"Can I come?" Fenn got to his feet and bounced in place as he looked at them with pleading eyes.

Alain crouched down and put a hand on the boy's shoulder. He affected a serious expression. "That would leave no one here to look after your sister. Your father and I are counting on you to protect her. I trust you know how to use the club we keep by the front door." Courtenay rolled her eyes as her brother puffed out his chest, but she didn't contradict him, thank the goddesses.

After throwing their cloaks over their shoulders, Alain and Boyce hurried outside and jogged down the path as the cacophonous roar to the west grew louder. Despite the horrid sound, the air stood so still not even a snowflake skittered across the recently cleared paths. Something was wrong—Alain felt in the way his teeth hummed, his hair stood on end, and cold ripples shimmied from his stomach up his spine—but he couldn't give it a name. Something moving through the air felt tangible, like sharp and frozen quills brushing his flesh, and it made his skin feel too tight on his body.

A cloud of dust rose, and Alain could no longer mistake the sounds for anything other than the screams of men and horses. Moments later, the first group of a few dozen riders cantered past the winery's gate, followed shortly by men on foot—probably a hundred men running for their lives.

"They're retreating," Alain observed, jogging closer to the gate to have a better view. "From the battle? What are they running from?"

Boyce, his skin waxen and white beneath his dark red whiskers, pointed to the northwest.

The sounds of regiments of soldiers barreling past their property slipped from Alain's attention as he stared at… at something he'd never imagined, let alone could identify. Maybe two miles away, at the very edge of their land, near the ridges where they could see the castle and even the lake on a clear day, a circle of black clouds had formed. Alain had heard clouds called black before, but he'd never really seen anything but the gray of a stormy summer sky. The perfectly round patch in the distance was soot dark, blacker than sin, sparkling like a fresh frost, and moving with an increasing speed in a funnel pattern.

Then the sky broke open, as if someone had pierced the firmament so the molten fire of the sun spilled to the ground, pooling, spreading, the brightness of it scorching Alain's eyes. He barely noticed Boyce pushing him to shelter behind him, grasping roughly at Alain's cloak to pull him back toward the house. He couldn't tear his eyes away as the fire spread across the land, washing over it like a flood, branching off and reaching out like the offshoots of a stream.

The bare trees and brush marking the northern boundary of their territory caught, forming a wall of flame at the limits of Alain's vision.

"Alain!" Boyce called desperately, his voice rough but sounding far away. "Goddesses, Alain! Come on! We have to get back to the house!"

"The whole forest to the north is burning," Alain said. "What about the vines on those hills? Goddesses, the people who live there? What do we do?"

Acrid smoke, dark as the Shades' Abode, grew thicker and thicker as it roiled down from the woods. In moments, Alain lost his bearings. He couldn't see more than a few feet in front of him, and he clung to Boyce's scratchy cloak as Boyce tried to shield Alain's head in the crook of his arm. People ran and screamed, just dark shapes flitting like phantoms through the noxious vapor, and the fire spread not only through the trees but across the sky. Clutching each other, coughing, Alain and Boyce stumbled to escape the chest-hurting smoke while the heavens blazed above them.

Metal screeched and stone shattered. A group of people—large men, maybe soldiers—ran past them, knocking Alain off balance, making him slice his knee on a sharp rock. Boyce grabbed him beneath his arms and yanked him back to his feet, trying to guide him—somewhere. Alain coughed until he tasted blood as more men rushed by them, trampling everything in their path. Bits of burning sky and balls of fire the size of apples arced through the blackness. Alain pulled his hood over his hair and tried to shield his face with his cloak. They had to get back to the house. Everything was burning, and soldiers had torn down the gate to escape the nightmare raining down on them. But Alain couldn't breathe. Every attempt felt like a knife to his chest, and he didn't even know what direction the house lay in. The world grew darker, smudged and incorporeal, though he didn't know if it was the smoke or his increasing dizziness.

Trying to keep each other standing, Alain and Boyce stumbled through the blackness and hail of fire, because it was all they could do. Shrieking people shouldered past them, and the burning thatch of cottage roofs poked holes in the gloom. The whole world was darkness pierced by flame and people crying out. Dying. Alain had to hold on to Boyce, get him to the house, get to the children…. He dragged feet that felt encased in stone toward the wall of fire in the distance, because the house faced south with the northern hills behind it, and the northern hills were burning. When he fell, he didn't think he could rise again. He felt numb, his mind leaking out his watering eyes, shutting off....

Boyce hauled him up. Children sobbed somewhere behind them. Men shouted and women wailed. The high nickers of horses and their hooves on the ground surrounded them, but it seemed like the smoke was clearing. Dozens of houses blazed, and the fields to the northwest were surely lost, but the air didn't feel so much like broken glass in Alain's throat.

He could see the house, a dark smear against the blazing fields. Not only farmers ran for the shelter of the strong, old building, but men in armor as well. People lay on the ground, some groaning and squirming, some still. Alain summoned his will and forced his body to obey him. A large group of nasty-looking warriors approached his home from the left, and they worried him more than the fire. The group knocked into their backs, but Boyce kept Alain on his feet. It was still hard to see, hard for Alain to perceive much beyond the clang of metal and armor jabbing and bruising him. He tried to grab at the men's arms, stop them or at least slow them down, but he only succeeded in letting himself be jostled away from Boyce, and in the chaos and smoke, he couldn't find him again.

Alain called out and Boyce answered, sounding farther away than he could possibly be. Looking side to side and stretching out his arms, Alain struggled to free himself from the mob. Something struck his leg, and he staggered. Booted feet hit the ground around where he fell, and he tried to shield his head. Someone stepped on his left hand and his wrist snapped. He cried out in pain and curled on his side to protect his wounded arm and his ribs and belly. He might survive the fire, but if he couldn't get back on his feet, he'd be trampled.

"Alain! Alain!"

Boyce. Alain lifted his head to answer him, but something struck his chin and he tasted blood. He wanted to tell Boyce to get to the children, get their people to safety, and he tried to push himself up on his elbow as people ran past him, oblivious to or uncaring of him huddled on the ground. When he attempted to push himself up on his hands and knees, his shattered wrist gave out and he fell facedown in the mud and ash. A sharp pain burst across his cheek and the back of his head, and churned-up soil filled his mouth.

"Alain!" Boyce sounded frantic, his voice frayed and tearing as he screamed.

Boyce. Alain tried to answer, but he was so tired, so weak, and he couldn't dam the glittering darkness oozing in at the edges of his vision.

Chapter Two

THE SOFT sound of sobbing registered in Alain's foggy mind even before the pain, but the pain followed a heartbeat later: sharp and throbbing in his wrist, in his head, his knee, his ribs. Pain bloomed every time he drew a breath and left his entire body a throbbing knot of agony. He tried to draw in air and coughed until he tasted blood in his throat and on the back of his teeth. He tried to sit up but vertigo knocked him back, and the gravel beneath him scraped the back of his head.

Boyce. He had to get to Boyce and the children. Another attempt to rise ended the same, and he lay looking up at an innocuous gray sky, tinged with pink and still smeared with smoke but clearing. Burning crops and buildings still crackled, and people shouted to each other. Cried. Water hissed and steamed against flame, making the air thick, wet, and warm. Like the air in the kitchen when water boiled to preserve jam, Alain thought, even as he realized it was an absurd comparison. How hard had he hit his head? Looking to the west, he saw the sun sliding toward the sea in the distance, leaving a watery orange trail in its wake. Night would soon fall, and it had been just before the midday meal when Courtenay had thought she heard the screams of crows....

Courtenay. Alain couldn't bear to think what the soldiers might do to her, or, goddesses help him, even Fenn. It gave him the strength to get to his feet, though he fell twice before he managed to keep his balance. Cradling his broken arm against his chest, he made a slow and agonizing journey toward the main house. It appeared undamaged, though the hills in the distance still smoldered. He would worry about his vines later, after he made sure his family was safe.

People were gathered on the porch: his people, not soldiers. Limping up the steps took the last of his strength, and Alain would have collapsed if one of the farmers, a big man called Denis, who had a thick golden brown beard, hadn't caught his elbow. Denis helped Alain to sit on the weathered boards of the porch and lean against the house wall. His wife, Marion, knelt next to Alain and offered him a clay carafe of wine. Alain drank straight from the pitcher. Goddesses, at least they had wine.

"My"—using his voice cost him a bout of painful coughing—"my niece and nephew?"

"They're fine," Denis said with a bitter but sympathetic smile, and something in Alain's chest unknotted so he could finally breathe. "Whatever in the Shades' Abode that was, it's over now. We're putting out the fires as best we can, but there's a lot of damage. Many people lost their homes today. Some lost family. Too many."

"We'll look after them," Alain said. "Pull together as we always have. Where's Boyce? I think my wrist is broken, and I need him to set and wrap it."

"Quite a few people are still missing," Marion said.

"Boyce is missing?" Alain took another deep swallow of his family's wine to fortify himself, and then he stood, grasping the porch lintel when a wave of nausea struck. He coughed until he retched and spit up a mouthful of phlegm on the frozen ground. The spell left his head ringing, but he still recognized Fenn's cries as the boy burst through the door, scampered across the porch, and threw himself against Alain so hard he almost knocked him down.

"I want my papa, Uncle Alain. Where's my papa?" He buried his tear-streaked, snotty face into Alain's cloak at the hip and wailed. Courtenay, standing by the open door, paled as she twisted the white apron over her blue dress into ropes.

Courtenay met Alain's eyes. Goddesses, she looked identical to Sabine at that age, and Alain as well, as many people had teased they couldn't tell brother from sister when the twins had been young. "Uncle Alain? Is Papa coming back?"

Alain nodded and willed the pain to the outskirts of his perception. "I'll go find him now."

"I'll come with you," Denis offered.

"Good. Marion, would you be so kind as to take my children inside? Give them some hot milk with honey, and a little dash of last year's D'Tiendo. Not enough to make them sick. They need something to calm them down, though. Maybe to let them sleep tonight."

Marion smiled and bowed her head slightly. "'Course I will, love. Go on, then, but don't tire yourself out. Your skin looks like curdled milk. Anyone can see you're hurt."

"Thank you." Alain hugged Fenn, kissed his teary cheek, and sent him into the house. Then he, Denis, and four other men who farmed the vineyard set out into the watered-down smoke, as wavering spears of rose gold light poked through the gray smudges. Alain's boots stuck in the newly thawed mud as he tried to keep up with the others. "What happened to the soldiers who broke down the gates?"

A gangly young man with an overbite looked at Alain over his shoulder. "'Spose they just wanted shelter from the fire coming out the sky. Most of 'em left as soon as it was safe."

"Just as well," Alain said. "But we'll have to keep on the lookout for stragglers. I don't want those people here. They're a threat."

As twilight descended, their group made its way slowly along the paths. Alain couldn't believe the destruction. Many of the cottages belonging to the people who had worked on the vineyard for generations had burned to the ground. Nothing but crumbling, blackened stone walls remained. All over the grounds, people, even children, carried buckets from the wells to douse the remaining flames. Where the fields still blazed, the farmers had loaded mule-drawn carts with barrels full of water, and they continued to combat the blaze as night fell. Alain felt a stab of guilt for not assisting them, but he needed to find Boyce, so he soldiered on with his small party. They encountered a few dead soldiers beside the trails, and Alain didn't know if they'd died in the fire or from injuries in the battle preceding it.

"We'll have to give these men a proper burial," Denis said.

Alain agreed, though a little reluctantly, goddesses forgive him. "We'll take a cart around to collect the bodies as soon as we know our people are safe and taken care of."

They passed a few more burnt-out shells of homes, but a quick look inside the collapsed walls told them the people living there had made it out and probably made their way to the main house. Seeing the fields of wheat, the apple orchards, and fields upon fields of ancient vines reduced to ash made Alain despair, but he pushed it into a box to open and worry over later. It would wait. His people came first. Once he knew they had survived, healed their wounds, rebuilt their homes, and secured shelter and food to see them through the winter, he'd worry over how any of them would grow enough grapes and make enough wine to sustain themselves.

The carnage grew worse as they moved into the northern hills. The vines had been decimated to bare soil, the rocks beneath the dirt left raw and exposed. Smoke still hung in the air as they passed cottages leveled flat by the flames. Heat had melted the stone walls into misshapen blobs, and if anyone had been inside, they'd find no remains. Even the ground had been scorched black and smooth as glass in places. Steam rose into the night as the people who had made Mountain Shadow Winery their home for generations threw water on the diminishing tongues of fire still threatening it.

"Where was Boyce last seen?" Alain asked, the cords around his heart pulling tight again, making it hard to drag air into his chest.

"Near here," Denis said. "After he lost you, he tried to save as many families as he could. One of these houses was burning, and there were children inside. Boyce went in to save them, carried out a boy and girl, took them to their mother. That's all I know. I think it was this house." He pointed to a pile of pitted stone, the thatch still smoldering, the stink stinging the lining of Alain's nose. The building had fallen in on itself, and anything inside was buried.

The rounded stones singed Alain's palms as he shifted them. He smelled his skin roasting, but he continued to hoist them aside. Something inside superseded the pain in his palms and fingers, even the pain of the wrist he'd done no more to set than to wrap it with a muddy strip torn from his cloak. "You're sure it was this house?"

The lanky young man nodded as he helped Alain move the rocks. "He ran in here, for certain."

A cold, smudged moon rose above them, turning the shadows from the decimated homes and burnt, twisted trees sharp and stark against what remained of the snow. The six men worked for hours to move the collapsed stone walls of the cottage, their breath misting around them like ghostly companions, their sweat freezing on their faces. Part of Alain recognized the futility of their exertions; no one buried beneath all that rock could still be alive. But though his whole body ached, shook, and wanted to collapse, he kept lifting stones, and the men beside him did the same. Though he couldn't articulate it, Alain felt grateful to those men for continuing to work when they must have known they'd accomplish little. When they managed to expose the packed dirt floor of the single-room dwelling, they found a charred corpse: an older man with a singed silver beard. In his arms, he held a child who could have been only sleeping except for the soot smearing its face and the blisters on the pallid skin. Though Alain choked on a sob, a small, dark part of him thanked the goddesses it wasn't Boyce. Damn him to the Shades' Abode, but he couldn't help thinking, better these poor souls than Boyce. He valued the people who lived on and worked the vineyard, but Boyce... Boyce had told Alain he was loved, and Alain, with his foolish, thick tongue, had only managed to thank him. How—why had he been too obtuse to let Boyce know he was also loved?

"Poor bastards," one of the men said. "They never stood a chance of making it out."

Alain cleared his throat; he had to say something. "Their families will want to know, want to bury them."

Denis nodded, looking meaningfully at Alain. "We should make our way back, resume the search in the morning."

As much as Alain's spirit wanted to protest, to keep looking, his body could no longer argue. He didn't know how he'd walk the miles back to the house. He scarcely had the strength to turn his head to gauge the others' opinions, but he forced words out his raw throat. "There's no one else here? In this house?"

Denis shook his head, but one of the others called, "Here, where the hearth collapsed. A boot."

Alain knew—he knew when he saw that scuffed leather tip, but for all his exhaustion, he bent and lifted blackened rocks, tossing them aside with an energy borne of desperation, of dread. He couldn't use his left hand any longer, and kept it tucked against his belly as he shredded his nails on his right hand digging under stones to push them away.

Alain had expected the sight that met him when they finished, but he wasn't ready. The sight of his brother-in-law, bluish, still, and crushed, sent him to his knees. Forgetting the others, Alain dropped to the rubble and let his face fall into his dirty, bleeding palms. No. It couldn't be. Even as he choked and slobbered into his hands, he couldn't accept it. It couldn't be true. He... he couldn't be alone. No. No. It was someone else. He'd find Boyce—

Alain didn't know how long he knelt in the ash and rimey mud, oblivious to everything but sorrow and memory, before Denis closed a hand around his shoulder. He didn't really care if he ever got up. "Tomorrow, we'll send them off to the goddesses. Tonight, you need to get home. Rest and heal. Be with your children. Alain—"

He clawed at his shoulders through his shirt. He didn't want to stand, didn't want to face life alone.... He couldn't. But Denis hauled him to his feet and steered him toward the path leading down the hillside. "Tomorrow."

Alain barely remembered stumbling down the path to the house. The others practically had to drag him. He felt nothing, his skin numb and his mind in a daze that couldn't distinguish reality from hope and denial. Denis helped him through the door and to the foot of the stairs. The house was quiet, the fires barely glowing in the hearths. "Thank you," Alain said. "I will be fine."

"We're going to need you," Denis said in a whisper harsher than the fires. "Everyone here will look to you."

"I know. Give me tonight."

"We'll stay. Marion and me. We can't have children, so we'll help. You don't have to go through this alone."

"Thank you." It sounded like such an empty platitude, but Alain meant the gratitude. He wished he had the eloquence to express it.

"Go on to bed, then." Denis patted his shoulder before Alain trudged to the sitting room inglenook to poke at the fire. Before he knew what he was doing, he was stabbing at it, thrusting the iron poker in, summoning swarms of sparks, and biting his lip as tears poured over his cheeks until he choked on them. He let out a strangled scream and smacked the poker against the old stones, making the iron ping and echo in the empty room that suddenly felt way too large and cold. Like it would never be warm again.

Denis had the grace and sense to leave the room. Alain heard his boots on the old floorboards, and when he turned away from the hearth, the other man was gone. Boyce's prayer book sat on the stand by the padded bench, a scrap of light blue ribbon from one of Courtenay's dresses marking his place. The reality that he was gone struck Alain then, and he sank down on his knees and held the little clothbound book to his chest. He could almost literally see Boyce on that bench, one ankle at the end of his long leg resting on his knee, a little crease between his coppery eyebrows, his white teeth tugging at the corner of his lower lip, the fuzzy, late-morning light decanting through the window, Fenn tucked under his arm and pretending he understood the words inked across the pages—

Boyce would never finish that book. Alain's chest hurt and his stomach cramped. He was just there—he'd been sitting there, it felt like moments ago, and at the same time, years. Part of Alain expected him to walk down the steps after tucking in the children and drop a soft kiss on top of Alain's head. Even as he swore he heard Boyce's deep laughter, his gentle voice, quick with a simple joke but slow to raise in anger, exchanging a few words with a farmer or one of the unattached women who came to help them keep house, he knew Boyce wouldn't be beneath the quilt Sabine had made when Alain went up to bed. He wouldn't mutter nonsense in his sleep or kiss Alain without even opening his eyes before throwing an arm around Alain's ribs and pulling Alain's back against his lightly furred chest. He wouldn't try to hold Alain in bed when Alain rose before dawn to do some errand on the vineyard. He wouldn't be in the kitchen cooking eggs or slicing bread and cheese when they came in from the fields. Not ever again.

Not ever again.

As he cried, Alain still couldn't accept Boyce wouldn't be coming down the steps, pestering him to get some rest, telling him to stop worrying about the grapes and come to bed. He had just been there. But Boyce wasn't there now; he was lying on the frozen ground, in the dirt, alone. He'd never allowed Alain to be alone, not even when Alain had accepted it as inevitable. But Alain had left him out there. He stood up and hurled the prayer book against the wall. It landed, splayed open to the page with the blue ribbon, and Alain grasped the table in front of the bench to get to his feet. He'd forgotten about his broken wrist until he tried to use that hand to hoist himself up. Pain shot up his arm, and he cried out before he realized the air had left his chest.

Denis ran into the room. "Alain? What are you doing, friend? I thought you were going to bed."

"I have to go get Boyce. I can't leave him out there. The foxes… the crows…"

"Alain," Denis said cautiously, "he can't get worse."

"He… he deserves better than to just be *left*!"

"Everyone we lost deserves better." Denis held tight to Alain's shoulders as Alain thrashed and tried to push past him. "Would he want you out there, getting hurt worse, getting sick, or here watching over his children? That girl and boy, they've got no one else now. You understand me?"

"I don't want him to be alone!" If Denis hadn't been so much larger, and if Alain hadn't been so achingly weak, he would have pushed past the farmer and staggered back to the cottage just to sit with Boyce all night.

Denis wrapped a big, rough hand around the back of Alain's head and forced Alain to rest against his broad chest as he stroked Alain's hair. "He's not alone. He's with the goddesses, and he's with Sabine. They're finally together again. Try to remember that."

The fight drained from Alain, but not the anger, and he went slack before breaking out of Denis's grasp and stumbling backward until he could sit on the bench and drop his head into his hands. "I understand."

"You should try to get some rest. Tomorrow will be long."

Alain nodded without lifting his face from his palms. Denis was right. Tomorrow, Alain had to tell Courtenay and Fenn their father was dead.

Chapter Three

THE PAIR of gray mules plodded over the rutted ground, with Alain holding the reins and Courtenay and Fenn sitting beside him on the hard wooden bench. He second-guessed his decision to let the children come along as Denis and a few other men piled corpses—some little more than charred bones—into the cart bouncing along behind them. But they hadn't wanted to be left behind, and Alain had just nodded, his voice caught somewhere between his belly and his throat. Maybe it was selfish, but having them beside him, their soft, warm little bodies pressed close, made him feel like he could face the next moment, because they needed him and he had no choice. If Courtenay and Fenn hadn't needed him—well, he thought he'd just wander out among his vines, sit on the ground—

They reached the cottage where... Alain couldn't even form the words in his mind, let alone say them. "Stay here with your brother," he told Courtenay.

"I'm coming with you," she said.

"Me too," Fenn agreed.

"No. I... I don't want you to see."

"I *have* to see," Courtenay said.

Alain caught her arm to stop her from hopping down. "No. He wouldn't want you to. I don't. Remember him as he was."

"Alain, I have to see!" Courtenay shrieked. Fenn started wailing and threw himself across the bench.

"Why?"

Courtenay balled her tiny fists by her hips, bowed her head, and spoke through trembling lips as tears flooded down her round red cheeks and dripped from her pointed chin. "Because. Because I woke up a dozen times last night, sure my papa was coming in to kiss me. I was sure he'd be in the kitchen at breakfast. I... I can't believe this is true. I have to see!" She screeched again, and Alain had never heard her raise her voice. She'd barely even cried as an infant.

Alain could only squeeze her hand and say, "It isn't pretty."

"I know."

As Fenn howled, and a lanky young man hurried to comfort him, they made their way toward the crumbled chimney. Alain felt like he wandered through a nightmare where nothing had solidity or meaning, but it had to be worse for Courtenay. Fenn would recover and forget Boyce, as Courtenay had relegated her mother to a role in a story she didn't really remember. But for Courtenay, the sight of her father—dead, bluish, smeared with ash and charcoal, skin burbled and scorched along an entire side of his face and body—would haunt her as it would Alain.

"Papa. Are you sure? Uncle Alain, are you sure it's him?"

"I'm sorry."

The girl broke free of his hand and went to the corpse. She knelt down and touched whiskers that looked obscenely red against the pallor. Too vibrant and alive next to the graying skin and sunken cheeks. Courtenay wrenched one of her father's stiff hands from his side, held it in her lap, and looked over her shoulder at Alain with shining eyes. Alain wished he had some idea what to say, but seeing them, knowing Boyce had lost his chance to watch his daughter and son blossom—he had to turn away, and he knew he was weak, and a coward, for not saying the things Courtenay needed to hear.

The men lifted Boyce into the back of the cart, and Alain hated the idea of him lying next to the same mercenaries and warriors who'd probably caused his death and destroyed their vineyard. Since he couldn't carry him, though, he couldn't protest. Elle, a widow who tended the sheep on the estate, had set his bone and wrapped it, but he still could barely use that arm. It hurt more than it had last night, but his heart hurt so much more for Boyce's children. They'd already lost their mother, and now their father. They had only Alain to depend on now, and he just didn't know if he could do it. How in the goddesses' names would he raise these beautiful children when all he wanted was to curl up by the roots of his vines, close his eyes, and never open them again? He didn't know if he had the strength to put his pain in a box, a box he'd open alone at night and masochistically finger the jewels inside, even if their edges cut his skin. But he needed the strength not to think of the cruel treasures in that box while he got the children back into the cart and pulled Fenn's tiny, trembling body onto his lap.

THEY BROUGHT all the bodies they'd gathered into a long, single-level stone building normally used to store hay for the goats and sheep. Before long, the reek of the dead covered the sweet, dusty scents of clover, alfalfa, and oats. Alain felt useless and pathetic, standing near the door where the air was freshest, as the others laid the corpses out on wooden pallets. They'd lost eight people and discovered the bodies of ten soldiers. A group of women, not priestesses, but devotees of the goddess Strella, began preparing the bodies for burial. The bitter herbal smell of the incense they lit did little to mask the reek of death. The other farmers left, but Alain stood watching as they cleaned and oiled the bodies.

He went over to Boyce's body and knelt down. The older woman with the night blue kerchief over her hair and the star pendant of her deity around her neck offered him a tired smile as he picked up a metal comb and dragged it through Boyce's hair. When he finished working out the knots, avoiding the places where the red tresses had been singed away and the skin beneath blackened and cracked, he dipped a cloth into the basin, twisted it to wring it out, and began wiping the mud and soot from Boyce's face. He got a little too close to the burns, and the skin fell off in darkened chunks. Alain choked on a sob as the hot, sour liquid in his stomach rose into his throat.

The woman across from him stopped cutting away the fouled clothing, set her shears down, and patted his hand. Alain hadn't realized it was shaking, his fingers white around the bloody rag. "You don't have to do this," she said, meeting his gaze with her blue gray eyes. "You can go home. We'll take good care of him. I swear."

Alain just shook his head, rinsed the cloth, and wiped his brother-in-law's body as the woman revealed it. Boyce's belly had already started to swell and distend with the vapors building inside. Alain had seen the dead before; on the vineyard, they took care of their own up to and including their final journeys, so he should have expected the swelling, the dark blotches where the blood settled, the smell…. He touched the trail of red hair below Boyce's belly button, running his fingers over it until he reached the top of his pubic patch. The hair was still soft and springy, but the skin beneath was cold, and Alain couldn't reconcile it. The skin should be warm, with a faint pink tinge, and Boyce should be teasing and chuckling as Alain toyed with that loved strip of hair.

"Tam." Alain had forgotten about the woman. "You should go home."

He had no idea how many moments he'd spent with his hand splayed just above Boyce's crotch, tears flowing unnoticed down his face. He had to be more careful. It wouldn't do to tarnish Boyce's memory, to make the people who had loved and respected him think of him with disdain. Alain pulled his hand away. Everyone would understand grief, but he couldn't let his sorrow divulge the truth of what his association with Boyce had grown into in the years after they lost Sabine. He didn't want anyone curling their lip when they thought of Boyce, or whispering his name with disgust. He didn't want that for the children—

He realized the woman was still talking. "It would help if you'd go back to the house, choose something for him to wear…."

Alain nodded. He couldn't trust himself or his reactions. Before he stood, he touched Boyce's ashen cheek, ran his fingers through his hair. On that side of his face, he looked peaceful, merely sleeping, while on the opposite, the skin was gone, exposing sinew and bone, his blue-green eye melted, the socket empty. With a choke, Alain looked away, down to his perfect, unmarred lips, lips edged in lines from so many years of smiling. Suddenly, Alain wanted to kiss him, one last time, to say good-bye. He just wanted to brush his mouth over those clay-cold lips and whisper that he loved him, as he should have done when Boyce could have heard. He wanted, needed that kiss good-bye, but he couldn't have it.

Feeling sick, hurting everywhere he could feel, he nodded to the woman, stood, and walked out of the building. As he made his way toward his home, he passed groups of men with shovels, singing hymns to the goddess Strella in mournful baritone, imploring her to guide the spirits of those they loved to rest. A cart carrying simple wooden boxes rattled down the path. The winery had several skilled carpenters. They were an insular community, self-sufficient, and death was part of life. All of them had done this before.

Alain found the house noisier and more chaotic than he'd expected. After hanging his cloak and removing boots caked with awful stuff, he followed the sound to the kitchen. At the bottom of the stairs, he found half a dozen women cutting meat, baking bread, and preparing all sorts of stews and pies. It tore Alain's heart a little further up the center to see Courtenay among them, her blonde ringlets held back from her face by a white scarf and her face pink and sparkling with sweat. When Sabine had died in labor with Fenn, Boyce and Alain had agreed Courtenay couldn't take her mother's place. They would do the cooking, preserving, and cleaning. They would even mend the clothes so she didn't have to become the lady of the house yet. They'd wanted her to have a chance to be a child.

Though he wasn't sure he had the strength to make his voice heard over the clang of crockery and utensils, Alain asked, "Courtenay, what's going on here?"

She set a large bowl on the table and wiped her sweaty brow, leaving a streak of flour behind. Her face looked drawn and exhausted, not like a child's face at all, but like a face weighed down by too many worries. "We're making a meal. For after the bodies are buried."

He knelt down and wiped her face with his sleeve, failing to force a smile. "You don't have to do this. You can go to your room and read."

She set her jaw and shook her head. "It's the right thing to do, and it's what Papa would want. He'd want us to show everyone we're still here to take care of things. He'd want us all coming together. We have to keep living, which means we have to eat. Someone has to make the food. Can we take wine from the cellar?"

He nodded. What else could he do? He just needed a day, and then he would take on the household duties, or he'd do what he'd always resisted and hire a woman. Courtenay *would* be a little girl, because that's what Boyce had wanted. "Where's your brother?"

"He's playing with some of the other boys. Marion's watching them."

He nodded again and walked numbly from the kitchen and through a house he could barely believe had felt like home just yesterday. He went to the second floor. Though they'd shared a bed most nights, Boyce and Alain kept separate rooms, because it wouldn't do for the children to get curious. Alain went into Boyce's room, and he was everywhere: in the pocketknife he'd left on the windowsill, the half-full cup of water and comb on the stand, a wool sock poking out from under the bed, his messy stack of books in the corner. The room still smelled of him, and some of his red hairs stuck to the pillow. Some of Alain's blond ones too. Alain sat on the edge of the bed, hugged the pillow, breathed in the scent of Boyce's hair, and cried silently for a long time before he could bear to stand and open the dark wood armoire. He stared at the simple garments inside, not seeing them so much as remembering Boyce wearing them. The vineyard was lucrative, and they wanted for nothing, but most of the clothes were worn and patched. Successful or not, they were farmers and vintners, and they saw no need for extravagant dress. In the end, since they'd buried Sabine in the pale gold gown she'd worn at their wedding, Alain found Boyce's marriage outfit in the back of the wardrobe, folded neatly in one of the wooden boxes they used to take bottles of wine to market. He tucked the brown trousers, linen shirt, and the doublet that had matched his sister's dress under his functional arm. Then he found Boyce's second-best pair of boots, because the pair from the wedding looked uncomfortable, and turned to make his way back to the barn.

THE CEMETERY stood near the center of the vineyard, atop one of the higher hillocks. As a child, Alain had been told they'd placed it there so the spirits of his ancestors could look out over the vines, orchards, and fields, so they could watch over everyone. Nine generations of his family rested here. As a hazy darkness fell and men without broken arms carried caskets to the holes in the frozen ground, Alain remembered coming here to inter his grandmother and grandfather, his parents, dozens of people from the vineyard, men and women who'd helped raise him and then toiled and bled beside him to harvest the grapes on time, Sabine….

Fenn sobbed and sniffled against Alain's thigh, and Alain couldn't even reprimand him for blowing his nose on Alain's nicest trousers. Courtenay cried stoically, chin trembling, and Alain just watched the mauves and lavenders of the winter sunset paint the sides of the ancient mausoleums and worn grave markers. Finally, all their people had been lowered into the ground beside their predecessors and families, and the soldiers put to rest in a barren patch in a corner shaded by an old arn tree. Though they were a faithful people, they weren't a formal people, and no priestess spoke and no one gave speeches. Relatives went to say private prayers by the graves of their loved ones, and Alain led the children to Boyce's resting place and looked down at the lid of the pale wooden box.

"I want my papa," Fenn cried. "Uncle Alain, bring him back! Make him come back!"

"Don't be stupid," Courtenay snapped. "*No one* can bring him back. He's *dead*. He's dead!"

Fenn wrapped his fleshy little arms around Alain's thigh, turned his face to the darkening sky, and wailed through an open mouth. Courtenay clenched her jaw so tight Alain worried she'd break her teeth. Goddesses, he hoped Courtenay wouldn't be like him: so full of pain and feelings but unable to translate them into language, into words others could understand. It made for a lonely life.

Swiping at his own tears, Alain knelt and picked up a handful of dirt to drop on the lid of the plain coffin. Courtenay did the same before turning to him with red eyes. "Is Papa with Mama?"

"Yes, my love," Alain managed. "Absolutely. He's at peace and free of pain. I'm sure he's happy, and we'll all be together again someday."

"When?" Fenn asked. "When do I get to see my papa?"

"I don't know. Hopefully not until after you've had a wonderful, long life here. He'd want that. For both of you."

"Does anyone get that?" Courtenay snarled, shocking Alain. Still, he couldn't bring himself to reassure her.

The goddesses granted them one boon that day, when a mix of soggy snow and fat, silver drops of rain fell to douse the errant fires that still sprung up here and there where they had failed to bury a few coals. At least now they wouldn't have to spare people to patrol the woods and fields.

BACK AT the house, fires burned in the hearths while people filled their plates from the impressive spread laid out on the dining room table and sideboards. Many of the wives who lived on the vineyard had contributed dishes. People ate, drank, hugged each other, laughed, and cried. They talked about the deceased, smiling and telling funny stories. Life went on. Alain wasn't ready for life to go on; his sitting room and dining room sweltered, and they smelled of onions, alcohol, and human bodies. Alain had to get away.

When no one was looking, he grabbed his old wool cloak off the hook and slipped out the door. The rain had let up, but it left a lingering fog behind, making everything run together and smudge like wet ink. As Alain walked, he felt like ink dripped off the edge of the world. So much of what had been solid and certain had melted and dribbled off the ends of the map. It all had to be drawn again, but who would draw it? Not him. Alain could only walk, ignoring the cold and the way the condensation in his hair turned to chilly rivulets that ran down the back of his neck. He made his way north, uphill.

Before he realized where his feet were carrying him, he'd reached the cemetery. The fresh graves stood mounded and dark against the watery new snow. Mud and frigid water soaked into Alain's boots, his socks. His breath came in white plumes, but he trudged to the center of the graveyard and looked to the northwest. From here, he could see most of the vineyard. Almost half of it, their most profitable crops of grapes, the verlaut and the sienscerre, had been decimated. One of the large apple orchards lay in ruins, unlikely to bear fruit for years to come. Alain sighed, and his exhalation froze and hovered like a specter.

Tomorrow, he would go into those fields and see if he could find anything living he could graft, nurture into taking root. Those fields, miles wide, would have to be replanted, and it would likely be many years before they bore a crop worthy of making even a barrel of wine. Goddesses, what would they do without those grapes? What would Alain do, with no one to share his worries with?

Since he didn't feel capable of being around people who would try to console him and wish him well, Alain wandered the narrow paths between the fields, taking stock of what had been destroyed and what was viable. The fire that had fallen from the sky—whatever that had been—had created such utter destruction that Alain would have to use cuttings of the strongest grapes, the verlaut and sienscerre, to try to replant. Even if he could coax them to take, it would be many years before they would yield a crop. Worst of all, he'd have to do it without Boyce, without Boyce assuring him he could make roses grow from ironstone—

How would he make them grow when he couldn't care if they thrived or withered?

Yet he would, because Courtenay and Fenn had no one else, and dozens of families who had lived on the vineyard almost as long as Alain's depended on him. It all fell on his shoulders, and now he had no one to help him carry that burden.

Alain wandered back in the direction of the house, but he didn't plan to go inside. When he went home, he wanted everyone gone, and he hoped Marion had put the children to bed so he could sit alone in the quiet and pick at his wounds. Because he was a coward. He barely had enough inside to keep himself going; he had nothing in reserve for others. The fire had left nothing.

He reached the orchard north of the house and found it had fared better than the one on the opposite side of their disorderly, ancient cemetery. At least half of the trees would bear fruit in the spring, and that meant they could make and sell cider. Though exhausted, he continued west, into an expanse of fierrine left largely intact. The fat red grapes, native to the island of Espero, were hardy, but the wine they produced wasn't to most Selindrians' tastes. Without the verlaut to blend with them, most of his customers would find the body of the wine too heavy to suit them. Strangely, considering new ways to blend the wines as he ran his fingers over the gnarled old vines soothed Alain. This problem he understood and could solve, given time. The rest of it—

Goddesses.

He could see the smoke from the chimneys of the main house, and it would be warm inside—warm, but full of ghosts. Alain thought he'd shiver less here among his grapes, and it was quiet, but not in the pregnant way the house would be. The vineyard should be quiet, but in the house, he'd be waiting for words and laughter that weren't coming. The house wasn't supposed to be quiet.

The vineyard was… but right now, it wasn't silent when it should be. Something thrashed, making the vines creak and rustle. Alain stiffened. Sometimes, though rarely, harrow-wolves made it onto the grounds. With the gates down and the wall collapsed in several places, the formidable predators could have found their way onto the property, lured by the flocks of sheep, dozens of chickens, and the few goats and cows some of the families kept. On his own, Alain would be no match for them.

Maybe it will be a mercy.

He didn't know what compelled him closer, but he picked his way along the neat rows of vines, his good arm held out in front of him. The vicious animals he expected never materialized. Instead, Alain found a man lying on the ground. He groaned and squirmed, though his eyes remained shut, and he clearly wasn't alert. Alain knelt down next to him and rolled him from his chest to his back. He wore armor: a battered chest plate and mismatched pauldrons over a chain-mail tunic. Like Boyce, he had been burned, and the blisters covered his left side to just below his ear. Part of his face on that side, along his jaw, had also been affected. The man's left arm jutted at a strange angle, clearly broken. Below it, his leather trousers had been burned away, along with the skin of his outer thigh and calf beneath them.

Alain didn't know what to do. Part of him wanted to leave this mercenary to his deserved fate, dying in the frozen mud, but he found he couldn't. The man had somehow survived the night, and the cold, out here abandoned. He was a young man, the skin of his face a deep olive, but smooth. Alain shook his shoulder, but he didn't respond. Without thinking much or considering his decision, Alain hurried to the closest barn and hauled a sledge used for carrying small parcels over the snow outside and onto the path back to the field. On his way, he passed a farmer returning home from the funeral feast. "Can you please go to Elle's cottage and ask her to meet me at the house? Tell her it's urgent."

"Of course I will, Alain," the slightly drunk man said.

Alain thanked him and dragged the sledge back into the field. It took some effort for him to get the larger man situated using only one arm, but he managed. Then he pulled the rickety travois up the path toward his house, making slow progress and leaving deep ruts in the frozen mud.

When he arrived at the house, he pulled the sledge up the front steps, opened the door, and dragged the wounded man inside. The house was still and quiet, just as he'd wanted, everyone either departed or asleep. He hauled the injured man into one of the bedrooms on the ground floor. It smelled musty after standing empty since before Alain and Sabine had been born. Some of his ancestors had had large families and even staff, but from the time of Alain's grandparents onward, at least half of the ten bedrooms hadn't been used. Alain struggled to get the injured man off the sledge and onto the low bed in the corner. It took probably a quarter of an hour and left him coated in sweat despite the chill. He would have to light a fire in the inglenook for the first time in decades.

As he stood looking down at the man, Alain's mind admonished him for what he'd done, bringing the soldier and probable sell-sword into the home where his children lived. This man fought and likely killed for anyone who offered a handful of coins, which told Alain he was dangerous and of dubious morals at best. While he wondered at having a person like this around Courtenay and Fenn, his heart wouldn't let him leave the wounded man behind. He surely would have died if Alain had left him. No matter what sort of man he was, Alain couldn't look in the mirror if he turned and walked away from a dying man. For at least a while, this man wouldn't be a threat. He could still die. Just to be sure, Alain would lock the door to this room from the outside.

Alain continued staring. While pale, the man had a naturally dark complexion and wavy, dark hair that fell across a smooth brow, eyes with thick lashes and black, slender brows, high cheeks that weren't too sharp, and a square but soft jaw lined in emerging whiskers. He had full lips that probably would have been a deep red brown if he'd been healthy.

A soft knock on the doorframe stirred Alain from his observations. Elle, the shepherdess and best healer on the vineyard aside from Boyce, offered him a tired smile as she came into the room and set a canvas satchel on the floor by the bed. Thankfully, she didn't question Alain, just told him to draw and boil water. He went to the kitchen to comply.

When he returned with his hands wrapped in cloths, carrying a steaming metal pail, Elle had pulled a wooden chair alongside the bed. She'd already removed the man's armor and the clothing beneath it and left them in a pile nearby. The man lay naked on his back, nothing but a small towel providing decency. He had a much more slender frame than it had seemed in his armor, but well-defined muscles and olive skin hid behind very little hair. Black, broken, and oozing skin spread from his left midthigh to his cheek just beside his ear. Over his waist, ribs, and chest, his mail shirt had burned its pattern into his flesh. Some other errant burns, probably from the sparks raining down, speckled the rest of his body.

"First things first," Elle said, ever efficient and never one to honeycoat things. "His left arm is broken in two places, along with his collarbone. They'll need set and wrapped. He has a nasty bump on the side of his head, which is probably why he's unconscious. We should get something cold on it."

"I'll go outside for some ice," Alain said. "Is there anything else we can do?"

Elle sorted through her bag and came out with some smooth wooden sticks and a spool of clean, white linen. "Not much with a head wound like this. Most people recover from them on their own, though that can take weeks. Maybe even months. We shouldn't move him unless we have no choice. Go and get the ice, lad."

Months, Alain thought as he fetched another pail and the spade to break up the ice lining the path. He hadn't bothered removing his cloak, so he went about his work clumsily with one functioning arm—a wound similar to the man who might be his burden for *months*. Alain didn't regret helping him, but now he wished he'd dragged him somewhere else. He could only implore the goddesses to heal the soldier sooner rather than later, and then Alain could send him back wherever he came from.

By the time he returned to the room, Elle had splinted the broken bones, propped the man's head up on a stack of pillows, and even started a cozy little blaze in the hearth. She wiped her hands on the white apron over her simple brown dress and looked meaningfully at Alain as she took some of the ice, wrapped it in a towel, and pressed it to her patient's head. "All that's left to do is clean the burns. It'll go faster if we work together, and you'll have to learn how it's done, because it will need to be done every day, or the wounds will go rancid and poison his blood."

"Let's do it."

She nodded without turning her gray eyes from his. "Get some towels, lad, and plenty of them. And get ready. You might want to fetch a bottle of wine. You might need it."

He obeyed, and then he shifted the man as she instructed so she could pile the towels beneath the burned places. Then she pulled the cork from a glass vial and poured some milky white liquid down the man's throat. "We don't want him waking up for this, by the goddesses," Elle said. "Get that pail of water." From her bag, she took a cake of yellow soap and two coarse brushes, like those used for grooming horses. She handed one to Alain, dipped her own in the hot water, and lathered it up before perching on the edge of the bed. The fury with which she began scrubbing the burns made Alain's hands tremble, and he sat down just because he felt weak. The blackened skin fell away in chunks, revealing what looked too much like raw meat beneath. Bile struck the back of Alain's throat and he barely managed to swallow it down. The room's plain wooden walls spun around him as Elle scrubbed until blood saturated the towels and fouled the water in the bucket.

"Go on and get fresh water," she said. "Then steel yourself up, boy. I need your help, and this will need to be done once a day. All the dead skin needs scrubbed off. You'll need to scrub until the blood runs just like this. You can't be gentle, and you can't be squeamish, Alain."

He found a new level of respect for the small elderly woman, her arms covered in gore to the elbows and her apron spattered with blood and burnt skin. She had a strength Alain didn't know if he could find in himself, but he had to try. Even so, he took her advice and opened a bottle of wine while he waited for the water to heat in the kitchen.

Somehow, they managed to scrape away all the dead skin, coat the raw flesh in a thick salve, and wrap the man in linen strips. Alain did most of it in a daze, his hands going through the motions without his conscious intent. He'd had to force himself to forget that skin was connected to a human being while he worked, because he couldn't comprehend pain like that on any level. Finally, they gathered up the bloody towels, and Alain took them to the small room beyond the kitchen. He'd boil them, along with the bandages he'd have to change, tomorrow, though he doubted the stains would ever come out.

He opened another bottle of wine, and when he found Elle in the hallway, both of them sank to the floor, leaned their backs against the wall, and passed it back and forth until it was gone. She left him with extra bandages, salves, soaps, and tinctures for pain—one that would ease the man's discomfort when he came to and one that would knock him out when Alain had to clean the burns.

As she got to her feet, a little tipsy, she placed a hand on his shoulder. "You have to scrub until the blood runs fresh, Alain. You have to keep the dead flesh from the living. Cut it away. Every day. Every time."

"I will," he responded. *Somehow.*

Chapter Four

THE SKIN along Breeze's left side felt stretched tight, torn and burning. Pain bloomed fresh with every floundering thud of his heart: on his side, in his arm, shoulder, chest, and head. Pherara, his damned head hurt like nothing he'd ever felt, and opening his eyes only made it worse. Even the low light in—wherever he was—stabbed into his eyes until he felt it at the back of his skull. He screwed them shut and fought the cresting nausea, breathing fast through his nose as he willed his surroundings to stop spinning. He waited many moments before he dared open his eyes again.

At first, he perceived only color: warm brown, white above him, shifting firelight and shadow. Fire. Goddesses, he smelled it. The smoke. It had been falling from the sky, the heavens burning, everything burning. Breeze bolted up as panic pierced his chest. Pain shot across his chest and down his left arm. His head throbbed until his world became a molten red rhythm of agony, respite, agony again. He collapsed against what he realized was a bed, and a clean one, judging by the smell. Somehow, he was inside, and the fire he smelled burned in a hearth. Fucking Shades! He was naked under the buttery-soft linens. What had happened to his bloody armor? If someone had looted it while he'd been unconscious, he'd find that son of a wharf-side slag and make him pay for it.

Breeze forced his eyes to focus and took in the small room—wood-paneled walls, plaster ceiling, rafters, stone hearth, single window, door. Bed. Table. Rough-hewn chair. Little else. His armor sat stacked in a corner.

Taking in his environment had exhausted him, so he sank back against the pile of pillows and focused on breathing as the vertigo subsided. As he lay staring at the ceiling, he took stock of his wounds. Arm broken. Collarbone too, probably. Certainly fucking hurt like it'd snapped. Burns, but someone had bandaged them. And his head— something was fucked rotten there. Something that made it hard to think or focus his eyes. Something that hurt like a *bitch*. Damn.

He didn't know how long he lay there before he summoned the strength to swing a leg over the edge of the bed and plant his foot on the cool, smooth floor. Getting the other to join it took more effort, and sitting up sapped him. Bleeding Shades, his left arm was fucking mangled. The pain when he tried to push himself up on it almost made him vomit, but he eventually got to his feet, naked as the damned day he was born, his bits and pieces on full display. On wobbly legs, he took the three steps from the bed to the door and grasped the worn brass knob. He tried to turn it, but it was apparently locked. Panic seized him again, and he tugged the sturdy door, making it rattle against the frame. It didn't give, and he pulled harder and harder, until dizziness welled up, and he was on his side on the floor before he knew he'd fallen. The impact exacerbated all his wounds, and he choked on sobs as he drew his knees toward his chest, only to feel skin ripping over his ribs.

The door opened, and Breeze tensed and scuttled back as best he could. He had no idea what to expect, and he might have to defend himself. *Fucking Shades, with what?* His sword wasn't among the armor piled in the corner....

Breeze relaxed a little when he managed to focus his vision on a plain man in homespun garments. Though pretty, with golden hair and big blue eyes, the lad had a simple look about him, an innocence. Probably a merchant or, more likely, a farmer. No one who posed Breeze any danger. The young man didn't look as though he'd ever picked up a weapon. He knelt to help Breeze back to the bed, and Breeze couldn't formulate a reason not to let himself be guided. The bed felt good against his back. It felt good not to struggle to stand, not to have the throbbing in his head and along his side magnified. This rustic boy couldn't hurt him if he tried.

"My throat's dry," Breeze said. "I'm hungry, and I've got to piss."

The too-pretty man with the pale golden hair forced a smile and retrieved the chamber pot. He pressed it against Breeze's groin and stopped just short of grabbing his cock to aim his stream into the basin. "Go on, then," the farmer said.

Breeze relieved himself. "Is there water? Anything to drink? Food at all?"

"Yes, just a moment." The farmer scuttled out of the room clumsily, long limbs tangling like a ball of yarn. Breeze huffed out a sigh; at least he was safe for the moment, though he'd found himself in the care of an inept simpleton. He supposed it could be worse.

The blond lad returned with water and chicken broth. Breeze sucked both of them down, and even remembered the courtesy to thank his host. "I owe you a great deal for helping me. I'll reimburse you if I can."

"That's not necessary," the pretty farmer said as he sat down on the edge of the narrow bed. He lifted a clay carafe to Breeze's lips, and the cool soothing liquid flowing down his throat felt amazing, soothing against the battered tissue. He didn't think he'd ever been so thirsty. He didn't know if the world contained enough water to slake it.

After drinking until the cool water started making his stomach cramp, Breeze studied the farmer. They looked around the same age; the farmer was likely a bit over twenty-five. He was a little smaller than Breeze, probably a little softer beneath his simple blue shirt and gray trousers. When he smiled, Breeze saw pain in the expression, but not guile. His straw-colored hair was too long, and his fringe hung in front of the bluest eyes Breeze had ever seen. He had a nice face, not too round but not too angular, and a little gold stubble dusted over his cheeks. Breeze felt even more confident the young man posed no threat to him, but there was still much he didn't understand.

"If you're not looking for money, why bring me here?" Breeze reached up to scratch his chin and noticed the thick whiskers. He'd shaved before he'd crossed the Starlight Bridge with his company. "Where is here, anyway?"

"You're in Lockhaven," the farmer said. "A few miles from the castle, on my family's vineyard."

Breeze didn't remember a vineyard. He just remembered his commander ordering the retreat, and all of them running as the sky burned and fire rained down. "How long have I been here?"

"A little over a moon."

"Fucking Shades!" His language made the farmer flinch and color. "A goddess-damned moon. The others must think I'm dead. How aren't I dead? How didn't I starve if I was out the whole time?" He had lost weight—he noticed in his chest and belly—but he certainly hadn't starved.

"You weren't out the whole time," the farmer said. "You had spells where you could take some water and broth, not much else. You mumbled a little in a language I couldn't understand."

"Fuck me. I don't remember a thing."

"You had a head injury. Our healer said it could take this long. She told me it could be many months still before you feel like yourself again. She said you shouldn't move around much if you don't have to. Some of the burns went beyond the skin, down into the muscle. They might bother you a long time, possibly for the rest of your life. The good news is, Elle says your bones are almost healed, and the breaks were savage, according to her. You'll still be here for a while, though. Of course, you can stay until you're well enough to move on."

Breeze hoped that would be sooner rather than later. He was safe, but he'd lose his mind on a farm, in this boring little room. He'd already become tired to the point he was having trouble concentrating and remembering everything he'd wanted to ask. The farmer watched him with what Breeze thought was worry but soon realized was empathy—it hurt him to see Breeze in pain. Breeze didn't understand; they didn't even know each other. "What's your name, anyway?"

"Alain Lamont. What's yours?"

"Fabrezio Orvina d'Caelus. Most of the boys choked on it, though, and they all just started calling me Breeze. It stuck, I guess."

"Breeze." Alain met his eyes and smiled. "I like that. It sounds so… free."

"Speaking of, why did you lock me in?"

"I couldn't leave you to die, but I also didn't know what kind of man you were. I suspected you're the kind who sells his sword to the highest bidder. I don't think I'm wrong, am I?"

"I suppose you're not," Breeze admitted, curling his upper lip a bit at the judgment in Alain's tone. "Do you have a problem with that?"

Alain looked away and shook his head, tossing all that golden hair around, but Breeze wasn't fooled.

"Look, if you can't believe I'm not going to kill your children in their sleep or rape your wife, I'll be on my way," Breeze said. "Thank you for what you've already done. It was more than most would have. I'll just get my things." He moved to sit up and a wall of vertigo hit him. He lost the room to a hail of gray fuzz for a few seconds. When his vision cleared, his head was back on the pillows, and Alain looked down at him with concern, all the disparagement gone from his features.

"You aren't fit to travel, and we both know it. Just... just stay in here. No harm will come to you. I'll bring you the things you need."

"Why?" Breeze didn't even try to lift his head. "Why do this, if you're not looking for money?"

"It's the right thing to do. You wouldn't understand."

"Why wouldn't I? Because I make my living by my sword instead of digging around in the dirt?"

"I didn't mean it that way."

"I didn't either," Breeze said, even though he had, at least a bit. This Alain was a strange man: kind, compassionate and generous on one hand, while the other half of him hated Breeze because of his vocation, wanted to lock him away from his family. It wasn't as though he was a Cast-Down assassin—not that locks did much against those. He shuddered. "Don't say much, do you?"

"No, I suppose I don't."

"Keeping secrets? Or finding me that lacking as a conversationalist."

Alain looked down at him and held his gaze for a few heartbeats. "Neither. I'm not good at it. Making people understand what's in my head."

"Maybe you try too hard."

"Maybe."

"Alain, what time is it?"

"The middle of the night. Why?"

"I'm starving. Do you have anything a little more filling than broth?"

"Elle says you should take it slow." As Alain stood up, he did something that struck Breeze as very odd: he touched the bandages at the center of Breeze's chest and let his hand linger a moment. "I'll go to the kitchen and see what I can scare up."

"I do appreciate this," Breeze said. "I'll find some way to pay you back, and that's a promise."

BREEZE FELT stronger and more alert after he ate the buttered bread and cold chicken Alain brought. The smooth, beautifully balanced red wine Alain opened alleviated some of the increasing pain along his side. He wasn't too addled to realize he was enjoying a very expensive bottle of wine. As he touched his wrapped skin gingerly, he found some of it hurt like a bitch while some of it was completely numb. The muscles in his left arm quivered with exhaustion after finishing the simple meal.

Alain, who'd been sitting in the chair by the bed, must've noticed something. "Are you hurting?"

"A bit. It feels... fucking strange. Burning and freezing at the same time. There're spots on my skin where I can't feel a thing. Do you think it will come back after time?"

"Elle said there's a chance it might not."

"Bleeding Shades. I'd like an hour in a room with that goddess-damned mage." Breeze clenched his fists but was too weak to hold them that way long. He wondered how many of the men he'd fought beside for the past several years had made it back to Rosecairn.

"What mage?"

Thinking back to the battle disturbed Breeze more than it should have. His heart sped and the room felt suddenly small and closing in fast. Alain poured a little more wine into his cup, and Breeze swallowed it in a few gulps, even though it deserved savoring. "I don't know, not exactly. Our commanders told us before the battle to be ready to retreat if they called for it. The knights and nobles told their men the same. Seemed, if I recall, and I'm not sure I do, they had some plan in place in case things went to the Shades'. Some damned mage, cousin of the prince, I think, ready to cast something big if it looked like our side would lose. Big. Fuck me." He was back, running hard.

How in the Shades' did you run from the burning sky falling down in fiery chunks on your head? He remembered fighting to breathe through the smoke, getting dizzy, smelling his own scorched skin. How did you run from the whole damned sky?

"I... I thought the world was ending," Alain whispered. "I thought the goddesses had decided to tear it all down." His hand jerked toward Breeze, but he balled it and pressed it to his lips, looking far away with the firelight reflecting off eyes that seemed wetter than before.

"You lost people," Breeze guessed.

"We did." They sat in silence. Breeze supposed each of them wanted to comfort the other, but neither knew how. Finally Alain spoke. "Elle gave me tinctures for your pain. Maybe you should take some so you can get back to sleep."

"All right."

"Do you want the one that will make you drowsy and take away the worst of it, or the one that'll knock you out completely?"

"I'll stick with the weaker one. I think I've had enough sleep. Fuck me. A whole moon gone."

Alain found the vial on the night table, pulled out the cork, and cradled the back of Breeze's head as he prepared to pour it into his mouth. Breeze chuckled as he caught Alain's wrist and held it gently. "I can probably manage to drink it on my own."

Alain pulled back and looked away. "Sorry. Habit, you know. I did it that way for weeks."

Weeks. This man had taken care of him for weeks, over a month, without expecting to get anything for his efforts? Who did something like that? Breeze took the vial from Alain's fingers and downed a gulp of the chalky yet astringent stuff inside. As he gagged and sputtered, Alain recorked the vial and returned it to the stand. He stirred up the coals in the hearth, added some more wood, then came back to the bed and pulled the soft linens and blankets to Breeze's chin and tucked them in around him.

Breeze, already teetering between wakefulness and sleep, laughed again. "Habit?"

"I suppose. Get some rest."

"Thanks, Alain."

With a nod, Alain left the room. The door latch clicked softly, and then with a louder, stiffer sound, the tumblers fell into place in the lock.

JUST AS the sun seeped through the old creamy-white curtains, Breeze woke to the door opening. The food Alain carried smelled better than a nobleman's feast, and the vintner had another bottle of that amazing wine tucked between his ribs and elbow. He set it down, along with the platter he had balanced on his opposite arm, the one splinted and wrapped in bandages, before gently helping Breeze sit and propping him against the pillows. Breeze couldn't hold back a grin as Alain spread a checkered towel across his knees.

"Smells amazing," Breeze said. "The little wife make this?"

"I made it." Alain set a rustic ceramic plate piled with eggs, strips of bacon, fried mushrooms, sausage links, and beans on Breeze's lap. Why would he have cooked all this? Could it be possible Alain's wife didn't know Breeze recovered in their home? And why would Alain keep him secret? Alain didn't seem capable of ulterior motives. Either that, or he could lie and deceive to shame the Cast-Down. Breeze would puzzle over it after he ate, but he wouldn't forget it.

After eating the best meal in his recent memory, Breeze flopped back against the pillows, rubbing his belly with his uninjured hand. Not long ago, he'd been able to finish three plates that size without blinking an eye, but he supposed his stomach had grown used to being empty, and he hadn't eaten half his breakfast.

Alain looked uncomfortable as he took the plate. He had the look of someone about to break bad news and reluctant to do it.

"What is it?" Breeze asked.

"I… I have to change your dressings. I do it every morning, but I've never done it while you were awake. Even when you were unconscious, I gave you a dose of the sleeping tincture, just in case."

"How bad can it be, changing some bandages?"

The way Alain pressed a shaking fist to his forehead and pursed his pale lips answered the question. He clearly hated doing it, dreaded it, and yet he'd done it every morning for a month. What about changing some wrappings had him ready to fall apart?

"You should take it—the sleeping tincture."

"Is it really so awful?" Breeze asked.

"It's the worst thing I've ever had to do. Please take it. I… I don't even want you to know."

Breeze took Alain's hand and squeezed it. The poor blighter, doing the worst thing he'd ever done, day after day, something so terrible he didn't even want Breeze to experience it. The worst thing he'd ever done, yet he wanted to shoulder it alone. "No, Alain. I'll take the other one, to dull the pain."

For a moment, as Alain tugged at his hair and scrubbed his hand over his face, Breeze worried he'd start screaming. Instead, the farmer pulled away from him, stood, and left the room, then returned a few moments later with a pail of steaming water, a small leather bag, and towels and fresh bandages heaped past his face. He wouldn't look at Breeze as he arranged them, packing layered towels beneath Breeze's burned left side. "Did you take it?"

"I took the one to dull the pain," Breeze said. "Alain, I will be fine. If you'd rather not do this, you don't have to. You have done enough."

"I have to." His gaze darted left and right, like a scared animal looking for a place to escape, but he took a small pair of shears from his bag and cut a neat, straight line through the bandages from Breeze's neck to the middle of his thigh. Then, slowly, watching his progress carefully though he clearly didn't want to, he began pulling them away. Bits—chunks, actually—of Breeze's flesh went with them, pieces of black and corpse-white skin clinging to the linen. Before he even knew he'd done it, Breeze screamed and beat his fist against the mattress. He'd never imagined such pain even existed in the Shades' Abode. "Bloody… Fuck. Fucking Shades!"

"Do you want to take it?" Alain pleaded.

"I'm… fine," Breeze said between teeth gritted so hard his jaw ached. At the moment, his teeth were the least of his worries. "Fuck. Just get it done."

Alain's breath came quick and shallow as he slowly peeled the bandages back. Though he couldn't bear to watch, Breeze felt his skin going with them, tearing off. It fucking hurt. He didn't know a profanity strong enough to express it, so he opted for repeating "fuck" over and over again.

Tears streamed into his mouth, and he trembled and felt frozen by the time Alain finished. "Thank the Thirteen Whores."

"Breeze, that's the least of it," Alain said. "Please take the sleeping tincture."

Breeze shook his head, though he didn't lift his forearm from his eyes. "If you can endure it, so can I. Go on then, Alain."

Alain didn't speak again, and Breeze soon forgot him against the onslaught of agony that followed. He lost track of his screaming, sobbing, and retching as Alain washed the burned skin, peeled the dead flesh away, and wrapped it in fresh cloth. No amount of pride could prevent him from bawling into his pillow like a child when the farmer finished. Goddesses, Alain had a strength in him to endure this day after day. This went so far beyond offering an injured stranger a bed that Breeze couldn't begin to think about it, the fortitude it would take to do it day after day, with no hope of recompense. Breeze opened his eyes a crack to Alain balling up towels saturated in and dripping blood to place them in the pail. He wanted to say something, but had to concentrate on not screaming his throat out.

Alain, covered in blood to the elbows, blood spattered on his face, sat on the edge of the bed and pressed a cool glass vial against Breeze's palm. "The sleeping draught. You should take it. Rest."

"I—" He wanted to say thank you, and that he'd take it if he needed it, but the pain distracted him from everything else. He could scarcely believe he'd survive it. He almost didn't want to. All he could do was nod.

"Good." Alain bent and brushed his lips over Breeze's forehead. Despite the pain and everything else, Breeze knew he'd remember the numbing tingle he felt at that swipe of mouth over skin. He wanted to say something, but by the time he'd even begun to order his words, Alain was gone.

Breeze held the little glass cylinder for maybe a few moments, maybe an hour—it felt like eternity—until he could take no more and downed over half of it. He slept for the next three days.

Chapter Five

EVEN THOUGH Alain brought breakfast, lunch, and dinner and sat talking with Breeze for an hour at each meal, after a week, he was ready to climb the walls. The room seemed smaller and duller with each passing hour. Breeze tried the leaded-glass bay window. Locked, from the outside. Just like the door. Fuck. Where would he go if he could get out? His meals and conversations with Alain exhausted him to the point that he needed a few hours' sleep after each one. Usually, when Alain changed his dressings after breakfast, he had to be roused for the midday meal, if he could wake at all. The only place he could go—Rosecairn—would take him several weeks to reach on foot. He'd never make it.

It didn't matter. Right now, he just needed out of this goddess-forsaken room. He tugged on the door, but it was old and sturdy. He let out a ragged yell of frustration as he paced the room, pulse speeding up and making his head hurt again. Throbbing in his burns. Looking down, he noticed nothing but bandages covered his body, and they didn't cover the important parts. He didn't find his pants among the bits of armor piled neatly in the corner. Why in the bleeding world had Alain taken his pants? He seemed anything but the sort to take advantage of an unconscious and injured man. If he wanted that, he could have done his business and then left Breeze to die. Breeze wished he didn't know such things happened, but he was a warrior, not a soft, simple farmer with a full larder, a warm house, and soft clean sheets waiting at the end of every day. Nice, soft, welcoming wife too, he had no doubt. Best damn wine he'd ever tasted. Had Alain done it as a way to ensure

Breeze couldn't leave? The thinking started to hurt his head, and he sat down on the edge of the bed and dropped it into his hands.

He'd been unconscious a month, and he'd been drinking water and broth, so…. How had he pissed? He recalled Alain holding the chamber pot and groaned. Habit? Had the farmer wiped his ass too? Damn. As humiliating as it was, Alain wasn't embarrassed, so Breeze couldn't be either. Maybe Alain was unnatural; he wouldn't be the first man with a wife who liked to play with the boys on the side.

Breeze didn't know. He knew he wanted his goddess-damned pants, and he wanted out of this room. He wrapped a sheet around his waist, went back to the door, and pounded on it with the fist he could lift. "Alain! Come on, friend! You can't keep me in here. I'm going out of my mind!" When he got no response, he kept pounding. When his arm got tired, he kicked at the door with his bare foot. Finally he heard muffled footsteps on the other side, then the tumblers in the lock disengaging. Out of instinct, he took a few steps back and looked from side to side for something he could use as a weapon. Breeze expected Alain, probably cross and all judgmental again, but when the door swung open, a little girl, nine or ten, had turned the knob. Her huge blue eyes went wide at the sight of his bare chest, and her cheeks turned as red as the sunset as she quickly averted her eyes. She looked just like her father: round cheeks, fair skin quick to flush, adorable button nose, and those blue eyes framed in long, curled, gilded lashes. "I did not mean to frighten you," Breeze hurried to say.

"You're not wearing anything," the girl said with a subtle superior tone Breeze was coming to recognize. He shook his head at how much she sounded like Alain, as a younger boy, a strawberry blond with greener eyes but still bearing the family resemblance, poked his head around the corner, grinned, disappeared, and then popped back out to observe them.

"Nothing to wear, I'm afraid," he said in answer to the girl trying to steal glances at his bare body. She may have seen men without shirts, likely had in the fields, but he had a warrior's body. She probably wasn't used to honed muscle made into a weapon. "Don't suppose you could help me out with that?"

The redhead popped his head back around the corner like a rabbit from a warren and pointed at Breeze. "You talk funny. And you're brown."

The sheltered little souls had never seen an Esperon, probably not even a southerner, even at a market. Breeze tossed his head back and laughed, realizing too late the movement tugged against his tight skin and made his head pound and ring like a hammer on an anvil. "You're a quick study, lad. What's your name?"

The boy finally emerged from his hiding place, though he stayed behind his sister as he almost fell sideways trying to look into the room. "Fenn. Do you have a sword, tam? Armor? Can I see them? I'm going to be a warrior one day! Then I'll have a sword, and I'll kill harrow-wolves and pirates and smugglers and bandits and mages and—"

The boy began waving both arms like a windmill until his sister caught his wrist. "Fenn, hush. We aren't supposed to be in here."

He stuck out his tongue. "*You're* the one who opened the door!"

"*I* thought something was wrong, simpleton." She turned her attention back to Breeze, raised her chin, and met his gaze with a quiet, defiant strength he'd also become accustomed to. "Is anything wrong, tam?"

Breeze smiled. "Only that I've been stuck in this room for almost a moon and a half. I feel a little crazed. Need some fresh air, you know. Stretch my legs."

"Do you have a sword?" If Fenn's eyelids peeled back any further, his blue-green eyes would pop out of his round little face.

"Had one," Breeze said. "A bow too. Daggers. All sorts of fun things. But there was a great battle, up to the north, near the castle, and I lost them. What I could really use is some clothes. Can you help out there, Tam Fenn? One warrior to another?"

The boy nodded till Breeze worried he'd break his neck, but when he turned toward the staircase behind them, his sister caught his arm. "We aren't supposed to unlock this door."

Breeze met her at the threshold, caught her plump little hand, and kissed the back. "Princess, I implore you. Show a poor soldier the goddess's charity. I'm indecent here!" He wondered if the girl's father grew red like that, all the way to the tips of the ears. "A shirt, a pair of trousers, and maybe some shoes are all I ask. And if you would be so kind as to escort me on a brief stroll, I would be in your debt, my lady…?"

She giggled, held out her rough-spun lavender dress, and curtsied. Children were so wonderfully simple. Be kind, a little playful, treat them like people, and earn loyal friends. "Lady Courtenay. Fenn, go up to Papa's room. Find Tam Breeze something to wear, a cloak, and some shoes."

The garments felt strange and scratchy against Breeze's sensitive skin. His left arm was stiff, and he had trouble extending it, so he kept it folded against him with his bandaged hand over his heart. Likewise, his left leg seemed to take shorter steps than his right, and it caused him to hobble along behind the children as they showed him the rooms on the ground floor of the house as if they were gilded chambers in King Agarick's Meritage estate. The place wasn't a palace, but a fine, old house, with good, strong bones cut from the stone of the mountains. Breeze could tell generations had loved it and called it home. The wooden floors shone from decades of feet, and baubles accumulated on the shelves, everything from old dolls to ax handles to sloppily thrown ceramic pots.

"This is the best room in the whole house." Courtenay threw open the set of double doors like a queen entering a ballroom. She even twirled as she entered the dimly lit space.

It smelled musty in a way Breeze recalled from a distant memory. Old books. Plenty of them, it turned out. Shelves lined the walls of the octagonal room, and late day sun seeped through the leaded glass of the many windows, lending the room a fuzzy glow as it illuminated the dust motes. Above, birds nested amongst thick, dark-stained rafters built in a starburst pattern. Coals smoldered in the three hearths, worn rugs covered the wooden floor, and benches with cushions strewn across them sat beneath the stacks. It reminded him of the Arcane University in Pala Reapaza, but much more intimate. More personal. Still, the family's collection impressed him. He wandered around the room, touching the leather-bound spines. In an alcove, he stopped to regard an ink drawing of a beautiful woman holding a bunch of grapes. He recognized the shy grin. Alain's wife? She looked more like his sister, but maybe he could blame the artist's skill for that, or maybe she was a distant ancestor: a grandmother or aunt. Other portraits hung between the stacks, all of them handsome and fair. The blood seemed strong in the Lamont clan, and Alain's children were no exception.

Courtenay tugging his sleeve roused Breeze from his reverie. The girl thrust a book toward his chest. "You might like this one. It's an account of Gar the Undefeated and his battles."

"I want to read it!" Fenn bounced on the balls of his feet, trying to reach the musty old tome Breeze held.

"You can't even read," Courtenay scolded.

"I can too—a little! I want to hear about the warriors cutting down the heathens to take the lands for the goddesses. Like this!" With an invisible blade, the boy demonstrated the ancient warriors' prowess.

Breeze chuckled. "You waste too much strength, young soldier. In a true battle, you'd tire yourself out and give your enemy an advantage. If you'd care to go outside, I can show you a few things."

"Courtenay, can we? Can we pleeeease?"

She gripped her white apron and shot Breeze an appraising look that seemed to ask: *Can I trust you?*

"It will be fun," he assured her. "We'll find some twigs, I'll show young Fenn here a few tricks, and get a bit of practice and fresh air for myself. My body is aching from being stuck in bed. I will warn you, I tire easily because of my injuries. I hope you won't be disappointed."

Fenn turned and ran for the door, calling, "I won't! We can practice every day! You'll be here at least until midsummer."

Had Alain told him that? Midsummer. No, he'd be back in Rosecairn long before then, back to his life and a world he understood. Looking at Courtenay, he saw his explanation had assuaged her and had the desired effect. She thought him too weak and hurt to threaten them.

"He'll be covered in mud if we don't catch up." The girl took Breeze's bandaged hand and held it as she led him down the hall and out into the glorious free air.

WITH THE spring came rain, and sporadic showers had kept Alain and the others from their labors. To make up the time they'd lost, they toiled well past dinner, into the gloaming, until dusk made it impossible for them to continue their work on the cottage they'd been rebuilding. Rubbing his sore shoulder as he took a step back, Alain was pleased they'd reconstructed the stone walls and placed the roof rafters. As soon as they got the thatch on, the family could move back in. Alain had insisted they see to the damaged homes before worrying over the barns and storehouses. People came first. Like a family, those whose homes the fire hadn't touched had taken in the displaced. Alain was now head of the family, and he had to take care of everyone. So he rose before dawn, put meat and vegetables in a cauldron over the fire for dinner, worked until the sun rose, went home to make breakfast and change Breeze's dressings… and sat talking to the man when he had much more important things to do. Though memories of scraping the dead flesh from Breeze's burns still stole his sleep, he found he looked forward to their quiet conversations, the stillness in the sunlit room as they sat together. He didn't trust the mercenary yet, but their time together let Alain distract himself from all the repairs still needing done on the vineyard, all the vines he'd lost and would have to replant.

Today, the setting of the sun made him sigh with relief. He didn't think he could lift another stone or board. It would be nice to get home, check on Breeze, and then enjoy a long meal with what was left of his family. Wives and children arrived to collect the men who'd been working, hugging and kissing them, taking their hands to lead them to their own hearths and dinners, and Alain felt hollow as he trudged up the thawing, slimy path on his own. He couldn't remember how many times he'd prayed to not be unnatural, but the goddesses hadn't taken his desire away. If anything, those yearnings grew stronger as the years passed, as did Alain's fierce longing for a partner, someone to stand beside him through life and help him head Mountain Shadow Winery. Boyce had been close, and with him gone, Alain knew he faced a life alone. He loved Fenn and Courtenay, but one day they'd marry and start families of their own. If only he could feel the way about a woman he felt about men, he might find someone to share his life.

That wasn't going to happen. Alain had tried. He wouldn't put himself or another poor girl through it again. He considered walking to the cemetery and sitting with Boyce a while, but his children would be hungry. Courtenay would want to tell him about her latest book, and Fenn would want to spin some fantasy about slaying a wyrm. They were grieving, and they had to come before his weakness. Breeze would be hungry; his appetite had been on the rise, and Ella called that a good sign. As he approached the house, Alain looked forward to sitting with Breeze, talking. They'd found much to discuss, even though Breeze clearly viewed life on the vineyard as boring, and Alain suspected Breeze found him sheltered and privileged. He couldn't understand Breeze's choice to build a life on shedding blood. Though Breeze didn't take much seriously and Alain doubted he could comprehend watching out for people other than himself, somehow they connected, and the hours passed quickly as they sat together.

The house was dark and quiet, and the creak and thud of the door closing echoed through the space. As Alain went to the hearths, stirred up the embers, and added wood to coax the flames, he knew eventually the house would feel this way every night. One day, he'd be all alone in the big manor. But now was no time to feel sorry for himself. Others needed him, and the children would be waiting in the kitchen for the stew that had simmered over the fire throughout the day. Alain was hungry too. For his family and everyone else on the vineyard, he had to go on living, and that meant food.

It surprised him to find the kitchen as dark and abandoned as the rest of the house. Worry welled up from his belly, and he hurried back up the stairs to see where Courtenay and Fenn might be hiding. The lack of light coming from beneath the double doors told him they weren't in the library, but he still checked among the shelves and in the alcoves. Then he went up to their bedrooms. Finding them empty, he started getting scared. When he unlocked the door to Breeze's room and found it dark and abandoned, his fear turned to a frigid panic in his gut.

Goddesses, he'd known exposing his children to a man like that was a mistake! As he'd gotten to know Breeze, Alain had never suspected the man would harm a child. Where could he have taken them, and what was he planning to do?

Alain ran from the house, his chest constricting. He needed to find someone who'd seen Breeze with his children, seen where he'd taken them. He had to find them. Courtenay and Fenn had no one else, and he couldn't bear the thought that he'd failed to protect them. Seeing no one between the front door and the main gate, he sprinted around the side of the house, toward the family's kitchen gardens, fruit trees, and berry patches. All that remained of the day was a pinkish smear to the west, and the rain made the berry fronds and high grass glitter while a thin mist blurred the dark trunks of the trees. Alain looked frantically from side to side, ready to scream. What had he been thinking, bringing a sell-sword into his home? He should have left him to die. He'd kill him himself if—when—he found him.

A bright laugh off to Alain's left cut through the chilly gloom quickly covering the world. Alain turned toward the sound and jogged in the direction of the chicken houses and a small duck pound, darting around the trees and neat rows of raised beds. At the edge of the vegetable patches, three fuzzy shapes approached him. "And then I'll go for the eyes, just like you showed me!" Fenn's high-pitched voice rang out, and it allowed Alain's heart to resume beating. Breeze laughed, and anger replaced Alain's fear. He closed the distance between them, fists clenched.

"What are you doing with my children?" Alain stopped with a few feet separating him from the trio.

Fenn ran to him and hugged his legs, smelling strongly of rain, soil, and sweaty boy. "Alain! I can't wait to show you what I can do! Breeze showed me loads of things! He's really smart, and a really good fighter! He even made me a beautiful sword!" The boy pulled a rough-carved branch shaped into a weapon from the belt over his tunic and waved it in arc through the gloom.

"Just a moment, my lad," Alain said, giving Fenn's shoulder a squeeze. "Courtenay, are you all right?"

"Why wouldn't I be?"

"You." He looked into the dark shadows of Breeze's face. "What do you think you're doing?"

"Going for a walk? Feeding the ducks and visiting Princess Courtenay's prized red rooster."

"I told you to stay in your room. I never said you could take my children anywhere. I don't want you around them."

"Why?" At first Breeze sounded confused, but after a pause, a sharp edge crept into his tone, bitter like wine gone to vinegar. "Son of a bitch. You honestly thought I'd *hurt your children*? Because I make my living as a warrior? I don't know what to say."

He looked down, clearly hurt, and limped past Alain with the aid of a stick Alain hadn't noticed.

"Alain, Breeze is really nice...." Courtenay's tone held a hint of scolding.

"What were you thinking?" Alain rebuked. "I told you not to unlock that door."

She planted her hands on her hips and jutted her chin out just as his sister had. "He isn't a prisoner. He's a nice man, he played with us all afternoon, and we had a really good time. It was nice to have someone to play with, Alain. And now you've made him feel terrible."

Goddesses. "We'll talk about this later. Take your brother back to the house and try to scrub some of the mud off him before dinner."

"Alain—" Fenn dragged his name into a long, low whine.

"Do as I say."

The children obeyed and headed down the path. They stopped to say something to Breeze, and Breeze patted Fenn on the top of the head. They hurried toward the house as the man, leaning heavily on his stick, took small steps with his right foot and all but dragged his left. It didn't take much for Alain to catch up with him.

"I'll gather my things," Breeze said without looking at Alain. "Leave for Rosecairn tonight."

"That is not necessary."

Breeze stopped and drew in a ragged breath. "I'm not staying under your roof when you think I'm going to rape your daughter."

"I don't think that," Alain said and meant it. "I was just worried, and I spoke without thinking. I do that often. I'm sorry. You don't have to leave. You're still injured."

"I can make it on my own," he said. "Been doing it a long time, friend. I appreciate what you've done, but it's clear I'm not wanted here, so I'll be on my way."

Alain moved to stand in front of him. He considered patting Breeze's shoulder but somehow couldn't do it. "I do want you to stay until you're well enough to travel. How long have you been out here? A few hours? And you can hardly make it back to the house. Stay."

Breeze arched one of his thin black brows. "So you trust me around your children?"

Alain wasn't sure, not completely. He honestly didn't think Breeze would hurt them; if that had been his goal, he'd had his chance. His influence might not be the best for them, but Alain would regulate their time together. "I know you wouldn't hurt them. Why don't you have dinner with us tonight, instead of in your room?"

"If I accept, will you stop locking me in?"

"Didn't do much good, anyway," Alain said, and both men chuckled briefly. Alain took the stick from Breeze and carefully wrapped his arm around Breeze's waist to support him.

Breeze prickled and stiffened a little. "I can make it myself."

"Don't be stubborn. I've had a long day, and I'm hungry."

Breeze laughed again and gave Alain his weight, and slowly, they made their way toward the hot meal and soft chair by the fire Alain's exhausted body craved.

Chapter
Six

"I DON'T think I can do the stairs, friend." Breeze looked pale beneath his dark complexion. Sweat beaded across his forehead, and his lips drew tight with pain amongst his thick dark whiskers.

"We'll just eat in the sitting room." Alain could tell the excursion had taken a toll on the other man. Breeze looked worse than he had when he'd first woken up. Alain helped him to the padded bench. He stacked some cushions for Breeze to rest his hurt arm against. Fenn sat down beside the mercenary, watching him with wide-eyed fascination as Breeze rested his head back against the bench, closed his eyes, and let out a sigh.

Alain and Courtenay went to the kitchen. She put bread, butter, apple jam, bowls, and utensils on a wooden platter while Alain fetched the stew and a few bottles of wine. They put both platters on the low table in the sitting room, sat down in the chairs on the opposite side from the bench, and Alain dished out venison stew that had cooked thick and tender since he'd put it over the fire before sunrise. Breeze, who'd fallen asleep, groaned with gratitude as he took a pull from the cup of wine Alain handed him. His brief respite had returned a little color to his cheeks, and Alain hoped a good meal would do the rest. All of them were hungry, and not even the children said much until they'd wiped the last of the delicious gravy from their bowls and dipped the crusts of the bread in their wine. Alain poured a second glass for Breeze and himself.

Fenn set his dishes on the floor and nuzzled up to Breeze, resting his head against Breeze's shoulder. Breeze gave him a tired smile. In the low light of the fires and candles, cuddling with Fenn and wearing Boyce's old clothes, Breeze reminded Alain so much of Boyce he had to look away. He didn't want anything to happen to Breeze, but it should be Boyce sitting there. Boyce had been a good man, a simple one like Alain, content to raise their grapes and their children. Warriors knew they risked death by choosing to live as they did. Alain thanked the goddesses Breeze had survived, but dammit, he couldn't understand the sisters' sense of justice.

"Will you come out and practice with me again tomorrow?" Fenn asked drowsily. The boy spent his days wound so tight, unable to cease moving, that he often nodded off after dinner, if not during.

Breeze stroked the side of Fenn's hair. "I don't know, lad. It took a fair bit out of me."

"That's all right." Fenn yawned. "You'll be here all summer."

"Well, I might be heading off much sooner," Breeze said. "Back home."

"It's got to be more comfortable for you to recover here than in a war tent somewhere," Courtenay said. "We have plenty of books. You won't get bored."

"Ah, princess. I'm a warrior; it's all I know how to do. I need to get back to it. Besides, Rosecairn isn't what you imagine. It's not all war tents and soldiers. We have houses and gardens, the same as you. Shops and bakeries. Lots of the men are married, and quite a few have children."

That surprised Alain. "Children? Isn't it dangerous for them?"

Breeze shot him a pitying, indulgent look he hadn't once aimed at the children. "Why dangerous? The Thorns of Rosecairn, the Roses for short, is one of the best and most respected mercenary companies. Who's going to attack us on our ground? If someone was fool enough to try, I promise you they wouldn't live long. And before you ask, our leader, Octavian Rose, doesn't take on disreputable types." He met and held Alain's gaze. "There's no place in the Roses for any man who'd hurt a child. There's no place for any man wouldn't give his life protecting one. Octavian won't permit rape or pillaging, and the villages around us know it. Believe it or not, the locals are glad to have us there. I'll wager Rosecairn sees less trouble from bandits and highwaymen than your Lockhaven."

"Are there roses?" Courtenay asked wistfully. "Is that how it got its name?"

"Yes, princess. In the center of our camp, which is really a village now, is a huge stone cairn surrounded by wild white roses. Do you know why?"

She shook her head, and Breeze took another swallow of wine before he continued. "It's a story you might like. Octavian told it to me when he agreed to let me join the company. I'm afraid I won't tell it as well as he did, though. A few hundred years back, instead of the cairn, a castle stood. Inside lived a kind and beautiful lady—"

"What was her name?" Courtenay moved into Alain's lap and put her arms around his neck and her cheek on his shoulder. Tears glittered on her round cheeks, and Alain held her tight. She had never cried, not even as an infant, but since the fire, Alain had noticed her off on her own, wiping her nose on her apron. Sometimes he thought he should approach her, try to talk, but in her position, he wouldn't want that, and he knew he was the worst person to try to say something to comfort her. At least he could keep her close and hope she knew he loved her.

Breeze chuckled. "I don't remember. Octavian told it better, like I said. I would call her Princess Courtenay, but I'd rather not, since I know how the story ends. Why don't you choose a name?"

"Sabine," Courtenay said in barely a whisper, punctuated by a sniffle.

"A beautiful name," Breeze said. "Lady Sabine was a beautiful young woman who lived in a beautiful castle. Unfortunately, her husband was a vile man, as cruel as he was ugly. There's more to it, but I'll tell you the rest when you're older. Lady Sabine was sad and lonely, because her husband kept her locked up in her chambers, and she had nothing to do but look out her window all day.

"One day, she spied a very handsome man, but low born, a common soldier. Even so, when he looked up at her window, she saw kindness in his eyes, and she vowed to find a way to meet him, so she begged her husband to be allowed into the gardens to cut roses to perfume her suite. Somehow she convinced him to agree, and it wasn't long before the lady and the young soldier fell in love. No matter how many moments they stole, it was never enough. They devised a system. If Lady Sabine could sneak out of the castle in the evening, she would drop a single white rose to the ground beneath her window. Her suitor would see it, and as much as he wanted to pick it up, he had to walk past it, pretending not to notice, and go about his duties until they could meet.

"They went on that way for many moons, until Lady Sabine became swollen with a child her husband knew wasn't his...."

"How?" Courtenay asked.

"When you're older." Alain kissed the top of her head.

"Aye." Breeze continued. "Her husband became enraged and ordered his wife beheaded. The soldier's beloved and unborn child died on the block that day. He was a brave and honorable man, and he couldn't let them go to the goddesses unavenged. He spoke to some of the other soldiers, and since he was well liked and respected, twenty men vowed oaths to follow him. Those men stormed the castle, and though they were outnumbered three to one, they brought it down. They killed all the knights and the cruel lord, though each man knew none of them would survive their injuries. The soldier found the head and body of his beloved, and even as their life's blood flowed out, the other men tore that castle down, razed it to the ground, and the stones that had once been its walls are now the cairn, a grand grave marker for poor Lady Sabine.

"Those twenty-one men died almost as soon as they finished laying the stones. The Thirteen Goddesses looked down on them and their sacrifice, and they made white roses grow all around the cairn. Tam Octavian is more of a poet than I, and he would say 'the briar fronds wreathed their bones, and blossoms opened in the sightless hollows where their eyes had once beheld the true meaning of honor and courage.' The white roses still grow there, fed by those brave men's bones. But sometimes, one of those buds opens, and the petals are streaked with red, because the soil remembers those men bleeding into it."

Courtenay scrubbed at her eyes with the heel of her hand. "I want to go to bed now."

"Did you not like my story, princess?" Breeze asked.

She stood, walked over, and kissed him on the forehead. "I loved it. I would love a white rose streaked with red."

"You'll have one," Breeze told her.

"Do you promise?"

"I do."

She grinned and kissed him again, and Breeze wrapped his arm around her brittle little shoulders before she broke away to head for her room.

"Why would a mercenary commander tell his men a story like that?" Alain wondered aloud. "It sounds like something for young girls."

"Think about it, Alain. Honorable, low-born men against a corrupt noble. Courageous men overcoming insurmountable odds. Octavian is a very clever man."

From the look on his face, Alain almost asked Breeze if loved the other man, this Octavian. His rich brown eyes glazed, a secret smile curled his lips, and he looked toward the windows and the night outside. Clearly, he held fond memories of his commander, and though Alain wondered why, instead of asking, he stood to scoop a snoring Fenn into his arms. The boy never woke as Alain tucked him into bed, though if the last few weeks were any indication, a nightmare would rouse him later.

Downstairs, Breeze breathed deeply with his head against his shoulder and his eyes shut. Alain gripped his shoulder gently. "Tired?"

The other man nodded, and Alain bent so Breeze could drape his healthy arm over his shoulders, and together, they made their way to Breeze's bed. Alain helped him strip off his shirt, lowered him into the bed, and pulled the blankets up around him. He turned to stir up the coals in the fireplace and add more kindling. It wasn't catching, probably because of the dampness the day's rain had left behind, so he knelt to blow on the flames.

"Alain, why didn't your wife join us for dinner?"

He stiffened and froze, crouched in an uncomfortable position. "I don't have a wife."

"I.... Oh."

Alain didn't stand or turn to face him. He couldn't. He clenched his fist tight around the poker and stared into the growing flames. "You would not understand."

"I might. You could try me."

"No." Alain got to his feet but didn't tear his gaze from the fire. "It's late. You need your rest. I'll see you in the morning." He hurried from the room and up the stairs to the cold, lonely chamber he had once shared with Boyce. Even after Alain lit the candles on the bedside table, his breath still misted around him. He went back to the sitting room and retrieved the small bit of wine he and Breeze hadn't finished, as well as the bottle they hadn't opened. Alain uncorked it, and then he went to kneel in front of his hearth.

The straw and twigs caught quickly when he sparked his flint, and a puff of smoke hit him in the face. The smell took him back to the day of the fire, fumbling in the smudged darkness with his hands held out in front of him, calling for Boyce and hearing Boyce calling him. Why hadn't they found each other? Would things have been different if they had? Was he a fool to think he could have protected Boyce?

A phantom pain in his chest made him cough, and he could taste the soot all over again. He went to the edge of the bed and flopped down, drained the inch or so of wine left in the first bottle, and took a few healthy gulps from the second. Since he couldn't bear to look behind him and not see Boyce sleeping or looking at him with a mischievous smile, he drank until half the bottle was gone. He remembered Boyce's coppery chest hair, how it felt beneath his fingers and against his back. He remembered the taste of his lips, how they'd felt against Alain's flesh. Goddesses, how selfish of him to long for the pleasures of his lover when two children had lost their father. Why did he have to be like this? He didn't want to be unnatural. He turned his face toward the rafters and the plaster ceiling and called out to the goddesses. "I want to be a good man. Why won't you let me? Take this away! Why would you do this to me?"

He cradled the bottle and drank from it between sobs. By the time he finished, he was tipsy and angry: angry at the goddesses, the mage who'd caused the fire, the soldiers who'd broken through their gate to escape it, the nobles and their petty conflicts, and at himself for not doing more. He was angry at the sorry little fire puffing acrid smoke into the room. He couldn't stand the stink of it, almost reminiscent of burning flesh. Alain touched some of the smooth round patches on his shoulder beneath his shirt, where the raining embers had singed his skin, and though the wounds had healed, he could feel it as if it had just happened. He could smell it. Boyce had reeked of burnt flesh when

Alain had seen him for the last time. He threw the bottle he held, and it shattered in the hearth, the little bit of wine in the bottom dousing the flames and replacing the smoke with fruit-scented steam. After kicking his boots off, Alain curled on his side on the bed, not bothering to cover up. The pillow he held against his chest and face no longer smelled like Boyce's hair. The bitter odor of the smoke had replaced it. Soon, he wouldn't remember the nuances of that wonderful scent, and he released all the tears he held in for the benefit of others. He had no one who could understand this grief. No one would console him over the loss of an unnatural love. He'd sworn he wouldn't defame Boyce's memory, so he cried alone, shivering, until the pain and alcohol combined to drag him into the numbness and dark.

Chapter
Seven

ALAIN LOOKED wan and pale when he came in with Breeze's breakfast the following morning. The dark crescents under his blue eyes made Breeze wonder if he'd slept at all. He suspected Alain's restlessness might have been his fault. He hadn't realized Alain had lost his wife in the fire. What an ass.

Still, Alain offered him a smile as he set a tray bearing some porridge, boiled eggs, a slice of ham, and a bowl of beans on Breeze's lap. He sat on the edge of the bed as he always did and poured wine. "How are you feeling this morning? Did you sleep well?"

"Better than it looks like you did. Why is that?"

"I'm fine."

Breeze put down the forkful of bacon-flavored beans he'd been about to shovel into his mouth and took Alain's hand. At his touch, Alain flinched and tried to pull away, but Breeze held firm, and eventually he relaxed. "Look, Alain. I'm just a sell-sword. I never claimed to be a scholar, but I feel like a stupid ass for not realizing you lost your wife in the fire. I hope that damned mage rots in the rankest pit of the Shades' Abode. But I'm sorry for being dull-witted, and for letting my tongue wag like the fucking fool I am. I know I hurt you, and I'm sorry."

When Alain looked at Breeze, tears glittered in his summer-sky eyes but didn't fall. He shook his head. "No, I've never had a wife."

"But Courtenay and Fenn?"

"My twin sister's children. My niece and nephew. My brother-in-law, their father, died in the fire. I'm all they have left now. I… I don't know if I'm good enough to raise them on my own. I love them, but I'm afraid I'll fail them."

"What happened to your sister?"

Alain caught the single tear he let fall on his fingertip and looked away to hide his grief. "She died giving birth to Fenn. Six years ago."

Breeze didn't know what to say, so he squeezed Alain's hand a little tighter, and Alain squeezed back. What he really wanted to know was how Alain had remained unmarried. Breeze freely admitted he was a handsome man, with his rose-and-honey coloring and those expressive eyes. And lips—pink, firm, and full without looking pillowy or slack. Add to that his estate, and he could have his pick of the buxom country girls. If he wanted help with the children, why not take a wife? Could he be.... Damn, out of nowhere, Breeze really wanted to know whose body Alain imagined when he slid into bed and slipped his hand into his trousers. He could see it: Alain's teeth denting his lower lip, red rushing all the way to the tips of his ears—

And he was a fucking pig for thinking about that while Alain struggled not to break down. Besides, it was none of his damned business who or what the vintner fucked, if anyone. Hopefully, in another month or so, he'd be long gone. On to better things. Still, he didn't like seeing Alain suffering. "I'm sorry." What a platitude. Breeze just wasn't used to men who needed comforting.

Alain nodded. "Thank you. You should finish your breakfast so I can change your dressings. Best to get it over with."

After a few more bites of food, Breeze asked, "Do you have a bathtub? I'm as rank as a whore's underpants, and I'd kill for a proper wash." He set his fork on his plate and scratched his chin. "And a shave."

He didn't know why that made Alain smile, but seeing it pleased him. "Why do you want to shave off your whiskers?"

"That's just how it's done in Espero. Men shave every day. The heat, I suppose. I'm just not used to these whiskers. Why, do you like them?"

Alain tensed visibly, and Breeze felt like horse's ass. Again. He was making this a habit. Why had he said that?

"I don't care about them one way or another. I just wondered. Most men in Selindria don't shave their whiskers."

"You do," Breeze observed.

Alain touched his soft-looking cheek with the fingers of his splinted hand. The way Alain worked and took care of him, Breeze found it easy to forget about the other man's injury. Truth be told, he bore it like a warrior. "Mine comes in all patchy. I can't grow a proper beard, just little scraps here and there. I look like a fool when I don't shave."

Breeze wondered if the hair grew in little golden swaths down the center of his chest, his soft belly, between his legs. Bleeding Shades, he had to drive off the pictures in his head. They'd make an Elvaran street slag blush. "So, could I trouble you for a bath? I'm sure you've had your fill of my stink."

"You'll have to come down the stairs, to the kitchen. We have an indoor well and a tub in a room just beyond it. I can help you, if you think you can make it."

"I think I can. I feel heartier than I have since I woke up." And if Alain looked beneath Breeze's sheets, he'd see plenty of proof. Probably best to get rid of that before Alain helped him bathe. He struggled to focus on his breakfast and think about anything else. Luckily, Alain helped distract him.

"So, I guessed you were from Espero. I haven't met many people from the island. How long have you been away?"

"About seven years."

"You must have been quite young when you left home," Alain said.

"Yes, I'd just come of age."

"Why did you leave?"

"Wanted to see the world, I suppose. Don't you?"

Alain laughed. "No! I have everything I need right here. This land has been in my family for nine generations—almost five hundred years. Since my ancestors accepted this property from the valen of Lockhaven, it's taken care of us. I love this place. I can't imagine leaving. Espero wasn't like that for you?"

"No." Silence fell between them as Breeze finished his breakfast. He didn't want to talk about Espero, and it wasn't anything Alain would be able to comprehend. "You don't want more for yourself?

Something grander? Adventure and glory for your name?" What young man didn't?

"No. I have no one to prove anything to. I love tending the grapes and the land. The goddesses have blessed us, and I'm thankful. My heart is here."

Sounds frightfully dull, Breeze thought, *if comfortable.* "No aspirations at all?"

"Maybe just… someone to share it with. But that won't happen." Alain seemed ready say more, but stopped himself and paused before rushing to quantify his statement. "Not anytime soon, at least. I have too much to do to get the vineyard back to where it can support us. Buildings need repaired, and over half of the vines will have to be replanted. I can only pray we'll be able to harvest enough come Berris's Moon to produce enough wine to sell next year. What we have to take to market this summer will barely get us by. Too many of the cellars caved in when the support beams burned. Luckily, last year was good, and we'll fetch a good price for what's left. And we have the ice wine. I'm sorry. You probably don't care about any of this."

To Breeze's surprise, he found he did, a little, and he caught himself imagining ways to help the vineyard thrive. Not that he knew a thing about it. "What is ice wine?"

"We leave the grapes on the vine until the frost, let them freeze before harvesting. The water in them turns to ice, and it concentrates their sweetness. We press them while they're still frozen, and it produces the most exquisite wine, as golden as the sunlight, sweet as honey, and with a taste of the mountains and the winter. It can be sold for exorbitant prices; the nobles here in the north adore it. Ice wine is risky, though. First off, if the frost comes too late, we chance letting the grapes rot on the vine and losing an entire crop. Secondly, the frozen grapes produce much less juice than they would if we picked them normally, so of course they produce less wine."

"That seems the thing to do, then. You might end up with less wine, but you'll make more gold in the long run, won't you?"

Alain wiggled his fingers in Breeze's hand like he wanted to tap them on something as he considered. "Possibly. Not all the grapes will work, though. And there's a good chance the goddesses and seasons won't cooperate. We usually only risk a small portion of the grapes for the ice wine, those we can afford to lose. If we made them all into ice wine, we would do quite well, but if we lost them to rot, we'd be doomed."

"Octavian always tells me destiny smiles on the bold man and ignores the timid."

"You speak highly of him," Alain said.

"He's a good man, as I explained. Shrewd, though. Sharp as a dagger. And, I suppose, he was good to me. Gave me a chance."

Alain looked at him intently, batting his long golden lashes, so Breeze continued. "He could have turned me away. I wasn't much of a warrior when I went to join the Roses. But I told him my story, and he told me his, and it turned out they weren't so different. He gave me a place to belong. Saw some worth in me that no one else ever had. I owe him a great deal."

"You didn't feel like you belonged in Espero?"

"No." Dammit, he didn't want to talk about this. He pulled loose of Alain's hand and took a long drink of wine to avoid speaking.

"Why?"

"I just wanted a different life from the one laid out for me there. Same as Octavian. I wanted to make it on my own like he did. He's not much older than us, you know."

"He sounds like a remarkable man." Alain looked like he wanted to say something else, but he busied himself with stacking Breeze's empty dishes onto the tray. "I suppose we should see to your bath."

Alain left the tray on the floor next to the bed and helped Breeze to stand. He arranged Breeze's arm over his shoulders, and Breeze caught his own scent. Goddesses, he really reeked, and he felt suddenly self-conscious.

The trip down the stairs and through the cheery kitchen hurt less than Breeze expected, but by the time they reached the small, whitewashed room at the end of the long corridor, the side of his left thigh trembled and threatened to cramp. Alain helped him to sit on a wooden chair while he filled three metal pails from the pump and suspended them over a raised pit of coals in the corner of the room. Then he picked up a pair of shears. "Oh no. I have to take your bandages off, and you didn't take your elixir."

Breeze laughed. "I can hardly wash and shave myself if I'm fast asleep. Or were you planning to do it?"

Alain colored. Goddesses, that was alluring, and Breeze wondered how far the dusky-rose color spread down his neck. Even his lips darkened when he spoke. "I have done it, you know. Bathed you."

"I know. Thank you. I was only teasing. I did not mean to upset you."

"I'm not upset. I just don't like doing this. I know it's necessary to the healing, but I don't like seeing you... seeing anyone suffering. I should go back to your room and fetch the tonic."

"I'd rather do without it," Breeze said. "I've had enough of feeling fuzzy."

"You really should—"

"Alain, I will be fine. This isn't the first time I've been injured." He didn't add that it was by far the worst, or that he wanted to experience what was about to happen without the haze of the elixir.

"I'll at least go the kitchen and get you more wine to dull the pain."

He returned with an open bottle, and Breeze drank. Goddesses, this would spoil him. This tasted like wine from Espero, bright and bold with notes of bitter cherry, currant, the black stone Pherara had pulled from the sea to form the island, leather, and tarberry. He almost moaned as it slid down his throat to warm his belly. "Amazing. You made this?"

"It takes a great many people," Alain said as he emptied the buckets into the round wooden tub.

"But according to your instructions," Breeze pressed.

"Yes, I suppose."

"You, my friend, are an artist."

"Thank you, but that's hardly the best we have to offer. Just table wine, really."

"Goddesses."

"Your bath is ready. I should take your dressings off. Drink some more."

Breeze didn't need to be told twice. After a few long pulls, he carefully rolled the loose brown trousers the children had given him to his ankles and lifted his feet out. Aside from the linen strips, he was completely naked. Not that he was shy—at Rosecairn, the men swam together in the summer and helped each other on and off with their armor. Besides, Alain had seen him, so he didn't bother covering himself. When Alain turned and saw him sitting with his legs open, everything on display, he blushed almost as burgundy as the wine and tossed Breeze a towel.

Breeze chuckled but draped it across his sensitive bits. "I'm sure you've seen it."

"I have seen it," Alain said a little shortly, "not that I was trying to look, or staring at it, or something. I kept it covered up when I could!"

"I never meant to imply otherwise, friend." Alain did *not* like being teased. Breeze was used to the back and forth jibes between the warriors at Rosecairn, and sometimes they grew quite vicious, but he didn't want to make Alain uncomfortable. "You know me. Not used to the company of civilized men. I apologize."

"That's not necessary," Alain said in a low voice. The haunted look had returned to his eyes, and for the first time, Breeze realized Alain should not be subjected to this. He wasn't a man comfortable with pain and blood, and he shouldn't have to become one. The world held enough men like Breeze.

Breeze reached to take the shears from Alain's hand. "Here. I can do that myself."

"You really can't. You don't know how, and you'll only hurt yourself worse. Don't worry; I'm used to it by now."

Though he could see it wasn't true, Breeze leaned back against the cool white wall and took another few pulls from the bottle while Alain arranged his tools, salves, and bandages on a low table. The coals kept the little chamber toasty warm, and though it could have smelled musty from the water, the only scent he noticed was whatever the family used to keep it clean, something like vinegar and citrus.

Alain cut a neat line from Breeze's midthigh to his underarm. He no longer wrapped Breeze's neck, and the skin there had healed to a whorled and mottled patch of pink Breeze knew would never completely fade. He'd wear the scars that extended in a thin strip up his face to his ear until he went to the goddesses. He wondered if it would disgust his future potential lovers as much as it disgusted Alain. Unlike some men, he didn't enjoy quick encounters in the dark, with both partners thinking only of release. He was far from a sentimental man, but he adored all the sensual pleasures of coupling, all the delightful things to experience beyond the act itself. He hoped the injury hadn't taken that from him.

Slowly, Alain began to pull the bandages apart as if he were opening a pair of curtains. Breeze hissed as the first piece of his skin came off with the linen. He clamped his eyes shut as chunk after chunk of flesh peeled from his body. By the time Alain finished, tears had run into his mouth and his nose dripped, but compared to the torture of the first time he'd endured it consciously, it hadn't been so bad. Looking down, most of the skin on his left side matched his neck and cheek: pink and closed but horribly disfigured. At the center, along his ribs, some open sores still oozed white puss, some blisters remained, and pieces of his skin looked hardened and yellowish.

Alain unwrapped the dressing from his leg and declared, "I think this is healed. I can have Elle look at it to be sure, but I don't think we'll have to keep wrapping it up." He ran his fingertips over the raw, sensitive flesh, its awful pits, peaks, and coils. It felt strange being touched on skin so exposed, but it didn't hurt. In some places, Breeze felt nothing at all and knew he never would. With his hand resting over Breeze's knee, Alain looked up and deep into his eyes. "This is a good sign."

Breeze stood and slowly extended the arm Alain had recently removed the splints from. It ached, the muscles weakened from disuse, and he didn't know if he'd ever be able to fully extend it. It was as if the muscles had bunched together, grown shorter. No, he couldn't accept that. Wouldn't. He might be stuck with the scars, but he needed his arm working so he could fight.

Alain stood only a few inches from him, big eyes wide and lips furled down in concern. "What is it?"

"Alain, am I hideous? Because of the scars?"

"I didn't know warriors were so vain about their battle scars."

"I'm not vain." He had to explain without divulging his fears in regards to physical intimacy. Discussing such things made Alain uncomfortable. "I don't want to be a prince in a velvet doublet with a lacey collar, but I don't want to be a monster either. I don't want to disgust people."

"You can barely see the scars when your clothes are on. And your hair covers the burns on your neck and beside your ear. Not that those are even that bad."

"And… what about when my clothes are off?"

Impossibly, Alain's eyes grew wider and his cheeks redder. After a second, he laughed softly. It wasn't something he did often. "You're worried about the reaction of the ladies. I understand they appreciate scars on a fighting man. I don't think you should be concerned."

"I'm not a grotesque?"

Alain stepped a little closer. With their chests almost touching, Breeze saw his recently awakened desire volleyed back at him from Alain's blue eyes. It took all the will he possessed not to groan, not to catch that full, flushed lower lip between his teeth and suck it into his mouth. Doing that might land him on his ass out in the cold. Or it might not. He'd seen the look Alain gave him on the faces of other men: raw desire. Was he a fool not to at least try? Just as he reassured himself with Octavian Rose's wisdom about destiny, said to the Shades with it, and leaned in, Alain stepped back. "You… you're like… anything but grotesque. You should get into the water. I didn't make it too hot, because of your burns, but ice cold won't be a holiday either."

Glad of the towel he kept pressed tightly against him to conceal his reaction to Alain, Breeze nodded and lowered himself into the water. Even the slight heat felt like a miniature lightning storm over his newly healed flesh, but he took a few deep breaths and waited for it to pass, which it did. Afterward, the water felt fantastic. He didn't think he'd ever been so filthy, so stale. Alain set a small round mirror, another cloth, a shaving blade, and a cake of yellow soap on the edge of the tub.

"I'm going into the kitchen to get something over the fire for dinner. Just call out when you're finished," Alain said.

"Oh… ah, thank you." Breeze, like the ass he sometimes was, had entertained a fantasy in which Alain lathered him up and whisked the bubbles from his skin with the cloth or the razor. He'd imagined lingering touches and caresses, Alain's fingers sliding through his wet hair. But he no longer needed the help, and Alain didn't seem to *want* to do it. Maybe he'd seen something that wasn't there. His head had been fucked silly since he'd woken up in Alain's little room. Nothing for it. He took the soap and the cloth and began washing and shaving.

He had really, really wanted Alain to shave him. That would have been just.... His cock stirred at the thought of Alain carefully scraping the sharp steel over his face and down his neck, and he wondered if he could get some relief beneath the water without Alain hearing. In the end, he decided to wait until he was alone in his room. He finished his ablutions and called for Alain, who appeared with a fresh set of clothes.

Alain gasped, almost inaudibly, when he saw Breeze without his whiskers. Though he knew plenty of women and men enjoyed a good beard, found it masculine, Breeze had always felt he looked better shorn, and Alain's reaction made him smile. He reached for the clothes, but Alain said, "Not yet. I have to check your wound and rewrap it, at least the part that's still open. Elle says it can go fetid if I don't. And if there's any dead skin...."

"I understand." Keeping himself carefully covered with the wet rag, Breeze went to the bench and sat down. Once again, Alain crouched next to him, this time holding a coarse, dry cloth and a pair of tweezers. The soak had turned the hardened yellow skin soft and almost liquid, sluglike as it crawled down his ribs, but it still hurt like a rotten, fucking whore when Alain caught the ends and slowly peeled it away. He apologized every time Breeze winced, and by the time he finished, admittedly much quicker than before, rivulets of blood ran down Breeze's waist, and he was cold, shaking, and sick to his stomach. Alain hurried to clean him up, slather him in that sticky, stinging ooze, and help him into his clothes. "We need to get you warm, and quickly."

Breeze held on and let Alain practically drag him to his bed. He collapsed, and Alain wrapped the blankets tight around him. He looked as pale and trembling as Breeze. Even after each of them downed a very large, and very welcome, glass of wine from the bottle Alain had fetched earlier, Alain still had a greenish cast to his skin. Though even his uninjured hand felt weak, Breeze reached up to squeeze the back of Alain's neck. He'd never felt so many knots of tension, and he knew they hurt. He did his best to help the other man relax, and it must have worked, because Alain's head lolled forward before snapping back up.

"Friend?"

Alain stammered out an apology. "I need to lie down a moment. I didn't sleep well last night, and I feel faint. If you don't mind, I'll just rest a few moments. There's still so much work to be done."

With his hand on the back of Alain's neck, Breeze guided him to the pillow. He curled on his side, so Breeze moved to his right side and draped an arm over Alain's ribs. When Alain shivered, he adjusted the bedclothes so they covered both of them. The next time Breeze opened his eyes, the room was pitch black and probably as cold as it was outside. Alain still slept peacefully beside him, his back curved against Breeze's chest and belly, Breeze's hand held tight and pressed to Alain's lips. Breeze's body awakened instantly, and he tried to shift his engorged cock away from the soft swell of Alain's backside before Alain noticed it.

This is a bad, bad idea, he thought. *I'm leaving, hopefully in a moon or less.* He had no problem with taking pleasure with no strings attached. Normally, he preferred it that way. But Alain… Alain was so lonely and fragile, and Breeze refused to hurt him more than he'd already been hurt. He had to get a handle on his heated blood and keep a reasonable distance between them from now on. This could *not* happen again.

Chapter Eight

EVEN WITH all the work that came with spring, the plowing of fields, the sowing of grain, the nurturing of the still-viable vines, and the coaxing of pieces of their roots to produce new plants to cover the burned fields, Alain tossed and turned in a bed that felt too big for a single man. He'd worked from before the sun rose to well after dark, but he still couldn't sleep. He scrubbed a hand over his face and readjusted his pillow. A shard of moonlight snuck between the curtains, but otherwise the room was dark. Finally it was warm enough to do without a fire, and instead of the smoky stench, Alain smelled freshly churned loam, new green growth, even some early flowers blooming. The scents of life and hope emerging didn't soothe him as they always had.

Giving up on sleep, he rose from the bed and pulled his trousers and boots on. His neglected hair had grown past his collarbones, so he tied it back with a scrap of twine before heading down the stairs and into the library. He lit the candles on one of the desks and sat down, staring absently at the portraits of his ancestors on the walls. By now, everyone knew what had caused the catastrophic fire. To stand against traitors to the crown, King Agarick had conscripted his nephew, the mad mage Yarroway L'Estrella, the same one he'd exiled for bewitching him into unnatural acts, to use a devastating spell against the enemy. Yarrow had done as commanded and won the day for the true king, but the king had not survived. The details of the king's demise were hazy, but his son, Garith, had ascended to the throne and married Princess Cothryn of Gaeltheon, uniting the two largest and most powerful kingdoms in the known world and ushering in the so-called Blessed Epoch, which nobles and temple priestesses promised would be an unprecedented period of peace and prosperity. To Alain, the promise felt premature.

He pulled a large leather-bound book, some scrolls, and some strips of parchment from a drawer of the desk and wet a quill in an inkwell. No matter how he manipulated the numbers, there just wasn't enough gold to go around. What remained in the communal treasury would barely buy a winter's worth of hay for their animals if they couldn't produce enough. They might need wheat to sustain the people living on the vineyard. Alain's attempts to grow new vines from scraps of root had been only partially successful; if the vineyard was to last, he had to purchase plants, and importing them from Elvara and Espero would cost. They couldn't afford to leave those fields unproductive for the years it would take him to raise fruit-bearing vines from root fragments. They needed to replace the barrels that had been destroyed when the cellar roofs collapsed. The vineyard boasted a family of skilled coopers, but the arn wood would have to be brought up from Everdale. And goddesses, glass for bottling cost so much.

Alain added and subtracted, hoping the coin he needed would somehow magically appear. Of course it didn't, and he had to make some hard decisions. Wheat, bread for the people, would come first if they couldn't grow enough. They needed a good season. Just one good season might see them through, but no one could predict the whims of the Thirteen Sisters. Buying wheat, and then hay for the horses, sheep, goats, and the few cattle they kept for milk and butter would drain the winery's reserves. No matter how Alain juggled the sums, purchasing the necessities to keep his people alive left nothing to invest in the vineyard's future—the future he would hand off to Courtenay and Fenn. To make wine, they needed grapes, and to raise grapes, they needed vines. Alain needed coin to buy those vines, and he just didn't have it. He couldn't buy vines without stealing the food from his peoples' mouths.

Goddesses, what do you want me to do? Help me. If not me, help the good people who have worked this land for generations. Please. Please hear me, just this once.

Beyond the open window, a night bird called out, and its mate answered, as if to remind Alain how alone he stood. He had called out, and no one had answered him. He'd been calling to the goddesses, begging them to make him a normal man, since before he'd even been a man. He'd never gotten a response, and he didn't expect one now. Looking around at the portraits of his ancestors, his parents and his sister Sabine among them, he swore not to let the vineyard fail. He didn't care how hard he toiled or what he suffered—five hundred years of family and tradition wouldn't sink with him at the helm.

He was so tired. The last time he could recall sleeping more than a few hours without a worry or a nightmare disturbing him was when he'd accidentally nodded off in Breeze's bed. He remembered Breeze putting an arm around him and how safe it had made him feel. The next thing he knew, he'd woken feeling ten years younger, having slept better than he had since lying next to Boyce.

Alain snuffed the candle wicks between his thumb and finger. The slight burn made him roll his eyes. This wasn't pain. Pain was the vestiges of his ancestors looking down on him, wondering if he would be the one to fail Mountain Shadow Vineyard after five hundred years. As their painted eyes bored into him, Alain wondered what would happen to Courtenay and Fenn. Courtenay would be a beautiful woman, like his sister, and she would find a prosperous husband to support her. Would Fenn be forced to live by his sword, as Breeze did? Alain didn't want such a coarse life for his nephew—

Or for Breeze.

He left the library and shut the doors. The house was quiet, though life—insects, birds, growing plants, and trees blossoming—sang softly beyond the open windows. In his bare feet, Alain padded down the hall and stood outside Breeze's room. The door hung open, and Breeze breathed deeply beyond it. Goddesses forgive him, all Alain wanted was to climb into the mercenary's bed and wind himself around Breeze like yarn. He had never slept so securely as he had in Breeze's arms, and that was strange, because he still didn't trust the man. Yet he wanted to get under the blankets with Breeze, twine his limbs around him, and feel the heat rising from his olive brown skin.

Had he grown so desperate? Breeze would be gone before the moon ended, if he had his way. Forming any kind of attachment to him would only cause Alain more pain. He leaned his head against the doorframe and listened as Breeze muttered in that language Alain didn't understand. He inhaled the scents of the honey-based burn salve and Breeze's sweat.

What a fool. He couldn't replace Boyce with Breeze. Was he so simple, so starved for affection, that he'd latch on to the first available man? That was pathetic, wasn't it? Breeze was friendly, but Alain didn't really know if his suggestions had been genuine. He doubted it. Anyway, it didn't matter. As soon as he could hobble across the Starlight Bridge, Breeze would join the rest of the Roses and continue his vocation as a sword for hire.

Goddesses, he smells good. Sweat and honey. Like wine and roses....

Alain leaned his head against the doorframe and closed his eyes for a few moments. He hated feeling sorry for himself, but he hurt. The gaping hole inside, the one he couldn't ever remember not festering, had just grown deeper, the edges more ragged and crumbling, with every person he'd lost. It hurt to know he'd probably never find anyone to fill that pit, that he'd be alone, but he knew he couldn't fill it with Breeze's lean muscled body, smooth dark skin, mischievous eyes, and easy smile. Amazingly, they'd become something like friends, but even that would end as soon as Breeze recovered fully. Losing the camaraderie would sting, but it would be for the best. Breeze had made it clear he could never be happy on the vineyard.

With a sigh, Alain turned and headed back up the stairs to his room. He undressed and flopped on the cool, scentless sheets of the bed. Whether he slept or not, he had to try to at least rest and let go of some of his worries, because tomorrow he had to pretend to be happy. Tomorrow wasn't about him, and he couldn't spoil it with his foul mood and self-pity.

BY THE time Alain got two of their shaggy ponies hooked to the cart with the help of the oldest son of the family who looked after the horses, the sun had risen, washing the vineyard in fuzzy pastels, lavenders, roses, and a faded blue that reminded him of one of Courtenay's old dresses. The emerging day, and the few clouds drifting lazily above him, seemed as soft, gentle, and quiet as the edge of a flower petal brushing against Alain's skin. He stopped the cart near the front door of his house, and the old animals just stood, content to pick at a few clumps of grass without being tied. Like Alain, the ponies had no desire to go anywhere else.

Inside, Alain tucked a few extra bottles of wine into the large basket he'd packed. Then he loaded it, along with a few folded blankets, onto the back of the cart. In the kitchen, it surprised him to see Courtenay, Fenn, and even Breeze dressed and waiting for him. The children sat at the table, Courtenay nibbling her lower lip while she read and Fenn bouncing on the bench like always. Breeze sat on a stool, doing a slow and clumsy but passable job of cooking half a dozen sunny-side up eggs. He looked over his shoulder and smiled at Alain, and Alain's heart floundered a few beats with a longing he couldn't name.

"Good timing," Breeze told him. "Go have a seat. It's almost ready."

Alain moved slowly to join the children, confused, hazy, for no apparent reason. It was the same old kitchen where he'd had his breakfast his entire life. Time moved thick and syrupy around him, the tune Breeze whistled as he flipped the eggs in the pan echoing through the room. He barely tasted his food when Breeze set a plate in front of him, just went through the motions of chewing and swallowing until it was gone.

"Is it time to go?" Fenn asked, tugging Alain's sleeve. "It's time, isn't it, Uncle Alain?"

"As soon as we clean up." Alain forced a smile. "It's a beautiful day already." He kissed the boy on the top of his head, where his hair was still wet and fragrant from his bath. Had Courtenay wrangled him into the tub? Getting the boy to bathe could be worse than wrestling a smooth, wet piglet into a crate.

"You lot can go on," Breeze said, struggling a little as he got to his feet to collect the dishes. "I'll take care of this."

A string in Alain's chest pulled taut and snapped, the broken ends whipping against his heart. "Why don't you come with us? Like I said, it's looking to be a gorgeous day, and you're always saying how you want to get out of the house."

Breeze shook his head. "I wouldn't want to intrude. This is a family affair."

"Then let's let the birthday girl decide," Alain said. "Courtenay?"

With a wide smile and a twinkle in her eyes, she said, "Yes, please. Come with us."

Fenn hooted, leapt from the bench, and jumped up and down, punching the air and making dried flakes of herbs rain down into his hair. "Maybe we'll meet some bandits along the road, and Breeze can come to our rescue and kill them! Chop their heads off or stab them in their bellies with his sword."

Breeze chuckled. "I'm afraid I lost my sword, young friend."

"I have mine, then." The boy pulled the wooden blade from his belt. He had barely put it down since Breeze had made it, and since then, Breeze had used a kitchen knife to continue working the wood, shaping it until it looked like a real weapon, and an ornate one, with swirling designs on the hilt and up the blade.

"Good man," Breeze said, winking at Fenn.

"Go and get into the cart," Alain told the children. "We'll be there as soon as we finish cleaning up."

After they ran up the stairs, Alain gathered the dishes and took them and a bucket of water to the sink. He scrubbed them with a coarse brush and handed them to Breeze to dry. "Fenn looks up to you."

"And that doesn't sit well with you," Breeze replied. "You need not say it. You rarely say what you think, and I've learned to guess at the rest."

"I just don't want him filling his head with foolish fantasies," Alain said, handing Breeze the iron pan. "He doesn't have a future as a warrior. His place is here on the vineyard. It will all be his one day."

"And if he wanted a different life for himself? Would you stand in his way?"

"I… I don't know. I know it seems dull to you, but our life here is a good one. I can't bear to think of either of the children in danger. The last thing I want for Fenn is to be a—"

"A man like me?" A corner of Breeze's mouth curled up, but it was far from a smile.

Alain shook his head, making hair badly in need of a trim fall across his eyes. "I don't mean it that way. I don't want *you* to be a man like you. It isn't disapproval, not completely. It's that every day you go out there, to fight, and you might not come back."

Breeze brushed the errant fringe from Alain's eyes, pinned it behind his ear, and let his fingers trace a slow path from Alain's cheek to his chin. "You must understand that I didn't choose this life out of desperation. I didn't join the Roses because I had no other option. I could have taken another path, back in Espero. This is what I *want* to do."

"It's difficult for me to understand," Alain admitted. Goddesses, Breeze had beautiful eyes, the rich, fertile color of the soil after a rain, with little golden flecks like the sunlight through the leaves.

"It's difficult for me to understand the contentment you feel here," Breeze said. "You had all this thrust upon you. You were never given a choice. I'd be bitter, yet you're not. It's hard for me to believe somewhere, buried deep, you don't long for more."

"Nowhere, deep or otherwise. I love this place, and my work."

Breeze shook his head, and even as he smiled, sadness and regret shone in his eyes. "We're just very different men, you and I."

"Yes." Now Alain intuited what Breeze left unsaid: there could be nothing between them. The loss of that possibility that was never a possibility hurt more than it should have.

"Do you want me to leave off playing at swords with Fenn?"

"No. He's just a boy. If I forbid him to do it, he'll just want to do it more. I can only hope it will pass, and that eventually he'll take an interest in learning about grapes and wine. We should go. They'll be gnawing holes in the cart."

"Is this a tradition?" Breeze asked as Alain helped him navigate the steep old steps.

"Going up to the lake for Courtenay's birthday? I suppose it is. My sister loved it there, and it's beautiful this time of year. We've been going since Courtenay was two. It's really our last chance for a day to relax before the real work starts around the vineyard."

"Real work?" Breeze sounded incredulous. "You're up before sunrise as it is."

Alain laughed as he helped Breeze onto the bench and climbed up next to him. The children looked comfortable in the back of the cart, so Alain took the reins and turned the horses to the gate and the road leading north. "Wait until Berris's Moon. When the grapes reach their ideal ripeness, we pick them and press them. We work until the work is done and all the juice is in barrels. Sometimes it takes three days and three nights without rest, sometimes more. Everyone picks grapes, and it can be grueling, but when it's done, we have a grand celebration, usually open a few barrels from the year before." Alain realized Breeze would be long gone by Berris's Moon, and he cursed himself. He was going to miss the other man.

"Well, if I ever grow wealthy, I'm coming here to buy all the wine for my estate. It's the best I ever tasted."

Alain struggled with the idea he wanted to express. His tongue felt thick enough to fill his mouth. "You could come back. Pay us a visit now and then. I'll give you all the wine you want."

"Alain...."

"Never mind. It was a stupid idea."

Breeze put his hand on Alain's knee for a moment. "No, it's a kind and wonderful idea, but life is unpredictable. I have no way to know where I'll be sent."

Alain didn't respond, and the silence that fell between them wasn't completely uncomfortable. He let the ponies plod along at a slow pace; for this one day, he didn't have to rush. The countryside along the road north from the vineyard toward Estrella Lake had suffered from the mage's fire. Most of the trees were blackened and twisted, though here and there new leaves struggled to burst from the charred wood. Grass sprung from the scorched ground, as sparse as the beard Alain had once tried to grow, but trying. Life struggled and fought against death, and slowly, it was gaining ground. The farther north they traveled, the thicker the hedgerows between the fields, the greener the copses of trees, and the denser the bracken and berry fronds growing alongside the road. Above them, a robin's egg sky dotted with puffs of cloud stretched toward the mountains in the distance. By midmorning, the sun grew so strong Breeze unlaced the front of his yellow shirt and rolled up his sleeves.

It took a few hours to reach the southern shore of Estrella Lake. As soon as Alain reined the ponies to a stop, Courtenay and Fenn vaulted over the side of the cart and hit the ground running. High-pitched squeals and giggles filled the air as they sprinted along the narrow path edged in high, pale grass and curling rushes, toward the water's edge.

"It's nice to see them happy," Alain said as he hopped to the gravelly ground to secure the horses to a tree stump. He went around to the back of the cart to fetch their feedbags and a few handfuls of grain. "There's so much to do back at the vineyard that I didn't know if we should take a day to come up here this year. I'm glad we did."

"Thank you for bringing me along. You didn't have to," Breeze said.

"I wanted to." Alain tucked the basket between his elbow and ribs and carried the blankets with his good arm. Seeing him with his hands full, Breeze swung his legs over the edge of the cart and carefully lowered himself down. Even hurt, he possessed a grace, an efficiency of movement that Alain delighted in watching. Breeze came around to the back and found his walking stick. One of the children must have packed it for him. Together, they made their way to the shore. Alain spread out the blankets while Courtenay and Fenn kicked water at each other and squealed.

Breeze shielded his eyes from the sun. "Goddesses, what a sight. I had no idea it was so vast. I cannot even see to the other shore. It's beautiful."

Alain joined him, the surface of the great lake reflecting the blue sky, clouds, and grand mountains wreathing it, the warm sun glinting off the ripples of the gentle waves. He took a deep breath of the scent of the water, the grass, and the evergreens growing thick farther up the shore. Holding it in his chest, he closed his eyes. "Everything here is so clean and pure. This lake is the heart of Selindria and Gaeltheon. It feeds the Kanda River, and the river feeds the rest of the land. Do you believe the tears of the goddesses filled this lake, as we're told in the temples?"

"Oh, I don't know. It's an amazing place, whether they did or didn't." Breeze leaned heavily on his stick. Bless him, he still tired so easily.

"Would you like to sit down?" Alain asked.

"I'd actually like to walk a little," Breeze said. "Could I trouble you for some help again?"

Alain was only too happy to agree. He took the stick from Breeze's hand and left it with their things before grasping his elbow. Taking slow steps, they strolled along the edge of the water, so close it sometimes washed over Alain's left foot and shocked him with cold. Breeze chuckled every time he shrieked. A few steps on dry land pressed the water out of the holes that held his laces with an obscene squishing sound, but his wool sock beneath clung to his skin. They walked a little way, taking in the rock formations and small islands extending out into the lake and even venturing onto an outcrop to catch a glimpse of the ancient temple to the Mother Goddess, the oldest sanctuary in the kingdom. It had been carved directly from the mountain rock, a massive structure, gray, simple in some ways, but towering, dozens of windows looking down on the holy lake, the mountain ledge serving as its roof held up by rough-hewn columns that dwarfed the oldest trees.

Before he considered his actions, Alain disengaged from the crook of Breeze's arm and took his warm, rough hand. He squeezed and Breeze squeezed back. They looked at each other, smiled, let their shoulders brush together, and looked back at the temple. Alain didn't know how long they stood together, but he felt more peace than he had since the fire, even alongside the hollowness of Boyce not being here. He missed him fiercely, but it didn't diminish his memory of what they'd had together for Alain to enjoy the beauty of the lake and the sun on his shoulders. In a strange way the edges of his current happiness collided with the emptiness of his loss, forming new patterns from the ripples they left over the surface of his spirit. The complex designs shifted and changed before Alain could study them, so he abandoned trying and just watched the swells and wrinkles, thinking there might be some beauty on the surface, if not beneath.

A piercing shriek made them both flinch and turn. Alain's initial worry evaporated when he saw Courtenay and Fenn fighting over what looked like a piece of driftwood. "I guess we should split them up."

"They'll be getting hungry, for certain," Breeze agreed. They walked together until they got within a few hundred yards of the children. When Breeze dropped Alain's fingers, Alain hadn't realized that pit inside had started to fill, maybe only a teaspoon at a time, until it reopened. Looking at Breeze, the strong sun lighting the planes of his body as he looked out over the lake, turning his skin to golden brown satin, and the hair Alain would have called black to a tapestry of chestnut, mahogany, and coal, with a few jewellike threads of crimson and gold on the topmost layer, just reminded Alain what he couldn't have. Breeze… Breeze was beautiful, and his friend, but they had not a single dream in common. Turning away, Alain crouched to smooth the blankets the light wind off the lake had rumpled into soft peaks and valleys, and then he began taking food from the basket while Breeze collected the children.

It being Courtenay's eleventh birthday, Alain had prepared and packed all her favorite foods: goat cheese soft enough to spread on herbed bread, a cold chicken salad with dried apples and raisins served on the spring's first miniature lettuce leaves, boiled eggs sliced into pretty little circles, and a honey cake topped with preserved berries and jam. Their location afforded them a view of the distant peak of Starmont, the fabled home of the Thirteen Goddesses, and even the highest peaks of the L'Estrella family's castle, poking out over the blue green forest off to the west.

"So, eleven years old," Breeze said, lifting his glass and making Courtenay's cheeks pink to match the wildflowers swaying in the light wind around them. "That's exciting. In Espero, your gift would be starting to manifest right about now if you were a mage, and you'd be choosing which schools of magic you wanted to study and meeting with mentors."

"I've read a little about Espero," she said. "It seems so strange. Is it true the ladies and the men all dress alike, and that they don't wear proper shoes?"

Breeze tossed his head back and laughed. "Well, it's much warmer, princess, so we—they—wear open shoes to let their feet breathe. Sandals. And yes, the women and men also wear loose, thin trousers for the same reasons."

"And the ladies walk around with their bare arms showing?" Courtenay lowered her voice at the scandal of it, and Breeze darted his gaze to Alain, as if wondering how much to say.

Alain offered him a nod and a smile, and Breeze said, "It's very hot, little love. I doubt you can imagine it."

"But lady mages can sit on the council. Isn't that right?"

"It is," Breeze said. "Magical ability and wisdom are more important there than the sex of the person possessing them."

"That seems like the way it should be everywhere." Courtenay looked at Alain, her eyes wide and her lower lip pushed out. "Why isn't it like that here? Why can't ladies here be important if they're wise?"

Alain didn't know what to say. When she phrased the question that way, he couldn't think of a single reason why they shouldn't. "Well, the priestesses of the goddesses are even more important than the king and his vassals."

She frowned and pushed her fair eyebrows together in an expression that made her look much older, wiser, and more cynical than her years. "That isn't the same thing. Espero sounds like a wonderful place. Is it wonderful, Breeze?"

A taint of bitterness flavored his tone when he answered. "Sure it is. As long as you're a mage."

After they finished their meal, Fenn grew bold enough to kick off his shoes, bunch his trousers around his knees, and wade to his ankles into the frigid water to try to catch the slippery silver minnows that lived among the shoals. Courtenay took her current book and wandered to a soft patch of sunlit grass, sat down, and arranged her simple skirts around her. She retreated more and more into the pages of stories, and Alain wasn't sure it was the best way for her to deal with her pain. But a little smile tugged at her lips as she read, so Alain decided not to make waves, not today. He dropped that stone into the waters of his mind and let it sink. The ripples of all the stones he'd plunked into that dark liquid overlapped at the edges and blurred until he couldn't separate loss and grief from the beauty around him, the contentment of a perfect day. He pulled his boots off and draped his socks over a stone to let them dry in the sun. He stretched out on his back, folded his arms beneath his head, closed his eyes, and listened to the waves lapping against the shore, the call of the birds, the wind in the needles of the trees, and the high-pitched giggles and squeals of Fenn as he splashed through the frigid water in pursuit of fish.

Alain didn't realize he'd nodded off until Breeze shifting next to him made him stir and lift his head. They lay facing each other, their foreheads pressed together, Breeze's parted lips just grazing the corner of Alain's mouth. He was deep asleep, but his eyes fluttered open when Alain sat up to check on the children. Courtenay still sat reading. At first he didn't see Fenn, but then the boy came running up the shore, his wet feet slapping against the sand. Giggling, he dropped a small cracked shell next to Alain, adding it to a little mound of crustaceans, smooth stones, and twisted bits of wood. When he ran off again, Alain flopped down on his back.

"Are you all right?" Breeze asked in a sleepy voice.

Instead of looking at him, Alain watched the feathery clouds slipping across the blue sky. "It's strange. I *am* happy. Just not as happy. I'll never be as happy as I once was, and neither will they. But they need this. They need to see life goes on, and even if it's been diminished, it can still be good. With everything they've been through, they need to know there's still beauty. Hope. Something to look forward to."

Breeze brushed the too-long hair back from Alain's forehead and left his fingers tangled in the strands. "So do you."

With a small smile, Alain closed his eyes again and let his head tilt until his temple rested against Breeze's shoulder.

Just before the sun set, they ate another simple meal of bread, chicken, and cheese, then packed up the cart to head for home. Before long, the children slumbered in the back of the cart, lulled by the gentle creak and rocking of the axles. It had worked since they were infants. Alain watched the stars blink alight one by one against the pink, purple, and blue layers of the darkening sky, lost in thought. He kept looking over, expecting to see Boyce on the bench next to him, as he'd been every year, and when he saw Breeze... it only confused him. Part of him had been buried with Boyce, and what had been torn away still screamed, oozed, and ached with phantom pains, but Breeze sitting next to him felt good. None of it made any sense. How could happiness and pain coexist like this? The concentric circles along the surface of his consciousness, their edges overlapping, forming hundreds and thousands of tiny little squares and elongated rectangles where the rings met, changed so fast, made such beautiful, intricate patterns, it hurt his head to try to keep up with them.

After full darkness fell, the chill in the air reminded Alain it was only just spring, and a little of the frost still lingered to bite the tip of his nose and the edges of his ears. An hour from home, he opened the last bottle of wine, took a swig, and passed it to Breeze. They moved a little closer together as they passed the bottle back and forth. The horses knew the way from here, and someone from the stable would be waiting to take them at the main house, just like Alain arranged each year for Courtenay's birthday. This wine, a good batch from several years ago, was strong and tasted of ironstone, green apples, and thick berry jam. Alain had hoped it would numb his pain, but it just splashed against the raw edges of that hole inside him, stinging. He thought of Breeze's wound, of peeling the dead skin away until the red blood flowed freely, and shuddered. They hadn't changed his dressings that morning, and now Alain worried he was too drunk. "Sorry," he mumbled.

"What?"

"Your dressings."

"Oh. I think they'll be fine till tomorrow," Breeze said. "They're almost healed, thanks to you. I know it hasn't been easy. I know you hated messing with the gruesome fucking things. I'm afraid I'd puke on my boots if I had to do it. I can't thank you enough."

"That's not why I did it," Alain said. "Not so you'd thank me."

"I know. You did it because you're a damn good man. I'm fucking lucky it was you who found me, or I'd be dead or worse. Don't think I don't know it."

"You should watch your mouth," Alain scolded with no real affront behind it.

"Sorry."

Alain shrugged.

"You don't like warriors much, do you?"

"I don't like being at the mercy of them, of battles that have nothing to do with people like me. Whatever the struggles between them that they feel are so important, people like us are just acceptable losses. We just want to live our lives. I want to grow grapes and make wine. Why can't I do that in peace without men with swords and bows pushing me to the wayside because whatever they're doing is so much more significant?"

"Me too?"

"Breeze… at first I thought you were worse, because you don't even fight for any misguided sense of righteousness. You just do it for money."

"And now? What do you think now?"

"I don't know," Alain admitted. "I see a good man when I look at you, but…. Maybe you were right. We're just too different." He reined the tired ponies to a stop near the steps to the porch, where a young man waited to lead them back to the stables.

Courtenay roused herself enough to sleepwalk up the porch steps and inside to her room. Alain expected to carry Fenn to bed as he did most nights, but the boy surprised him by jumping from the cart and stumbling inside, his polished wooden sword swaying like a tail behind him and bouncing off the edge of each step with a clatter as he ascended. Alain unloaded their basket, blankets, the yarrow flowers Courtenay had wrapped in a towel, and the pail of shells, twigs, and a few dead fish Fenn had collected, and set them just inside the front door to worry about in the morning. Then he went to the cart to help Breeze step down. The long day, no matter how pleasant, had left Breeze moving so stiffly he struggled with the few stairs leading to the house, and once inside, he leaned against the wall by the door and panted with strain.

Alain combed some sweaty hair from where it clung to his forehead and cheek, trailing his fingertips down the hot, sweat-slippery planes of Breeze's face until he felt the faintest hint of emerging stubble along his jawline. He let his tentative touches move to the gnarled skin beside Breeze's ear and along his long, elegant neck. At first Breeze flinched, but then their eyes met, and he tilted his head to let Alain explore, exposing his damaged parts. The bravery and trust in the gesture made Alain's breath snag on its way out, and before he knew what he was doing, he'd bent in and let his lower lip graze the whorls of tissue below Breeze's earlobe, his mouth trembling against their texture. The faintest flavor of Breeze's perspiration lingered for his tongue to flick away as he drew back, breathing hard.

"Alain...." Breeze grasped his biceps and twirled him, reversing their positions, and pressed Alain against the wall next to the open door. His teeth gleamed white in the moonlight spilling in, and his eyes glinted as his breath crested hot and wet over Alain's lips and chin. "Please forgive me."

Before Alain could question him, Breeze pressed his chest against Alain's and ran his hands down Alain's arms until he could grasp Alain's hands, squeeze them tight, and pin them next to his hips. Their lips crashed together like the water against the shore, lapping, caressing, pulling away, and sliding back together. Breeze drew Alain's lower lip into his mouth, tugged at it, released it, and licked across the sensitive flesh before tilting his head and sealing their mouths together. Alain flexed his thighs to still the wobbling of his knees as the tingling at the root of his body spread to his fingertips and toes, alighting every inch of his skin until it felt like his hair stood out from his head and thunderstorms moved through his veins. Breeze released his hands to wrap his arms around Alain's waist and pull him closer. Alain reached up to curl his fingers in the springy hair at Breeze's nape and hold on as Breeze pushed his tongue past the seam of his lips. Alain curled his tongue out to meet it, taste it, wrap around it. One of them, or maybe both, groaned as Breeze slid his hands up under Alain's shirt to knead the small of his back. Alain melted under his touch, his body hanging from Breeze's like a limp rag thrown over a hook. He tasted so good—smelled good too: pure water, sunlight, evergreens, yarrow, and pungent, aroused man. When Breeze pulled away from Alain's lips to nibble across his jaw and lick the sweat from his neck, Alain wriggled free of his grasp.

"I'm sorry, Alain. I had to. I had to know what it would feel like to do that. What you'd taste like. I… goddesses." He reached for Alain, but Alain darted away around him to the foot of the steps.

"I… I can't. I'm sorry." He didn't hear how Breeze responded, because he hurried up the stairs and into his room, where he closed the door and collapsed on his bed. This room was still too quiet, too cold. It had once been full of Boyce's sounds, his scent, just the comforting feel of his existence. Every time Alain entered it, he expected that familiar, accepting presence and it pierced his heart every time he realized it was gone forever. It had been a little over two moons, and already Alain was forgetting the exact shape of Boyce's eyes, the timbre of his low chuckle against Alain's belly. Too soon, all evidence of him, beyond his ink portrait in the library, had started to fade, and Alain couldn't hold on to it any more than he could hold on to the morning mist as the sun burned it off. What was wrong with him?

He wasn't betraying Boyce, he reminded himself as he touched the swollen center of his lower lip and remembered Breeze's teeth and tongue on it. Boyce was gone. "He's gone. He's really gone. Goddesses, what do you want from me? I know I am to be alone. Why do you feel the need to taunt me? You're as wicked as the Cast-Down. Worse, for your illusion of caring. At least the Cast-Down admit they delight in cruelty."

He wanted to go to his kitchen or cellars for wine, get so drunk he couldn't feel a thing, not even the draw to be near Breeze that drowned out all the other feelings, the confusion and pain incinerated in the passion he felt for the exotic mercenary. He wanted to crumble in an inebriated heap and clutch his knees and just let life move along and leave him behind, hazy and oblivious on the floor. But there was work to be done on the vineyard and people depending on his guidance, so he took his clothes off and settled beneath his blankets, staring at the dark ceiling beams and white plaster until they blurred into unconsciousness.

Chapter
Nine

BREEZE FINISHED cleaning the breakfast dishes and set them on a towel beside the sink to dry. As usual, Alain had barely spoken to him during the morning meal. Since they'd kissed after their outing to the lake, Alain had made sure to spend no more time than absolutely necessary in Breeze's presence. Even when he'd changed his dressings that morning, he'd been silent and unwilling to meet Breeze's eyes. It fucking stung. It hurt more than Alain peeling up the few remaining chunks of dead flesh.

It was time Breeze did something about that, or, more importantly, something to repay the people who'd given so much to nurse him back to health when they could have left him to die. His fortune waited back in Rosecairn, but while he was a guest at Mountain Shadow Vineyard, he'd do what he could to square his debt. He didn't like an unfulfilled obligation dangling over his head, so he made his way to the foot of the steep stairs, feeling weak. He hadn't been sleeping well, tormented by visions of flaxen hair, acres of creamy skin, the hint of the lithe muscles he'd felt against him, and goddesses, those eyes—like clearest summer sky, but so much deeper, complex, layered like the wine he made....

His lips. Innocent and vulnerable, yet yielding. Wanting. Starved, even. Scared, though. But why? Alain had drunk from the fount of Breeze's lust like a man who'd just crossed a desert, but then he'd run. Why? Breeze was determined to find out, and to give as much as he took from this vineyard. After finishing the dishes, he grasped the whitewashed stone wall to drag himself up the steps. His left arm and leg still didn't work right, but to the Shades' with it. He'd make it. He'd overcome worse.

He made it up three steps before the outside of his thigh cramped and he couldn't lift that leg. Wedging his right hand under his knee to force his stubborn foot to the next stair accomplished nothing, and after several moments of struggling to get his leg to lift the few inches to the next ledge, he swore with frustration.

The distant echo of his mother's voice resounded in his head. *Put some effort into it, you idiot boy. If you actually tried, you might manage something close to useful.*

He put effort in, he tried, but his leg wouldn't budge. Fucking Shades. Fuck, fuck, fuck! He couldn't even make it up a staircase.

Useless and lazy. That's your problem. His father's scathing tones this time. *Too content to lounge around. This is going to take some work, you slug. Don't you have any pride?*

He had pride, too much pride to be undone by a narrow flight of stairs. Too much to prove. Gritting his teeth, he made that leg lift his left foot, even though a shuddery pain shot up his inner thigh and groin, into his belly and ribs. The side of his boot scraped the edge of the stone step, but he managed to drag it to the next, and the next. Three steps before he had to rest his back against the wall and wince against the throbbing in his leg, ribs, and head.

Is that the best you can do? You make me sick. His mother.

"Fuck you, bitch." He bent in half and grasped the steps above him, stepping with his good leg and dragging the injured one behind. By the time he emerged from the kitchen, his arms wobbled from the strain. He was really fucked up, but he was healing. It would take time, maybe more time than he wanted to spend on this boring scrap of land at the base of the mountains. But it didn't mean he was useless. He wasn't fucking worthless, just hurt! At the top of the stairs, he sank down to the floor to sit and stare at the sun pouring through the windows along the front of the house. He allowed himself a moment to close his eyes and lean the back of his head against the wall, at least until the world stopped spinning around him and his arm and leg didn't feel like a stretched bow string ready to snap.

Bleeding Shades, he wanted Alain. As much as it disgusted him to depend on someone else, he wanted Alain to come through the door, help him up, and drape Breeze's arm across his shoulders. Alain didn't pity him or find him wanting, like his parents and family had. He just understood Breeze was injured. No one had ever taken care of him as Alain had, without any hope of recompense. Breeze had been sure, at first, that Alain must have expected something from the effort. Maybe just to feel important, to experience the power of having someone at his mercy. Gratitude to make him feel special. But he didn't. Alain had helped him because he'd needed it. Simple. Simple, but so bloody damned complicated and confusing.

Breeze grasped the heavy wooden trim around the doorjamb to hoist himself up and took a moment to close his eyes until the sparkles faded from behind his lids. One thing he knew for certain—he'd fucked up his friendship with Alain before it had been allowed to grow. Smashed it like a tender little vine under a soldier's boot. He had to make it right.

He found a flurry of activity outside: an old woman guiding a flock of ewes and lambs with a supple switch, a man driving a cart stacked with bales of hay, a trio of girls with white kerchiefs over their hair carrying pails from the well. Goats gnawing at the bracken. Geese honking. Children laughing, shrieking, and chasing each other up and down the muddy paths. Fields full of people.

Breeze didn't see Alain anywhere between the house and the gate, so he wandered around toward the fruit trees and gardens, past the duck pond, and across the bridge spanning the frothy little stream. His determination faltered when he looked out across the fields. Alain had told him many of their crops had been lost, but seeing the miles and miles of scorched ground, left rutted and inky by the recent rains, made his heart sink into the hot, churning mess in his belly. These people hadn't deserved that. They'd had nothing to do with King Agarick, the Roses, cursed, cat-shit mad Yarroway L'Estrella, or the battle. He added another line to his list of things he had to make right. But first he had to find Alain.

When he asked them, a group of men with spades and hoes pointed Breeze to the southeast. Taking slow, careful steps, he headed in that direction, but before he'd made it even a few hundred yards, he had to stop and rest, sitting on a stump. After he recovered his strength, he walked a little farther, then sat down again. At this rate, it would take him days to get to Alain. Luckily, a hay wagon passed on the road, and Breeze waved down the old man driving it. Breeze felt stiff and cramped by the time they reached a sprawling field untouched by the fire, green and full of life. Full of people, all of them bent down over the vines, working so intently they didn't notice him wandering aimlessly between the rows. That was probably for the best, since even Breeze's short walk had left him feeling like something a rabid dog shat out, and more than likely it showed. He wished he'd brought his walking stick along as he looked out over the expansive field of vines. Pherara, it must have been glorious before the fire. If he could, he wanted to help it return to its former splendor. He didn't know why he cared—beyond repaying what he owed Alain—but he decided to ponder it later.

Sweat soaked his borrowed shirt at the armpits and darkened a V down his chest by the time he finally spotted Alain hunched over a thick, gnarled vine with a grin on his face. Breeze stopped to watch him a moment. Alain smiled, happy and distracted. He really did love his work. Fuck, he was beautiful with the sun glinting off his spun-gold hair. Breeze had never meant to kiss him that night. He'd had no right, but goddesses, he'd looked irresistible with his cheeks and the bridge of his nose painted apple red by the sun at the lake, smelling of wine, wildflowers, and sweet sweat. And he'd touched the ugly scars on Breeze's neck without recoiling, and then he'd put his wonderful mouth on that sensitive, newly birthed skin—

Alain paused in his work, mopped his berries-and-cream face with his sleeve, and took a few swigs from a leather canteen on his belt. Gawking at him and entertaining filthy fantasies would do no good, so Breeze walked over, rubbed at his stiff thigh, and clumsily crouched down next to him.

Alain jumped, clearly startled. The sun had burned his nose beet red, and it would peel before evening. He should have a hat, something to protect his fair face....

"Breeze, goddesses! What are you doing out of bed? How did you get all the way over here?"

He smiled past his pain and dizziness so he wouldn't worry Alain, but he accepted the canteen and drank. Handing it back, he said, "I'm climbing the walls in that house, friend. Besides, there's work to be done. What are you doing, anyway?"

"Trimming the vines. We need the ones we have left to be as productive as possible, and, well. With the people we lost and those who are hurt, it's quite an effort."

"I'm here," Breeze said. "You can use me." Damn, he hadn't meant that the way it sounded. "I mean, I want to help. Tell me what needs done."

Alain eyed him with concern, and Breeze forcibly let the tension out of his shoulders. "Alain, I want to help you. Show me what to do. You just said you need people, and I'm here."

"All right." Alain reached into one of the leather pouches on his belt and handed Breeze a heavy pair of shears. "But if you get tired—"

"Goddesses. Just tell me what to do." Fuck, even that sounded like a dirty suggestion to Breeze, but Alain didn't seem to notice. They knelt down in the moist, sucking soil together, and Alain snipped off a little tendril sprouting three leaves and let it spiral down to the dark soil. He continued clipping along the crusty vine, as thick as his wrist, cutting off everything newborn and green, save a few broad leaves near the base. "I don't understand. How does this help it grow?"

Alain turned his head and smiled. For the first time in days their eyes met and held. "You have to cut it back to the bare stock, Breeze. You can't coddle the vines, just let them sprawl all over. You have to make them fight, make them focus everything they soak up from the rain, the sun, and the land into grapes and not leaves or pretty spirals. Give them the bare minimum to survive, and they won't waste their energy. We need grapes out of them. Go on, then. Try."

Wielding the shears in his right hand, Breeze focused as he cut the fresh offshoots from the ancient brown vine. It seemed sad to cull the new life, but he trusted Alain, and he wanted to help, so he trimmed as much as he thought he could.

Alain shook his head. "More. Leave it just enough to keep itself alive. That will make it fight. Look at it. If you try, you can see its essence, that part it needs to *be*. See that, and cut away everything extraneous to its purpose. That way the vine isn't distracted. It knows what it needs to do."

Breeze understood that. He'd left Espero with nothing but the will to survive and prove himself, and the singularity of purpose had helped him shape himself into someone worthwhile. He moved to the next vine and cut until he thought he'd destroyed it. Alain nodded, said, "Good."

Together, they moved to the next pair of vines, and the next. Though he grew tired quickly, and his muscles twitched from hunching over, Breeze found a sense of satisfaction in the work. He turned to Alain. "You're good at this. You're really an artist. Painting masterpieces with the blood of these vines. Hah! You're even rubbing off on me. That was rather poetic, wasn't it?"

Alain smiled, met his eyes. "I appreciate you thinking so highly of our wines. And I appreciate your help, Breeze. How are you feeling?"

Strange. Satisfied. Fulfilled in the work. What the fuck? "I'm fine for now."

"Well, let me know if you're not. You were hurt really badly."

"Aye. And you healed me. Alain, you're my friend. That's important to me. I… after the lake… goddesses, I'm sorry for what I did." He leaned a little closer so the other workers wouldn't hear his next words. "You were just so beautiful, and I needed something good… I needed to remember life could be good. And you… you are *so* good. Damn. I don't know what to say, other than I shouldn't have done it, and I apologize. I don't want you to feel strange around me. Is there any way we can just forget it?"

Alain chuckled. "Forget it?" He snipped a curled tendril from a vine. "No, I can't do that."

"I should go."

"No, Breeze. You're not ready. Not to fight again."

It was true. He'd barely managed to ascend a staircase and cross a field. Yet, "I don't want to stay here if I make you uncomfortable. You have done so much for me. You mean a great deal to me. I want us to be friends."

"Then we will," Alain said without looking up from the vine he tended. "We'll be friends. Until you're well enough to return to your life at Rosecairn. And then we'll just be good memories for each other. Memories of friends."

Goddesses, he sounded sad. Broken. Breeze wanted to do something, but he didn't know how, so he trimmed vines alongside Alain until the sun plummeted into the western sea and he could barely rise from his knees. Thankfully, a passing cart gave them a ride back to the house, because pride or not, Breeze wouldn't have made it on foot.

THEY SPENT the next several days pruning, and then the time came to fertilize the fields. Alongside Alain, Breeze helped spread the pungent mixture of goat, horse, sheep, and cow shit, combined with the skins of last year's grapes, around the healthy vines and over the burnt fields where Alain hoped to plant the roots he'd been coaxing. The following week, they worked with scythes to mow the soft swards of grass growing between the rows of vines. Then it came time to trim the plants again. In their short hours of spare time, they took care of the kitchen gardens and fruit trees. They worked from dawn until dusk, bathed, ate dinner, and fell into bed. Breeze slept better than he ever had, feeling, at the end of each hard day, that he'd accomplished something important. Helped. Paid Alain back, at least a little.

And if Alain didn't linger or steal glances while he bathed, if they never again fell asleep pressed together, at least they spent their days talking, sharing things, and being friends. *Friends*. Friends that would one day be only memories.

FIGHTING AND waging campaigns had nothing on farm work for conditioning Breeze's muscles. He sat down to dinner in the sitting room aching and gratefully drank from the wine goblet Alain passed him. He never remembered being so hungry, or a simple pork stew with turnips smelling so delectable. "What's on the table for tomorrow?" he asked between slurps of the delicious gravy.

"Tomorrow we have to start preparing for Y'Airns Market," Alain said, dabbing the corners of his mouth with his napkin.

"I want to come along," Courtenay said.

"Me too." Fenn scrubbed some thick broth from his chin with the back of his hand.

"I'm not sure that's a good idea," Alain said. "It's a long journey and days of sleeping in a caravan. It's hard work."

"Oh, come on, Alain!" Courtenay protested. "There's so much to see at that market! It's one of the biggest in the area. We don't want to miss out and be left here alone."

He looked into his wooden bowl and scraped little circles and swirls against the bottom with his spoon. "You won't have much chance to see all the things offered for sale. I'll be at our stand from the opening of the market until it closes, letting patrons taste the wine and hoping they'll buy some. That's the point of going, after all."

Surprisingly, Breeze found himself excited by the idea of going to the market and showing the children the exotic goods. He imagined Courtenay's wide eyes as she perused the cloth and jewelry and Fenn bouncing and darting from stall to stall. They'd have books. Weapons. Armor shops. Not that he had any coin here in Lockhaven. Still, he'd been isolated on the vineyard since the fire and he itched for some excitement. Maybe he could even convince Alain to let go of some worry enough to enjoy himself.

"Alain, I hope I'm not out of line here, and of course the decision's yours, but if it would help, I'd be happy to come along. I can look after Courtenay and Fenn, and I'm sure I can do something to assist you as well." Goddesses, every word he said to the man sounded like an obscene proposition, even though he wasn't doing it on purpose.

Alain tapped his spoon against the rim of his bowl, staring down into his lap for so long Breeze wondered if he'd upset him. Maybe he had no right to offer to help with the children. They weren't his family, but he couldn't help liking the little blighters. Finally Alain looked up, candlelight reflecting off his eyes, and smiled. "I…. All right. Thank you, Breeze. This could be fun, couldn't it? Goddesses, I just hope we can sell most of what we bring to market. That would take a lot off my mind, and maybe even give me some coin to work with getting this place productive again." He lifted his glass, twirled the stem in long, graceful fingers Breeze thought about more often than he should, and stared into the rubicund liquid. When he spoke again, it was to himself. "Even the root cuttings I've managed to nurture won't bear so much as a cluster of fruit until next season, at the earliest. Some of the best vintages survived the fire. If we can get a good price for them, maybe I'll have enough to have some vines delivered from Espero and Elvara…."

Fenn had grown bored enough to pick apart his bread and drop doughy little clumps into his own cup of watered-down wine, but Courtenay narrowed her eyes and set her spoon down without making a sound. "Alain, is the vineyard in trouble?"

He colored and trapped a trembling lower lip between his teeth. Breeze wished he could clasp Alain's hand for comfort. To support him as his too-clever niece glared. He stammered before answering her. "Many of our crops were damaged. You know that. I've taken root cuttings, and they're growing. I'll be able to make them grow."

"And until then, we don't have enough grapes to make the wine for next year," the girl deduced. "We won't have enough wine to sell to buy the things we need for the vineyard, or to pay the people who work on it. I'm not stupid."

"It's not for you to worry over," Alain said. "You're a child. The vineyard is my responsibility. Just mine."

Breeze wanted to reach over and touch his shoulder. He wanted to tell him he didn't have to bear his burden alone, but he left the hollow words unsaid. By next year, he would be long gone, with troubles of his own. By then, he would have likely forgotten all about the alluring vintner and his wonderful children. Yes, this place and these people would soon be a distant memory.

"What's going to happen to us?" Courtenay demanded.

"You need to calm yourself," Alain said in a tone Breeze had never heard. Disciplined and demanding. "I told you it isn't your problem."

"It will be if I starve! I wish my pa was here."

"Well, he isn't, now, is he? No. I'm afraid I'm all you have left!"

"I hate this place!" She hurled her wooden bowl against the stone inglenook behind Breeze and Alain. It bounced and thudded against the floor, spewing brown broth. Alain stared with wide eyes as she stood, gathered up her skirts, and ran sobbing up the stairs.

Fenn dove against Alain's chest, howling and sniffling. "I want my papa! He's never coming back, and we're all going to die!"

Petting the boy's hair, Alain shushed him. He opened his mouth to speak, but then he closed it again, wrinkled his eyes shut, and held his nephew. Soon, tears sparkled on his long, golden lashes.

"There, now," Breeze said, patting the lad's back. "Nobody's dying or starving. Your Uncle Alain here is brilliant at growing grapes. Before you know it, this place will be crawling with vines, grapes just dropping off before you can even pick them. You have to believe that, 'cause I have no doubt. Alain won't fail. I know he won't."

"Really?" Alain looked up and met Breeze's gaze with sparkling eyes.

"No doubt. And little man, you be strong. There's nothing wrong with missing your pa, but you have to learn to get by on your own and help take care of your family. Remember to act in ways so he'll look down from the goddesses and be proud you're his son."

Fenn stood and squared his shoulder, a determined expression on his face that added years to him. "Yes, tam! I will make him proud, and you and Uncle Alain too. I can be a man, and I can help with the grapes."

"Good man. Now, why don't you get these dishes gathered up and take them down to the sink? After they're cleaned up, we'll go out to the orchard and practice for a while."

With a wide grin, Fenn scooped up the bowls and bounded toward the kitchen stairs.

Alain heaved a sigh. "Thank you, I suppose. Even you have a better idea what to say to them than I do. At least you made him feel better. How am I supposed to raise them? Goddesses, maybe I should have you talk to Courtenay as well."

Breeze slid a little closer but didn't touch Alain. "I will if you ask me to, but I don't think it's a good idea. She'll be fine. She's a lot like you from what I can tell. Holds everything in. Won't ask for help. Do that long enough, and it builds up until something has to break. Let her cry it out. She'll feel better. Sometimes you just have to let go, you know? You should try it."

Again, the double entendre he hadn't intended whisked right over Alain's head. He turned his hands over, rested them on his knees, and stared into his empty palms. "I'm scared. I'm going to fail, lose this place. It's been here for over five hundred years, and I'm the one who's going to let it fall." He clenched his hands to trembling fists. "Boyce always used to say I could make anything grow, roses from ironstone, and I guess I can, but I can't make them grow any faster. And now he's gone, and it's all on me. I'm… I'm alone, and I don't know what to do."

Fuck it. Fuck it to the Shades. Alain was hurting, so Breeze held him. He wrapped his arms around Alain's shaking shoulders and drew Alain's head to his chest. At first Alain struggled, but then he collapsed against Breeze as if he no longer had the fortitude to support his own body. He grasped Breeze's shirt and choked back sobs. Breeze raked his fingers through Alain's soft hair and moved his hand down his back, rubbing what he hoped were soothing circles over the overwrought muscles there. "Go on, friend. Just let go of it. It's just me and you here, and I won't think any less of you. Go on, Alain, you need this."

"I... I can't fail all these people. I don't know what to do. Boyce is gone, and I have to do it all alone. Why did he have to be taken? We were supposed to stand together. Now... now—goddesses." He crumpled against Breeze and cried softly, his whole body convulsing with his pain over past loss and fear for the future. For probably half an hour, he choked, hiccupped, and mumbled against Breeze's chest, until he'd soaked Breeze's shirt with his snot and tears. Breeze held tight. Alain needed this. Needed to get it out.

When his sobs died to sniffles, Alain sat up, scrubbed at his cheeks, and wiped his nose on his sleeve. Breeze looked at his reddened, streaked cheeks and puffy eyes, and Alain turned away, clearly ashamed. "I feel like a fool. Goddesses, I shouldn't be blubbering like a child. I'm... sorry you had to see that."

Breeze chuckled softly and raked some damp hair off Alain's forehead. He caught a pair of straggling tears on his thumb when Alain blinked them loose. "I'm sorry you had to help me take a piss, scrape the rotten pus off my burns, and likely wipe my ass. I think you've seen me in a sorrier fucking state than I've seen you. Do you hold it against me?"

Alain let out a fractured breath that ruffled Breeze's hair and enveloped him in the scent of wine and herbs. "You were hurt."

"So are you," Breeze said, absently twisting a clump of Alain's hair into a point at the end. Then, in barely a whisper, he said, "I wish I could take care of you like you took care of me." He could take such good care of Alain, make him forget all his troubles for a few hours, make him think he'd gone to the goddesses. But he couldn't. Alain wanted lasting companionship, not a meaningless tumble. If Breeze couldn't offer him that, he had no right to toy with the poor man's already tangled emotions. Still, he brushed his lips across Alain's forehead before standing. "Go on to bed. I'll take care of the dishes and see Fenn gets his bath after we practice."

Alain stood and looked at Breeze across the few feet of space separating them. For a long time, they just stood looking at each other, the crackle of the fire the only sound in the quiet room. "Thank you," Alain finally said with a scratchy voice.

Breeze felt the frayed edges of Alain's husky tone move up his spine, raising gooseflesh and peaking his nipples. One step would close the distance between them, and he could have Alain in his arms again. Instead, they both stood still until Breeze reluctantly moved past Alain, brushing his fingers down Alain's arm on his way to the kitchen. If he couldn't give Alain all of him, he wouldn't tease him with scraps. As much as he wanted the beautiful winemaker, he didn't—had never—wanted the mundane life of a farmer. The sooner he moved on, the better it would be—for both of them.

Chapter
Ten

EIGHT WAGONS, all of them so full of wine their wheels sank into the fecund soil, waited in a line just beyond the gate. After going through the house one final time to check everything was in order, Alain jogged down the road and hopped onto the bench next to Breeze, in front of the enclosed caravan where his family would sleep during the four days of the biggest market in the north. Though he still worried about how much they'd make selling the wine, he felt lighter, less encumbered, after falling apart against Breeze.

The sun's blush had just started creeping up the dome of the sky as they started off, Alain's caravan leading the other eight teams of horses. Though they made slow progress down the rocky mountain paths left gouged by the spring rains, Alain couldn't complain. The newly birthed vines he'd raised from the root cuttings needed this rain, as did the rest of the vines. Goddesses willing, by summer the weather would dry up to help the grapes ripen and keep them from rotting. As he guided his ponies carefully down the mountainside, he wondered what the ash in the soil would impart to the grapes he'd recently planted. Grapes were marvelous things, he'd often thought, soaking up everything around them and transforming it in something almost like a mage's spell. If one knew what to look for, what to taste for when sipping wine, one could tell how hot and wet the season had been, what the winds had been, and what kind of soil or rock had nursed the clusters of fruit. Everything the grapes experienced while on the vine shaped the character of the wine. That was why they trimmed the vines so mercilessly, because pampered grapes made for cowardly wine.

Breeze understood, and he'd become quite good at pruning; he even seemed to enjoy it and would look down on his work with a proud little smile as he wiped the sweat from his face.

Alain turned his eyes, but not his head, to look at Breeze without being noticed. The mercenary tilted his head toward the rising sun, and the soft rays tickled his hair, bringing out all the colors in the long, wavy strands. He'd closed his eyes, and his thick black lashes cast spiky shadows on his sharp cheekbones. With his brick-colored lips slightly parted, he smiled at either the warmth on his face and the fresh scents of verdant growth, or something playing out inside his head.

Just forget it, Alain told himself with a suppressed sigh. *There's no point in imagining something that can't be. He isn't for me. He doesn't want any part of my life. He doesn't owe me, and he has every right to live the life he's chosen.*

But he was so beautiful, and just thinking about him made Alain's insides shudder and tighten. Looking at him made Alain feel light and, well… breezy, like leaves tumbling along on a warm wind. Looking at him made Alain grin like a fool until his cheeks ached, even as it reminded him what he couldn't have and how hollow he'd probably always feel. He'd always known he was unnatural—that he admired men the way the goddesses intended for him to admire women—but no man had ever inspired such a powerful *want* in him. Guiltily, he acknowledged not even Boyce had made him feel this way, even though he had loved Boyce with every fiber of his being. He still loved Boyce—probably always would—but Breeze sparked so much lust in him. He wished he could banish it or ignore it, but he couldn't.

They ate their midday meal on the road—bread, cold ham, and cheese from a basket. By sunset, they'd left the foothills and emerged upon the northern edge of Everdale. Having been born in the mountains, Alain would never get used to the gently rolling hills, the little green patches of high, swaying grass separated by hedgerows. Large herds of sheep and goats dotted the landscape with white and gray, mirroring the clumps of clouds moving slowly across the darkening sky above them. Most of the people who accompanied them were men, either unattached or with wives at home waiting with the children. Blessed Epoch or no, the roads could be dangerous, and when they found a flat patch to stop for the night, they kept the carts in a tight circle. Some of the men lit fires to roast meat or simmer stews, but Alain and his family contented themselves with more cold meat and cheese before falling asleep in the back of the caravan.

By the next evening, they'd reached the pretty little village of Y'Airns, nestled in a shallow valley at the point where Lockhaven, Everdale, and the bairny of Windwake overlapped. Many merchants had made their fortunes since the place had been a simple trading post, and stately ironstone homes with spear-shaped leaded-glass windows stood on either side of the cobbled streets. Alain and his people made their way to the large open space at the center of the town and found a place to set up their booth. Alain wanted it done before they retired, so he'd be ready to greet his earliest customers. Together, the men from Mountain Shadow Winery made tables from boards laid over barrels. They unloaded barrels of wine and arranged them according to vintage and varietal as Alain checked the paper labels he'd placed on them carefully. Then they set up a few canvas canopies to shield their patrons from the sun and keep them comfortable while they perused the goods on offer, as Alain arranged bottles of their best wine on makeshift shelves, then dusted them off with a rag so they'd gleam in the sun. He opened some of the wooden boxes with the vineyard's seal burned along the sides and arranged the contents alongside brass goblets for sampling.

Morning came too early. Worry and wondering had stolen Alain's rest, but he splashed some water on his face, tied his hair back, and went to stand with his wine as the market began to fill with patrons. Soon musicians, acrobats, and other performers lured people, those who lived in Y'Airns as well as the many who'd traveled to visit the famed market, into the square. He opened a few bottles for potential buyers to try and waited. He was no good at drawing people in, engaging them in light conversation. Boyce had always been the one to charm and make small talk. As for Alain, he could make wine, but he was rubbish at talking it up and selling it. Hopefully, after people tasted what he'd created, his wines would sell themselves.

He'd sold several well-aged bottles and a dozen barrels to local taverns and inns by the time Breeze, Courtenay, and Fenn joined him. For a surreal moment, Alain expected Breeze to put a hand on the small of his back and give him a subtle kiss on his cheek, like a partner. Of course he couldn't, and Alain shook off the strange and unexpected fantasy. His lack of sleep was catching up to him. "People are buying," he told the mercenary. "Buying the older, more expensive bottles, and even some of the ice wine is selling. I don't know if it's just their faith in the promised prosperity of this so-called Blessed Epoch, but they're willing to part with their gold. The inns and taverns who normally buy from me have already purchased several barrels of the coarser stuff, and they didn't balk at the small increase in price."

"That's good news," Breeze said. "Hopefully you were worried over nothing. Now, tell me. How can I help?"

Before Alain could answer, an older woman in an expensive-looking gown covered in fine embroidery, along with what looked like her three daughters and two servants for each of them, came up to the booth. The youngest of the girls ran her finger along the cut glass of one of the bottles of ice wine. "This is so pretty. It almost looks like a jewel."

"If you fancy the outside, my lady, you'll never believe the magic it holds." Breeze stepped forward, lifted the bottle, and held it out to her.

All four of the women focused on Breeze, and the one he'd addressed blushed slightly. "Is it really that good?"

He nodded and moved a little closer to the group. "Like suckling at the teats of the goddesses, and that's no exaggeration. It tastes of honeysuckle, roses, and violets, and it's as sweet as sunlight on your tongue. But, please, don't go on my word alone." He poured a few drops of the ice wine into four thimble-sized silver cups and handed them out.

After sipping it, all of their eyes grew wide, and they looked at each other, as if each of them wanted the others to confirm they'd tasted what they had, and not tumbled into a daydream.

"Now, tell me," Breeze said, leaning his elbows on the makeshift counter. "Have I spun tales or told you lies?"

"It's amazing," the matron said. "We must buy some of this to serve at our banquets."

"I know of nothing that will impress high-born and sophisticated people like Mountain Shadow Winery's ice wine. Few vintners have the skill to produce it, and few climes are warm enough to ripen the grapes yet frost early enough to create this marvel." Breeze leaned a little closer and lowered his voice conspiratorially. "The ladies you entertain will be quite envious."

"And what is the price of this wine?" she asked, raking her eyes over Breeze with very thinly veiled appreciation.

He blinked twice, slowly, his attention never leaving her face. "How much are you interested in?"

"Do you have three dozen bottles available?"

Someone could have knocked Alain over with a feather. He'd brought eight dozen bottles, but would have been happy to sell a dozen. Breeze, though, never flinched. "Well, for that quantity, we can offer a discount. How about fifty pieces of gold per dozen?"

Alain almost interrupted him; he usually asked thirty-six and would negotiate for less. Before he could say anything, the woman had motioned a male servant in clothes almost as fine as her own to count the coin into Breeze's hand. He deposited it in the locked chest beneath the counter before moving around it to take the woman's elbow. "And now, m'lady, let us discuss the other needs of your household. For a good, everyday table wine, let me recommend our signature blend. It's a mix of verlaut, sienscerre, and a little splash of fierrine, a wonderful little grape from my homeland of Espero that adds a tantalizing touch of heat and spice." He pulled a goblet from the barrel, and the woman brushed her fingers over his as she took it from him. "Twenty barrels of this vintage should keep you well supplied for the year, although, for more important feasts, you may want a few barrels of the older vintages. The character of this particular wine becomes quite elegant and complex with age."

Alain gaped. Breeze had just sold twenty barrels of wine as easily as if he'd asked for a copper piece for a loaf of bread. The women seemed happy as their staff loaded the barrels onto a cart. Dumbly, Alain put the ice wine into wooden boxes and nailed the lids shut. By the time they drove off, Breeze had already approached his next patrons, a group of cooks and servants tasked with filling the cellars at Greyrclif Castle. By the time he'd finished with them, they left with three dozen barrels of wine, and Breeze looked over his shoulder to tip Alain a wink.

Sales lulled by evening, but Alain couldn't believe what he stared at as he examined the tally marks and figures in his little leather-bound ledger. Breeze flopped onto the ground next to him. "Good?"

Alain shook his head. "It's been an amazing first day. I can't believe it. How did you do that?"

"I understand the politics of wealthy families. Foremost in their minds is always outdoing other wealthy families. Other than that, I suppose I was just being nice."

"You were very nice to the ladies." So... *nice*, in fact, Alain had started to think he'd imagined Breeze's bone-melting kiss those few weeks back.

Breeze leaned closer and spoke in a scratchy voice near Alain's ear. "If I'd known I could win you by making you jealous, I'd have tried it a moon ago."

Alain's spine snapped straight, and his fingers tightened around the quill he held.

Breeze let out a long-suffering sigh. "It was only a joke, my friend. I forget how sensitive you get about being teased. Why is that?"

"You... you should not say such things, in jest or not. What if someone heard you? Please, try to think about what my children would have to face if people started talking, if they thought I was...."

"I'm sorry, Alain. I'm hardly a cultured man. I suppose I'm not terribly fit for polite society."

Letting himself relax, Alain closed his book. "Fit enough to know how much wine a noble household requires for a year. Why is that?"

Breeze laughed and bumped his shoulder against Alain's. "That's simple. My family's rich. Most pretentious bunch of gits you'd ever meet."

Alain wanted to know more, especially to know why Breeze worked as a sword for hire if he'd come from a wealthy and respectable family. The son of a noble household, or even a prosperous one, would usually gravitate toward the knighthood if he wanted to fight. Men only resorted to selling their skills to the highest bidder out of desperation. What had made Breeze that desperate? Could it have been his... proclivities? The ones Alain suspected they shared? He'd almost mustered the courage to come out and ask when Courtenay and Fenn came running beneath the canopy and crashed onto their laps. They'd been playing with the large brood of children belonging to a baker, presided over by that family's eldest daughter.

"There's a stand here selling used books." A fine layer of dust covered Courtenay from the top of her faded muffin-style hat to the tips of her battered boots. The sun had nipped her cheeks and nose red, or maybe it was her excitement. "They have everything. Do you think we can look them over before we go home? I'd be happy to take the ones without the pretty covers. They cost less."

Alain smoothed down her springy yellow curls. Her hair smelled like sunshine and fresh air. "And did you look for someone selling cloth like I asked you? You're going to need a few new dresses by winter. That one you're wearing is already too short. Both of you will need new boots. Did you take the time to look for those?"

He knew the answer, knew she'd passed the entire afternoon running her fingers over the spines of books, leafing through their crumbling pages, and even reading as much as the proprietor would allow.

"Oh, I forgot about that. Sorry, Uncle Alain. It's just the first day. I'll look tomorrow, I promise."

"All right, my love."

Fenn, on Breeze's lap, looked ready to break in half by the time his turn came to speak. "Breeze, Breeze! There's a weaponsmith here! Not just a blacksmith like Guy back home, but a real swordsmith! Armor too! Spears, shields, mail shirts, and steel boots! It was amazing. Tomorrow, I'll take you there so you can tell me how to pick out a good sword. Oh, and there's another shop selling bows and arrows. I'd sure love to have a bow."

"I have to admit," Breeze told him, talking as if to another warrior and not a six-year-old, "I feel naked without my sword. I wonder what happened to it. Some fff-ilthy son of a who-hole in the ground probably took it when I couldn't defend myself. Don't feel quite whole, quite myself, without it. It was a damned good sword."

"Language," Alain chided around a contented smile. He felt happier, more at ease, than he had since before the fire. In the back of his mind, he knew he had to have a talk with his children, make sure they knew Breeze wasn't planning to stay. Fenn, especially, had grown quite attached to the mercenary, and if he wasn't expecting it, losing Breeze so soon after losing his father could devastate him. It was going to devastate Alain, no matter how he prepared for it, but he wasn't a child, and he had no one but himself to blame. He'd let himself get attached even though he'd known it was a terrible idea.

"I saw a lovely inn just beyond the market," Courtenay said. "They had tables outside, under arbors covered in flowers. Do you think… do we have enough coin to maybe eat our dinner there?"

Alain smiled. He set Courtenay on her feet, stood, and reached out a hand to help Breeze up. "I would love for us to eat our dinner there."

BY THE last day of Y'Airns Market, they'd sold almost everything they'd brought, and Alain had taken orders for the next season he hoped he'd be able to fill. He would have to sit down and puzzle through the figures, but he felt optimistic he'd be able to give his workers their stipends, purchase wheat and apples to replace what had been burned, and have enough left over to buy some mature vines that could produce fruit as early as next year. For the winery to stay afloat, they needed to replace their hardiest, most versatile grapes: the sienscerre and verlaut. At least now they had a chance.

Courtenay and Fenn had had a lovely time at the bazaar, though by the midday meal on the fourth day, both children looked tired. Alain still needed to talk to them about Breeze, make them understand he'd chosen a different course for his life, and that it didn't mean anything was wrong with them, but he'd yet to figure out how to order those necessary words, and he didn't want to pop the happy little bubble they floated in. Having some extra money gave him ideas, and he itched to put them in motion.

"Can you look after the booth for an hour or so?" he asked Breeze. "If you wouldn't mind, I have some shopping to do before we leave Y'Airns."

"Why don't you take him with you?" Courtenay asked, a twinkle in her eye. "I can look after things here. I know how to count coins, and I grew up on the vineyard. I could describe the difference between fierrine and verlaut by the time I was two. Not that we have much left to sell. Go on. Have a little fun. Fenn can load the crates if we sell the last little bit."

To demonstrate, the boy rolled up his shirtsleeve and flexed his tiny bicep. "You can count on me!"

"All right, then. I'll have some of the other vineyard workers come round and check up on things. Most of them are camped a little ways behind the booth, where they can see to the stock and load carts for customers, so if you need something, don't be afraid to find someone." Alain waited until they'd passed beyond the children's hearing before he turned to Breeze. "Courtenay is wise beyond her years. They're growing so fast."

"They're wonderful," Breeze said. "Happy and loved. You're doing a terrific job raising them, Alain. Don't worry so much. They're going to turn out fine. You make them feel worthwhile, and I can't think of anything more important than that."

His simple words reassured Alain, let him believe things might turn out well. Thanks to Breeze's charm, Y'Airns Market had been more lucrative than it had in years. Alain had a little extra coin to spend. "I want to get something for them. To reassure them the vineyard isn't sinking. I also do have to get that cloth, and the boots."

"Need any soap or oils?" Breeze canted his head toward an apothecary stand.

Oils. That sent Alain's imagination soaring, but he shook his head. "Some of the women on the vineyard get together now and then to make soap. There isn't much we don't provide for ourselves."

"Well, here's the cloth stand." Breeze put his hand on Alain's shoulder to guide him into the tent where bolts of fabric sat piled to the peak. "What are you looking for?"

"Something sensible to make a dress or two for Courtenay, maybe a new pair of trousers for Fenn." He went to a roll of heavy brown cloth and pulled a few feet of it out to inspect. It seemed durable, and he motioned to the woman watching the shop.

"Courtenay should have something feminine and pretty," Breeze said. "She'll be a young woman soon. What about this?" He pointed to some pale blue cloth dotted with embroidered pink flowers. "Roses. She'll like that."

Alain balked a little at the price, but the brown cloth was a good bargain. He could use it to make two pairs of trousers for Fenn and a simple everyday shift for Courtenay. Then he could use the fancy cloth to make her a dress for special occasions. Breeze was right; she deserved to be a young woman and feel beautiful. What was he going to do when he didn't have his mercenary to point out the obvious? He selected some thick evergreen cloth that would make a nice warm vest for Fenn and another simple gown for Courtenay, and then some thin, beige fabric—nice and cheap—for petticoats, underpants, and shirts. He paid the proprietress, and she folded the cloth neatly and placed it in his basket.

Next they bought shoes for the children, and then Alain made his way to the sprawling bookseller's. He didn't even know where to begin, and his confusion must have shown on his face, because Breeze approached the tiny man with the white beard who ran the shop, and said, "A little girl's been here, probably every day. Probably stealing every word from you she could read before being driven off. Round red cheeks and yellow hair. Blue eyes like the best day of your life."

The wizened shopkeeper leapt from his stool, grinning beneath his thick beard. "Ah, yes. I remember the lovely lass. Let her read all she wanted, I did. Follow me. She seemed particularly interested in tales of mages." He plucked a fat tome with a pale purple leather cover from one of his bins. "The tale of Emperor Fane's life and battle against the Thirteen Goddesses. An old account, written by the preeminent scholar on the subject at the university in Pala Reapaza, in Espero. An odd choice for a young lady, as it's a scholarly account, but she kept coming back to it. If you don't want to spend as much coin, I have a copy with a plainer cover."

"No," Alain said. "We'll take the one with the pretty cover." Breeze clearly approved, and he smiled. "Is there anything else she especially liked?"

"Here." The small man plucked a narrow green book from a shelf and handed it to Alain.

He looked at the worn cloth cover, surprised. "But this is a book of spells. For mages."

Breeze leaned over Alain's shoulder. "Aye, it's a simple course of study, much like those young sorcerers are given in Espero. It teaches how to control the arcane flow, focus it. It's more techniques for meditation and concentration than anything else. It's harmless, really. But so are all spells in the hands of someone without the gift."

"Why would Courtenay want this?" It cost next to nothing, but Alain didn't understand. "She's no mage."

"Perhaps she just longs to understand," the old shopkeeper said. "It's a fascinating subject, especially with fewer mages born every generation."

"No matter. It's just a book. We'll take these two." Alain paid the man, and he wrapped the two tomes in brown parchment. Alain put them in the basket with the cloth. "And now a gift for Fenn."

"What are you thinking?" Breeze asked.

Alain couldn't believe what he was thinking as he walked toward the archery stand. "If I buy this, will you teach him how to use it? Otherwise he'll be shooting the chickens, the grapes, and likely my workers." He picked up a tiny, harmless-looking bow that seemed about the right size for his nephew. "Maybe this isn't a good idea."

"It's a fantastic idea," Breeze said, earning a nod from the lanky ginger lad manning the booth. "It never hurts to be able to defend yourself, and if he doesn't need it for that, he can hunt. Do it, Alain. It'll make the boy feel strong, in control of his destiny. That's how I felt the first time I held a sword, and bows are better. Less dangerous. The archer keeps out of the thick of things."

"Will you teach him how to use it?" Alain looked down at the supple curve of pale wood. "Because I have no idea."

"Aye, I will. I should be able to show him enough before I'm off back to Rosecairn."

Alain paid for the tiny bow, half a dozen arrows, and a green leather quiver. He tucked them into his basket, hiding them beneath the fabric. He and Breeze walked back toward their booth in silence. Alain could think of nothing to say, because his time with Breeze was coming to an end, and all he wanted was for it to last forever. "I have a few last things to finish up. Would you mind going back to check on the children? I don't like leaving them alone this long."

With a sultry smile and theatrical bow, Breeze said, "I will do anything you ask of me." In spite of his injuries, he turned and wove his way through the throng with a liquid, feline grace Alain couldn't stop staring at until he disappeared. Then he made his way to the weapons stand.

Courtenay had a customer when Alain reached their pavilion, and he looked important: an older man in black and burgundy velvets with a gold medallion around his neck and three bodyguards standing behind him. Courtenay stood behind Breeze, clutching his hand, her face flushed. Some women from the vineyard huddled together a few dozen feet away, leaning close to exchange words hidden behind their hands, and some of their men stood holding hammers and shovels, looking uncertain. Alain knew something was wrong. Had Breeze offended a potential patron with his coarse language and innuendo? Goddesses.

"Is there a problem, tam?" he asked, regarding the man's crooked nose, haughty expression, and greasy, thinning hair. "We've sold out of most of the wines we brought to market, but if you'd like to place a custom order, we'll do our best—"

"I am well acquainted with your wines," the man said in a nasally voice. "I'm much more interested in your lovely daughter."

"My—what?"

"Allow me to introduce myself," the man said. "I'm Tam Wagonnier Almes, a respected merchant and trader from the city of Felgard. Recently, the goddesses called my wife away, and I've been looking to replace her. Unfortunately, I have found nothing but coin-grubbing harlots and women too used up to meet my needs. But when I set eyes on this lovely young woman, I knew she'd do nicely. I am a man of means, and if you'd like to sit down, we can negotiate a price."

Alain thought he'd be sick, thought he'd plummeted into a bizarre nightmare. Courtenay cried silently, her face buried against Breeze's back. "She's not of age," he managed to stammer.

"She is close enough," Tam Wagonnier said. "Her breasts are beginning to swell. Has she bled yet? I'm sure it will not be long."

"No." Alain trembled; he wasn't sure if it was rage or disgust. "She's a child, and she has a place at the vineyard. No. We aren't interested."

"Who do you think you are, farmer?" The man stepped close to Alain and bared his small, stained teeth. "I am an important man, and I'm offering to do you a favor, taking this useless little wench off your hands and paying for the privilege."

Alain shoved him before he knew what he was doing. "I said no. Get out of here. You're a sick, awful man. She's just a little girl!"

"You'll be sorry you did that, you simpleton!" Almes snarled. "I was willing to pay for her legitimately, but if you're going to be an ass and forget your place, I'll just take her." He motioned to the three big men standing behind him, and they moved around him, toward Courtenay.

Before Alain could even formulate a reply, Breeze moved between the three men and his niece. "I'll tell you once, and only once, to get your sorry asses the fuck out of here."

"Or what, farmer?" The man nearest them reached for Courtenay, but Breeze caught his wrist, brought his knee up, and snapped the man's arm at the elbow. The crack of his bones echoed through the tent, and he sank to his knees, howling and cradling his ruined limb. Breeze crossed his arm in front of his chest and silenced the man with a vicious backhand swing. He sprawled on his back, blood oozing from his lips and nostrils.

"You little bastard," one of the remaining man swore, running at Breeze. With a tilt of his head, Breeze dodged his fist while bringing his own up to punch the larger man in the throat. His companion tried to catch Breeze off guard by rushing his side, but Breeze drove his knee into his enemy's ribs, kicked him in the face when he doubled over, and smacked him twice in the back of the head with his fist before he fell facedown. The man he'd hit in the neck kicked at him, but Breeze caught his ankle and twisted his foot with a sickening snap of bones. As the man arced backward, Breeze drove the heel of his hand against his ribs, and Alain heard them break.

"You need to hire better help, you pitiful old fool."

"How dare you," the merchant hissed, running at Breeze. Faster than Alain could even follow, Breeze grasped his arm, twisted it behind his back, and forced him to his knees.

Breeze swatted the back of Almes's head, twice, making his fat chin smack his ill-defined chest. Then he leaned down and spoke near the old merchant's ear. "You ever fuck with my family again, if I ever see your ugly face again, I'll tear your heart out and shove it up your flabby ass. Do we understand each other?"

When Almes didn't answer, Breeze grabbed him by the thinning hair and bounced his face off one of the shelves. "Do we understand each other, you fucking piece of shit?"

"I—yes," Almes managed while choking on the blood flowing into his mouth. Breeze released him, though he gave him a swift kick in the ass as he scampered away, sending him down on his chest with a mouthful of sod.

People—patrons and other merchants—had begun to gather by the time Almes slunk off with his hirelings. The three bodyguards could barely manage to drag each other away. Once he was well out of Breeze's reach, he turned and poked a fat finger at the mercenary. "You're going to be sorry, you filth!"

"Bring it on, old man! Anytime! Though you might want to hire some men who know the difference between fighting and playing with their cocks!" Breeze grabbed his crotch and made a gesture so rude Alain wished he could have covered Fenn's eyes.

Instead, the boy ran to the edge of their booth, stood next to the mercenary, and brandished his toy weapon. "That's right, whoresons! Bother with us and you'll be sorry. I'll stick my sword right in your bum!"

Goddesses. Alain tingled, torn between wanting to hit something and wanting to curl up and hide. Breeze had been… frightening, amazingly capable. Sisters, Alain knew Breeze was a warrior, but he had never pictured him so adept. He'd moved so fast Alain had barely been able to track it, and in moments vanquished three armed men. Now he was kneeling down in front of Courtenay, wiping the tears from her eyes, pinning her mussed hair behind her small ears and promising her everything would be all right. He'd somehow managed to make her smile past her frightened tears.

Help me, Alain beseeched the goddesses. *He's amazing, and I love him. What do you want me to do? I love him, and I can't pretend I don't. Why do you insist on making me suffer?*

Chapter Eleven

EXCITEMENT FLOWED through Alain as he lay on the floor of the caravan next to Breeze. His children snuffled softly, deep in sleep, but respite eluded Alain. After an hour of tossing and turning, trying to position himself so he couldn't feel Breeze against him, he rose and ducked out of the small set of doors at the rear of the caravan. In the quiet of the warm night, he wandered to their booth and found a bottle of their best wine: pure, aged fierrine, mellowed in burnt arn-wood barrels. He peeled the wax from the neck of the bottle and pulled out the cork. Then he wandered to the center of the market square and sat down in the dewy grass.

Before long, Breeze joined him, and Alain handed over the bottle. Not a word passed between them as they finished it, and Alain went to fetch another—a delicate white, primarily breumaurinier—grapes native to Lockhaven, but sweeter than the typical patron preferred. Breeze seemed to like it; his Adam's apple bobbed as he took a few deep swallows, and Alain couldn't seem to tear his attention from his throat.

"It's like a dessert," Breeze commented, licking the sweetness from his full, terra-cotta lips.

"It's a wine the ladies like," Alain said.

"What does that mean? Alain, I don't understand you. But I do enjoy you, and if you're saying you want me to play the part of the lady—"

"I'm not saying that," Alain interrupted. "I'm not unnatural. I'm a good man."

"I would never imply otherwise," Breeze said. "Goddesses, I was poking fun at *myself* that time."

Alain took another swig of the wine. He blamed it for the mutinous words that escaped his lips when all he'd planned to do was apologize to Breeze for being too sensitive. At least he had the presence of mind to look around and make sure they were alone. "Have you... done that before? The lady's part...? Goddesses, never mind. I'm so sorry. I should have learned by now to keep my mouth shut."

Breeze pushed Alain's unkempt hair back and traced the tip of his aquiline nose up Alain's cheek. "You can say whatever you like to me. Don't worry if it comes out wrong. It's only words. They can't hurt. I would rather you just let go. Perhaps you'd have less trouble expressing your thoughts if you didn't think so much before you spoke."

Alain shook his head. Breeze's nose had left a trail of heat up his face he was sure would blister. "I've made an ass of myself too many times."

Breeze's chuckle ruffled his hair and cooled the edge of his flushed ear. "Doesn't stop me. Do you want me to answer your question?"

If his face got any hotter, Alain's skin would boil, melt, and drip from his bones. "If you want."

Leaning closer, putting a little of his weight against Alain, he said, "I have, in fact. Though not often. I like playing around as much as any man—hands and mouths—but that, for that, the man has to be special. He has to be someone I can trust. I haven't met many men like that."

"Aren't you afraid someone will find out?"

Breeze shrugged and took another pull from the bottle. "Things are different in Rosecairn. The men I fight with, we have to trust each other with our lives. You learn fast that if you can depend on a man to have your back, drag you out of a mess, and look out for you if you can't look out for yourself, well, that's all that matters. Hardly matters who he wants to lie next to at night."

"Is that why you.... Ah, forget it."

"Goddesses. Ask. I've been waiting moons to get to speak to you like this. Usually, I can figure out all the things you leave unsaid, but it can be taxing. Spit it out."

"You wanted to talk to me?"

"Yes!" Breeze sounded both amused and exasperated. "There's far more to you than the simple farmer I expected. I want to know you."

"Why?"

"It's not enough that you saved my worthless life with no hope of recompense?"

"Your life isn't worthless, Breeze."

"Depends who you ask." A hint of bitterness crept into his voice, and he washed it away with a healthy gulp of the wine before passing the nearly empty second bottle back to Alain. "Another?"

"Why in the Shades' not," Alain said. He went to fetch another bottle of the fierrine, since it was Breeze's favorite, surprised at the difficulty he had in walking a straight path back to their booth. When he returned and plunked back down in the grass, Breeze was rubbing his bad shoulder, and Alain knew he'd strained himself more than he'd admit, fending off that oily merchant and his hirelings. Alain opened the bottle, leaned it between Breeze's spread legs, and took over massaging his knotted mound of muscle. "Thank you."

The mercenary snorted. "Those entitled fucks. I enjoyed it."

"Not just for that," Alain said, moving his fingers around the back of Breeze's neck. His dark hair hung in loose waves, but at the base of his skull, it grew it tiny, tight, springy curls. Alain found the texture delightful. "For everything. I thought this market would be a misery. Everything I used to do with Boyce is... hard now. I keep expecting him to be here, to look over and see him, but I don't. But you... you're here, and, and...." He sniffled and choked back a couple of drunken sobs. What a fool he was, and the wine had broken through the wall his pride had built around his grief.

Breeze pulled Alain against his chest, and Alain didn't even fight him. He let Breeze wrap an arm around his shoulders and rake his other hand through Alain's hair. "You have nothing to be ashamed of by missing him. I'm going to botch the fuck out of this, but Octavian told me something like 'There's no greater measure of a man's life than who mourns him when he's gone.' If someone like you is mourning your brother-in-law, that tells me he was an extraordinary man. Anyone can see the two of you were close."

"I loved him." Alain admitted it so quietly, with his lips mashed against the hard planes of Breeze's chest, he had no idea if Breeze heard. It had hurt him more than anything not to be able to express his loss, not to be able to make anyone understand the scope of it. If he'd lost a wife, no one would begrudge his mourning, but since Boyce had been a man, he had to hold it inside. He'd prayed hard for someone who could understand, and he had Breeze now. Breeze had been with other men, and he didn't even mind Alain rambling and tripping over his own tongue, so Alain just let the words purge out of him.

"I loved him. I didn't tell him, and, and when I saw his body, all I wanted to do was give him one last kiss, but I couldn't. He was so wonderful to me, putting up with me, even loving me back though he wasn't unnatural.... He, he was a good man, and I thought I'd have someone to stand beside me through everything. Through life. Someone to grow old with. Do you want that, Breeze?"

Breeze held Alain tighter and rested his cheek against the top of Alain's head. "Most mercenaries don't grow old. I wish I had something better to say to you. I know it hurts. I'm not the man to tell you he's with the goddesses, that he's better off, 'cause that's shit. Fact is, life's shit sometimes."

"He thought I was beautiful." Alain closed his eyes. "I remember when we first.... It had been two years since my sister died, and we were in the kitchen cleaning up. Boyce said, 'You look so much like Sabine, but you're so beautiful in your own right.' I asked him if he was thinking of her. 'Not just now,' he told me. He said, 'I will always love Sabine, but I have room to love you too, and I think I love you.' He said he wanted to show me, but he had no idea what to do."

"You did?"

Alain could formulate no reason not to tell him. If Breeze hadn't run from him in disgust yet, he wasn't likely to turn away now. "Yeah. I had desires. Now and then, when I was making a delivery, I'd find my way to a roadside inn, get way too drunk, and just... just kind of let any man who wanted to have a go. I barely remembered most of their faces by the time it was over, and I always felt sick with shame. Until Boyce, I thought that was all relations between men could be, just that—that sick, savage sating of unnatural urges. But we loved each other. It went way beyond what happened in bed, because, goddesses, he was bloody clueless about *that* at first."

"Yeah?"

Alain nodded at the bittersweet memories and drank more even though he sure as the Shades didn't need it. "He treated me like a woman at first, sucking my nipples forever, caressing my legs... just too soft. He caught on, though."

"Don't like your nipples sucked?" Breeze asked.

"I like it fine. But I'm not delicate."

"Like it a little hard, then?"

Hard. Alain's cock was hard, and if he didn't have so much alcohol numbing his senses, he might have come in his pants. "Yes, sometimes." But he wasn't expressing himself right, again. "It wasn't just what happened in the bed. That was nice, sure, but what I wanted, what I want, is someone who will always stand beside me. Someone for life, you know? You don't. You don't have to worry about it, because you want to go out in a flash of glory on a battlefield somewhere."

He expected Breeze to deny it, take offense, but he said instead, "Aye, I guess that's always been the plan."

"That makes me sad."

"Why? I'm a warrior. Plenty of men are."

"Don't you want a life? A family? Children and grandchildren by your bed to hold your hand when you die?"

"I guess I never really thought about it," Breeze said, leaning back in the damp, fragrant grass and pulling Alain with him.

Alain felt sleepy, safe and content, too drunk to question the source. "But you had another life. A wealthy family. But you walked away. Was it because... because of being unnatural?"

Breeze combed his fingers through Alain's hair and pulled Alain against his chest so he could speak softly next to Alain's ear. "First off, I don't like that word. I'm as natural as the next man, just the way the goddesses made me. But no. I left because I wasn't a mage. My parents were disgusted when I couldn't manifest the gift. It's been in our blood since forever. They thought I was just lazy. Useless. It wasn't that. I tried so hard. I wanted them to see me as worthwhile. I prayed, every night I prayed to the goddesses to let me have just a little magic. They didn't listen, though, and I didn't have much future in Espero. After a while, my family just pretended I didn't exist. No one would acknowledge me when we sat at feasts. They all talked to each other and ignored me completely. Didn't even respond when I tried to join in the conversation. My father, he thought my only chance would be becoming a scribe, a servant to an important mage, someone to take down notes for them and dust off their books. My mother didn't think I was worthy of cleaning a mage's chamber pot, and she told me so every chance she got. They'd had high hopes for me as their only son, and they never let me forget how I'd failed them. By the time I was twelve and it was certain I'd never make a mage, they turned their attention to my sisters. I didn't want to be a servant. I wanted to show the world I was worth something, so I found my way aboard a ship, got off Espero. Good riddance."

"Why?"

"There are two kinds of people on Espero, Alain: mages and the people who take care of their needs so they can read, lark about, and do useless, sparkly things with their fingers. I thought I could do better, make a name for myself. Maybe I just wanted to prove my parents wrong. I don't know. Doesn't matter."

"Sorry," Alain mumbled. Beneath him, Breeze was warm and alive, his heartbeat and breath loud in Alain's ears, his scent enveloping Alain.

"Life's shit, like I said. No matter. I had the good fortune to meet Octavian Rose, and it turned out he'd been in my position, stuck facing a shit life he didn't want, and decided to make it on his own. He really took pity on me too, 'cause I was a shit fighter at first."

"Not now," Alain said, tracing the prominent muscle of Breeze's neck down from his ear to his collarbone. "You were so fast I couldn't even follow you. Four men, like it was nothing."

"Those bastards were shit." Breeze's vocabulary had devolved with his inebriation. "Your lad could have taken them."

"I couldn't," Alain said.

"You should learn." Breeze drank and then passed the bottle to Alain. Goddesses, when had they finished it? "To use a bow, at least. I could teach you. Least I could do."

Alain nuzzled against him, drinking in his heat and wonderful smell as he pictured Breeze standing behind him, guiding his stance and his hands on a warm, supple piece of wood, whispering instructions next to his ear. Though he could never say it aloud, he loved him, loved him in a different way than he'd loved Boyce, a way that inspired him to recklessness, to shout it to the stars and tell anyone who didn't like it to go to the Shades. If his love for Boyce had been the comfort of a hearth fire, his passion for the exotic mercenary—the capable but kind man, the man who loved his children, who couldn't resist risking Alain's ire to tease him—made Yarroway L'Estrella's fire look like a fleeting flicker.

Chapter
Twelve

I LOVE you. I shouldn't, but I can't help it. You're like a fire I'd wander into even if it killed me. It surrounds me, and I can't escape. Don't want to. I wish I could keep you.

Breeze didn't think Alain remembered the words he'd mumbled drunkenly against his chest shortly before passing out, snoring and drooling, against him, but they'd been seared into Breeze's mind, and he heard them again every time he looked over at the vintner guiding his ponies toward home.

He wanted Alain, sure, but Alain *loved* him. He wasn't worthy of that. Nothing good would come of it. They were just too different. Too different in what they valued and desired from life.

The effects of the drink they'd shared were as clear on Alain's face as Breeze felt. Alain looked pale, and dark circles ringed his brilliant blue eyes. Even so, he seemed lighter; it had done him good to get out the poison he'd been holding inside. Breeze realized he'd done the same, and he hated it. It wasn't like him to whine about his family, and he hoped it was as forgotten as Alain's declarations. It was over and done, and he didn't care anymore.

Fires burned holes in the sultry summer air as they stopped the caravan in front of the gate. Alain jumped down from the bench and handed the reins off to a young man. Breeze followed him, his hurt leg protesting when it struck the ground. He reached for Alain to steady himself, and Alain patted the hand Breeze draped over his forearm. "What's going on here?"

"The festival of Tyrinna and Tyrinnius," Alain answered, looking much more animated and alert than he had on the journey home. "The twin deities of the vine. Do you not know their story?"

"I'd like you to tell it to me," Breeze said as Alain moved to the back of the caravan to fetch his basket. It seemed like he'd wait for tomorrow to unload the rest. That was good. Good to see him letting himself take some time to enjoy life. They'd worked hard at Y'Airns Market, and Alain deserved a break. Breeze fell into step next to him as they made their way toward the circle of wooden tables piled with food and drink beneath dangling glass lanterns and garlands of grapevines and wildflowers. At the center, a rough-hewn stone statue of a young man and woman, barely covered by gauzy drapes, sat surrounded by flowers, fruit, and candles. A large goblet waited by its base.

Alain took an open bottle of wine from one of the tables and splashed a little into the vessel with a smile and a small bow of his head. "Tyrinna and Tyrinnius are the twin children of the harvest goddess, Berris. The siblings were close, and so every year, on this day, to celebrate their birth, they competed to see which could give the other a finer gift. One year, Tyrinna created the first grapevine for her brother. She was sure she'd won their little game, but then Tyrinnius squeezed the juice from the fruit, let it age, and made wine. At first they thought to keep their creation to themselves, solely for the use of the goddesses and their children, but eventually they chose to share their gift with mankind. We celebrate this night to thank them."

Alain handed Breeze the bottle, and he poured a tinkling little dribble into the cup. They took a seat on a bench while Courtenay and Fenn went in search of their friends. Before long a group of the vineyard's children had gathered around them to hear about the wonders of Y'Airns Market. "When we were young, my sister Sabine and I used to play." A regretful smile touched his full pink lips. "I'd scour the woods and fields, trying to find something amazing, coming up with feathers and rocks, maybe an interesting piece of wood. She always managed to get me the most wonderful things. I miss her."

Breeze remembered the presents Alain got for the children, and now he understood why. He wished he'd known to get Alain something, especially when the people from the vineyard began coming up to him to clasp his hands and present him with little trinkets, mostly useful things like candles, soaps, jars of preserves, and tins of baked goods. Alain put them in that ridiculous huge basket he'd been lugging around.

As they ate and drank, some of the farmers and laborers brought out instruments, mostly flutes and drums, though one girl had scared up a lyre, and she actually played it quite capably. Some people danced while others gathered in groups to sing along with the musicians. Alain sat silently, resting his elbow on the tabletop and his cheek in his cupped hand, watching. Blue eyes sparkling. Smiling a little, but sad. So sad. Breeze thought he understood. All Alain wanted was a partner, someone to greet him with a kiss when he returned from market, someone to tell his troubles to, someone to dance with at feasts. He would never have it, and that made Breeze angry. Goddesses, it was a sad world indeed if someone like Alain would never get to dance.

"What do you say we round up those little devils you call your children and give them the gifts we... I mean, the ones you got at the market?"

"All right. They'd like that." He caught Courtenay's attention and waved her over from the table where she sat with some other girls her age. Breeze thought, from her mischievous grin, she probably knew what was coming, and she hurried over to kiss Alain on the cheek. "Where's your brother?" Alain asked, wiping a bit of jam from the corner of her mouth.

"Must I get him? He's been playing with the Tooley brothers, up by the pond. All of them are probably filthy and covered in duck shit."

"Courtenay!" Alain colored. It took so little to pink up his face, and it took everything Breeze had not to press a finger to his heated cheek. "Young women do not say that word."

"Breeze says it all the time."

Well... well *shit*. How would Alain respond to that?

With the truth, turned out. "He is a grown man, and to be quite blunt, outside the rules of polite society. This is not a war camp. You are my daughter, not a mercenary, and you won't speak like one."

She rolled her eyes the way girls her age did. "It was only one little word, Alain. I'm sorry, all right?"

"Go and find your brother."

"Sorry about that," Breeze said as soon as she'd gone.

To his surprise, Alain met his gaze and smiled. "You've shown them more good than bad."

"Have I?"

Alain nodded but didn't elaborate.

Breeze wondered if he would have if they'd been alone. He wanted them to be alone, so Alain could say what he felt without worrying. Yet the thought of being alone with Alain Lamont scared the piss out of him, because he didn't know if he could stop himself the next time the vintner curled up against him and asked him if he liked to take a cock inside. Fucking Shades, just the memory of that conversation had Breeze squirming on the bench, trying to position himself so his dick didn't poke him in the belly. It had been too long since he'd gotten any relief. When he got back to Rosecairn, he'd find at least a few men willing to have some fun, and he'd indulge himself until he couldn't rise from the bed. That fantasy, while it started pleasant, turned his thoughts to Alain and his trysts at roadside inns, and that broke Breeze's heart, because he could picture the sweet, delicate farmer manhandled and used by men who didn't care about him and wouldn't give a fig if he enjoyed it. Breeze wondered if he'd resume his habits, now he'd lost his brother-in-law, and it made him want to hurt someone.

Fenn hurtling himself onto Breeze's lap shattered the vision in his head and dispelled the foul mood it had conjured. As he mussed the boy's hair, he knew Courtenay had been right—Fenn was quite pungent. He'd need a bath and a fresh set of clothes before bed. Breeze laughed at himself. When was the last time he'd concerned himself with something like that?

Breeze turned the boy around and swiveled so they faced Alain and Courtenay as Alain rifled through his basket. "Both of you were so good at Y'Airns, and you helped us so much, me and Breeze thought we'd get something for each of you."

Breeze hadn't expected that—Alain including him—and his chest tightened. Alain handed Courtenay the books, and her eyes went wide as she hugged them to her chest. "These are the ones I wanted most. Oh, thank you so much! I can't wait to read them." She wasn't lying, because as soon as she'd kissed Breeze and Alain on their cheeks, she bypassed her group of friends in favor of some soft grass beneath a low-hanging branch and a lantern.

"And for you, my fine lad." Alain held out the bow, but kept it out of Fenn's reach, even though he stretched for it frantically. "Now, this isn't a toy for a child. It's a real weapon, for a young man, and you have to respect it, Fenn. There's no taking it out on your own, at least not for a while. Breeze is going to teach you to use it, and you must do exactly as he says."

"'Course I will." Fenn finally succeeded in snatching the little bow, though without the arrows, he couldn't do much damage. "I always listen to Breeze. I want to be just like him!"

Alain furrowed his brow but nodded. "Go on, then. I know you want to show off to your friends."

Fenn laughed as he ran away, and soon a group of suitably impressed boys surrounded him, each waiting his turn to hold the wondrous weapon.

"Sorry for that one too," Breeze said.

"He could do worse."

"You're the one he should be looking up to," Breeze argued. "The things you can do, keeping this place going, making things grow, mixing that extraordinary wine… that stuff's beyond a simple son of a bitch like me. Shooting a bow and hacking at shit with a sword's got nothing on that. He's a clever lad. He'll see it soon enough."

"I hope so."

For a few hours, they ate, drank, and watched the musicians and dancers. Alain managed to pull Courtenay out of the pages of her books for a dance, and Breeze smiled as they moved together across the grass, their identical pale gold hair tossing around as they jumped and skipped, and matching color on their cheeks. A few comely lasses invited Breeze to dance, but he declined. He enjoyed watching Alain, catching his gaze when Alain looked over, smiling, and raising his cup. Besides, though he wouldn't say it aloud, his brief scuffle with that pack of simpletons and a night sleeping on the ground had left him stiff and aching.

By the time the half-moon rose to the center of the sky, most of the food had been packed up, and many of the families had gone home. Those remaining got pleasantly drunk, but being good people, and simple, they did nothing more untoward than laugh a little too much and sing a little too loudly, or dance a little clumsily with wives and husbands they clearly loved. Breeze and Alain abandoned any hope of wrestling an irritable and exhausted Fenn into the tub, and they settled for stripping him down and wiping away the worst of the grime before letting him stumble off to bed.

When they came up from the kitchen, spattered in mud, shirtsleeves rolled to their elbows, and soaked from trying to clean up the cranky boy, only a few embers glowed in the hearth, and other than the moonlight pouring in the windows, the room was dark. Outside, someone played a slow, lilting melody on a flute. In the solitude of the sitting room, Breeze reached for Alain, wound his arms around his waist, and guided him as they swayed to the distant song. "Alain, dance with me. I want you to get to dance."

Breeze expected anything but the way Alain melted against him, pressed their chests and bellies together, pushed his hands up under Breeze's shirt, and rested his head on Breeze's shoulder. They moved together, slowly, rocking from side to side. Goddesses, Alain fit perfectly against him. It felt so good to hold him close, breathe the scent of his hair, feel his muscles bunch and lengthen as he moved. Breeze closed his eyes, pressed his cheek against Alain's, and let the rest of the world disappear. Nothing else existed for Breeze but Alain in his arms, warm and content, moving his hands up and down the muscles of Breeze's back.

They clung to each other, swaying, until long after the music of the flute faded away. Both of them lifted their heads at the same time, and they caught each other's gaze. Alain smiled. Breeze returned it, and then he brushed his lips over Alain's mouth, barely making contact. Still, it made Alain shudder, made his lips gape open, so Breeze did it again, pressing a little harder, letting the tip of his tongue flick out to touch the center of Alain's upper lip. Alain groaned and sank his nails into Breeze's shoulders. As he arched backward and pressed his belly against Breeze, Breeze moved his fingers into Alain's hair and gripped handfuls of the soft golden strands. Then he kissed him for real, tilting his head to the proper angle and pushing his tongue past Alain's teeth into the soft, silken recesses of his mouth.

Alain's tongue surged out to meet him, and they bumped, twisted, and curled together. More of a dance than a struggle, and that was what Breeze wanted. He didn't want to fight Alain or throttle him into submission. He wanted to make him feel good. Spoil him. Treat him like a prince—the way he deserved. Before he could, he had something he needed to say.

He pulled their lips apart with a slurp and a wet pop. Alain panted against Breeze's chin, his hands wandering over the backs of Breeze's thighs and his ass, kneading into the muscle, and goddesses, it felt good. Almost as good as the sucking pecks Alain trailed down the side of his neck, leaving his skin chilly wet, tingling, and likely bruised. Not that he gave a damn.

He had to stop him. Had to be honest. Couldn't risk causing him pain. Breeze used Alain's hair to gently pull him back, and then he held Alain's shoulders and looked into his lust-darkened eyes. "Alain. Goddesses, Alain. I want this to happen. I really want it to happen, but you have to know that I'm still going back to Rosecairn. I don't want to deceive you, but I want you. Want you like I've never wanted anything in my life."

"Me too." Alain ran the edges of his teeth along Breeze's chin and pressed his swollen cock against Breeze. He wriggled his hand under the front of Breeze's loose shirt to toy with the sparse trail of hair at the center of his belly, and then the rim of his belly button. Lower. Into the thicker hair, at least as thick as it got on Breeze. "And I know you're leaving. Your life is somewhere else. I know. So, your room?"

It was the closest. Breeze wished he could pull Alain's thighs up around his waist and carry him to the bed, but his body hadn't recovered enough yet. He settled for pressing his tongue into Alain's mouth again, lapping at the sweetness of the wine over the even sweeter taste of Alain as he guided them into the hall, holding Alain's hips as he staggered backward. As soon as he could, Breeze shoved his elbow into his bedroom door to slam it shut without lifting his lips from Alain's. How many nights had he spent dreaming about the taste of his lips, what his body would feel like pressed close? And, goddesses, it was better. Alain responded to his every breath and touch, going pliant, malleable beneath his hands. Breeze had no doubt he could bend the vintner over his bed and fuck him into oblivion, but Alain wasn't an ordinary fuck. He was… he was *Alain*.

"Why don't you get comfortable while I light the fire?" Because he needed to be able to see. When Alain just twisted the hem of his shirt in his hands and stared at his boots, Breeze pried his clutching fingers away from the fabric and kissed him again, kissed him until he felt all the tension run out of Alain's body. "I'm asking you to take your clothes off." He tugged at the strings lacing Alain's shirt shut up the center. "I'll get it nice and warm in here. Will you undress?"

Alain's throat worked as he swallowed hard. "Yeah."

By the time Breeze coaxed a weak blaze from the twigs in the hearth, Alain was naked in his bed, the linens tucked up beneath his chin. Breeze pulled the loose shirt he wore over his head and tossed it into the corner. He couldn't help being aware of the burns, healed now, but still hideous bumps and swirls of mangled skin. He expected Alain to flinch, but he didn't. His gaze never left Breeze's face as Breeze toed his boots off and shed his trousers. Then he caught Alain looking down and licking his lips at what he saw.

"Come here." Alain pushed the sheet aside, exposing a slim, beautiful body Breeze had dreamt of night after night. He sprawled across the bed, his head on the pillow and his arms folded beneath it, and Breeze hurried to cover Alain with his body. He wiggled a little, just to feel their skin catch, feel those little patches of hair he'd imagined since Alain had mentioned them. Their legs knotted together like vines. Then he found Alain's mouth. It opened to him like a flower, and he pushed his tongue inside as he circled his hips to rub their cocks together. Their tongues twined together, and Breeze moved his hands down the divine smooth skin of Alain's ribs as Alain wrapped his legs around Breeze's waist. "The salve—on the night table—"

Breeze chuckled against Alain's needy, swollen lips. "All in good time. Not yet." He stopped Alain's question by pulling the skin of his neck between his lips, stopped his clutching hands by grasping his wrists and pushing them into the mattress. He dragged his mouth down Alain's chest, biting at the errant patches of hair, pulling on the pale strands with his teeth. Alain truly had nipples a man could suck forever—pale pink, tiny, and hard as pebbles. Breeze circled each of them with his tongue and couldn't resist pulling one into his mouth and stretching the rosy flesh, sucking hard until Alain cried out and jabbed his groin up into Breeze's belly. Goddesses, the taste of him was divine, his skin like his ice wine, something to be sipped at, savored, rolled over the tongue before swallowing slowly. Like his grapes, Alain had absorbed the sun, the goodness of the soil, the strength of the ironstone, and the sweetness of the rain. He was complex and delicious, and Breeze took his time drinking from him, tasting along his waist, burying his nose in the light fur of his underarms, burrowing his face between his heavy, pink sac and his inner thigh. He kissed Alain's legs from his anklebone up to the musky patch of golden hair around his long, pretty cock, and back down. He couldn't get enough, drunk on Alain and wanting more.

"Turn over. Please, will you turn over?" He didn't wait for Alain to answer before flipping him onto his belly and pulling his hips up. He had to keep tasting him, so he dragged his palms up the soft hair on the backs of his legs and spread his cheeks. Then he ran his tongue over the hot, wrinkled skin of his cleft, smelling and tasting his essence distilled, strong and overwhelming enough to make him see stars as he stabbed his tongue inside.

"Goddesses!" Alain cried. His muscles clenched around Breeze's probing tongue, and Breeze pressed a palm to the small of his back to steady him.

He lapped at Alain's hole until he got it dripping wet, and then he wriggled a finger inside him while still circling his rim with his tongue. The way Alain moaned and trembled beneath him almost made Breeze embarrass himself. He'd never been with such a responsive man, one who could appreciate all the sensual teasing he enjoyed so much. He pushed a second finger into Alain and felt his muscles tug him deeper.

Breeze looked at Alain's head on the pillow, his folded arms, golden hair tousled around his face, cheeks as red as the wine he made, eyes clamped shut, lips puffy. He needed to kiss him, push his tongue into him, get closer. He lifted his damp face from Alain's flesh and guided him to his back. As soon as he could, he joined their lips, and they shared each other's air as they ground against each other with short, desperate thrusts, both of them drizzling moisture against the other's belly.

"Can I be inside you?" Breeze huffed out when he broke from Alain's lips. "Alain—"

"Goddesses, yes. Breeze, do you know how I've dreamed of this? Imagined this? You taking me... your cock deep inside me... I touched myself, imagining it. I put my fingers inside myself, imagining they were yours...."

Fucking Shades. Breeze had been close enough to spilling his seed onto Alain's belly before he heard that. Alain wanted him too; he hadn't been the only one suffering. Yearning. Goddesses. "Show me. Show me how you put your fingers inside yourself while you thought about me." He reached over to the table, unscrewed the lid from the salve, and smeared a generous quantity over Alain's elegant, long fingers. Then he sat back on his heels between Alain's splayed legs. "Show me how much you wanted me."

Flushed from his heels to the tips of his ears, Alain tilted his pelvis up and teased at his wrinkled, red opening. Breeze watched, enrapt, as he pushed two and then three fingers into that tight hole. He gnawed at his bottom lip, his brilliant blue gaze never leaving Breeze's. Then he threw his head back and moaned. "Shouldn't you be doing this? I don't want my hands. I want yours."

Breeze leaned down and sucked the dusky pink head of Alain's cock as Alain continued to fuck himself on his fingers. He just wanted Alain to come apart, forget everything but pleasure. Besides, it was fucking amazing to taste his dick while listening to the obscene sounds he made as he pressed his fingers inside himself. Alain hadn't even touched Breeze's cock, but already, this was the best fuck of Breeze's life. If it went no further, Breeze would be satisfied to rub his tongue against the veins and ridges of Alain's cock and let Alain spill down his throat. If he needed that, Breeze would give it to him.

"Want you," Alain keened. "Please."

Breeze drew his mouth slowly up Alain's shaft before letting it slip from his lips. He peppered reverent kisses over the golden curls between his legs and grazed his thighs with his fingertips. "No begging. I would do anything for you, and all you have to do is ask. Or order. I don't care. Goddesses, I'm fucking yours."

"Inside me." Alain grasped Breeze's hair with both hands to pull him up and kiss him. Their bodies lined up without much conscious effort, and Breeze's cockhead nudged at Alain's slicked hole. He gave a small, tentative nudge, and Alain dug his nails into his hips in response. "Oh, please, goddesses, yes!"

Breeze pushed, breaching Alain's slight resistance, and found himself swallowed in heat and pressure. He stilled, waiting for Alain's body to acclimate to the intrusion, sprinkling gentle kisses along Alain's jawline and neck. "Is it all right? I'm not hurting you?"

"No." Alain drew his knees into Breeze's underarms and curled his body up, pressing Breeze deeper into him. He rocked slowly, and

Breeze thrust down to meet him. They moved gingerly, testing, slurping at each other's lips as their bodies got to know one another. Breeze found the angle where he could hit the sweet spot inside Alain, and he drove his cock against it again and again, swallowing the sweet sounds of bliss Alain made, delighting in the way Alain's muscles tightened around his cock. Goddesses, he wanted this to last forever. For the first time, it meant more to him to look down Alain's blissful features, his slack, compliant body, than it did to find release.

Eventually, both of them grasped at each other, their movements clumsy, quick, and desperate. Breeze tugged at Alain's cock, wishing he was flexible enough to bend down and suck it while he thrust into Alain. He contented himself with nipping and suckling Alain's gorgeous lips as he finished with a few short, savage strokes. Just as he almost blacked out from the force of his release, Alain shot so hard he coated his chest in white ribbons, and even spattered his chin. Breeze leaned down to lick it away, swirling the sweet nectar around in his mouth before he swallowed. He kissed Alain. "It's never been like this for me. What did you do?"

"I—nothing. I just really enjoyed myself. You really know what you're doing. You're amazing."

"It was because I—" *Fuck!* "It was because I wanted you so much. Wanted to make you happy. Goddesses, Alain. I could eat your ass forever. It's even sweeter than your wine."

"I'll have to see if yours is the same. I look forward to finding out." He tangled his fingers in Breeze's hair and kissed him, wet and sloppy. "I want to taste your cock, Breeze. Could I do that soon?"

"Bleeding Shades." How had he gotten so lucky? This almost made the burns and the horrible scars a fair price to pay. It wasn't until that thought crossed his mind that he realized Alain was absently touching his disfigured skin, lightly tracing the ledges of the deepest whorls over his ribs. All worry Alain would be disgusted peeled off and fell away, dead and forgotten. Breeze kissed his sweaty forehead. "I'll do my best, friend. Anything to please you."

Hours later, after Alain had sucked him dry and sprayed his seed all over Breeze's face, they lay sleeping, Alain caged against Breeze's chest, snoring softly. "Damn it, friend. That was good." Alain, slumbering, didn't respond. "Good, because I fucking love you. Goddesses help me, I love you. I need to get the fuck out of here."

Chapter Thirteen

SOMETIME BEFORE daylight, with silvery lavender light shining hazily through the windows, Alain rose from Breeze's bed and stretched his arms over his head. His back crackled and popped, and he kneaded the muscles just above his ass with his knuckles. Goddesses, he was sore. Even the back of his throat hurt.

He dressed as quietly as he could so he wouldn't disturb Breeze, who lay stretched out on his back, a forearm draped over his eyes and the balled bedclothes barely concealing his best parts. Alain smiled and pulled the covers up around him as he'd been doing since he dragged him in from the fields. Then, he hadn't known if he'd brought the mercenary into his home just to die, and a buried part of him might have been relieved if he had, to spare Alain from the horror of culling the dead flesh from his wounds. He had never imagined a man could suffer as Breeze had and not die. Now he'd healed almost completely. The swath of burbled pink skin still stretched from his neck to the middle of his thigh, standing in stark contrast to his smooth, deep olive skin, and it probably always would. It hardly made Alain find him less beautiful. He reached down and brushed away a wisp of dark hair that had fallen across Breeze's lips. Looking at those lips, Alain wanted to kiss him again, immerse himself and drown in Breeze as he had the previous night.

He was the worst kind of fool.

Since it would be hours before he needed to start breakfast and he couldn't bear the thought of going to his cold bed alone, Alain poured himself some water from the pitcher on Breeze's nightstand….

Breeze's nightstand. Breeze's room and Breeze's bed. How long after he returned to Rosecairn would Alain keep calling them that? Would this space ever feel like anything other than his?

Alain closed his door because, suddenly, looking down at him hurt too much. He crossed the foyer and noticed the basket of things he'd bought at market. He had forgotten to give Breeze his gift, and now he wondered if he'd been stupid to buy it. Had he made another mistake?

Outside, the light decanting through the clouds and the mist rising in translucent sheets from the ground lent a blurred, gray quality to the vines, trees, hedges, and grass. The whole world felt muddled and soft, almost dreamlike. No wind whispered through the vegetation, and no birds had yet woken to serenade the sun. Alain knew he could find some work he needed to do, or he could just walk. Without really making a decision, he wandered around the back of the house, past the gardens, and over the bridge with the burbling brook beneath. The vineyard was beautiful, and looking at it, breathing in the richness of the loam and the playful, peppery scents of the patch where Boyce's medicinal herbs still grew soothed him. No matter who came and went from his life, this land would be here to nurture and provide for him. It would be with him until they laid his bones at the hillock in the center, and then he'd become fully part of it.

It would be enough.

Alain continued walking north. The farther he got, the more wounded and exposed the fields looked, so different from the lush greenery in the southeast corner of the vineyard. The fire had reduced their apple orchard to blackened, twisted ghosts of the trees where Alain had once spent endless summer days climbing with his sister. He would have to replace them, or lose a significant source of their winter stores, not to mention the cider for themselves and to sell. Only tiny specks of green showed in the fields of verlaut: the first leaves Alain had coaxed from those few bits of root he'd found alive after the blaze. He didn't even want to think about the vast expanses of sienscerre that occupied most of the north of the estate. They were gone, and it would take Alain the rest of his life to regrow all those vines from cuttings—if he could even find enough viable root stock.

He'd felt so hopeful at the conclusion of Y'Airns Market, and they had done well. He'd be able to purchase some vines and maybe some seedlings, but nowhere near enough to replace what they'd lost. With the money from the wine he'd sold and what he could expect from his regular patrons—inns, taverns, and wealthy households who bought in quantity—he could buy enough wheat to get them through the winter. They would be all right for another year, but he couldn't be sure about the next. Goddesses, he might have to sell off some of the land that had been in his family for nine generations just to keep them all alive. When he could no longer stand to think about it, he made his way to a toolshed and tucked a pair of pruning shears into his belt.

As he knelt in the dark, damp soil among the verlaut vines, snipping at errant tendrils, Alain thought about the act of cutting. He'd been taught since he was old enough to understand that paring the vines made them strong, that ridding them of extraneous leaves and shoots made them fight. Even what Elle had told him about Breeze's burns made sense—the dead tissue had to be cut away to allow the living to grow. Letting things long dead remain, things that had passed their time, made everything they touched stagnant and poison. Alain understood, but he couldn't let go of the deceased things he clutched close: his parents, Sabine, Boyce. Somehow he didn't think excising them would let him heal. He couldn't even slough off his ridiculous dream of finding a man to love him, raise a family with him, and stand beside him to guide the winery back to prosperity.

People were waking up, coming to the fields to work, and Alain didn't want to speak with them. He didn't feel like going to breakfast, either, so he stood and wedged his shears back beneath his belt. He kept his head down as he walked briskly to the west, hoping those he passed would think him in a hurry to do something important and not trouble him. He mostly succeeded, making it to the path at the bottom of the cemetery without much more than a few terse nods to the friends he passed.

His thighs ached by the time he reached the top of the hill, and he dropped to his knees in the pillowy grass next to Sabine's and Boyce's graves. For a little while, not long, he wondered if they looked down on him from beside the goddesses, if they were together. He wished he could believe it, but all he knew for certain was that they were gone. Anything else took faith, and Alain didn't have much. After all, the goddesses had ignored the one prayer he'd repeated over and over—to take away his unnatural longings. If only he could cut the abnormal part of him out so something good could grow, then he could be whole.

His mind went blank after a time, and he sat staring at the unremarkable stones that were all that remained of his sister and Boyce. He didn't look up when boots swishing through the grass approached him, or when Breeze sat down next to him and brushed his fringe out of his eyes. After moments of silence, Breeze said, "I thought I might find you here when you didn't come to breakfast. Courtenay fed the chickens, and she and Fenn have gone off to play with those Tooley boys and their sister. Planning to make mud pies, I think."

Alain groaned at the thought of the mess, and then the silence stretched between them again until Breeze cut through it. Leaning his head on Alain's shoulder, he asked, "What are you doing up here, anyway?"

"Thinking," Alain said. "Worrying. Feeling sorry for myself."

"Regretting?" Breeze asked in a small, uncertain voice. Alain had never heard him sound so vulnerable, not even while he screamed and sobbed as Alain tore chunks of flesh from his body. "Regretting what happened last night?"

Was he? Why should he? People—men and women—lay together for nothing more than pleasure every day. He could enjoy it without getting attached; he had to.

"Alain?"

"No. Last night was very nice. I enjoyed it."

"So did I. Very much. What has you looking so troubled, then?"

Alain rubbed his soil-caked fingers across his sweaty forehead. "I just—my head's so full of things, things I don't have any way to figure out, things I don't even know how to put into words."

"Try," Breeze urged, drawing little circles on the inside of Alain's wrist. "Just tell me the first thing you think of."

"Your skin."

"Well, I'm flattered. I would have preferred those thoughts made you smile, though."

"No." Alain tapped his fist against his forehead. He didn't know how to say it. "I was thinking about when I had to scrape off the dead parts, so you could heal. I... I think I'm holding on to dead things. I can't cut them away so *I* can heal."

"Oh, you poor, beautiful man. People you loved aren't the same as putrid chunks of skin. It's right you should hold on to the people you loved."

"Not people. Dreams."

"What dreams?"

Alain had no intention of trying to coerce Breeze to stay with him out of guilt or obligation. Nothing good could grow from that poisoned soil. He didn't want Breeze staying out of pity, either. "Dead ones. Nothing. It doesn't matter. I have wasted enough of the morning sulking up here like a spoiled child. There's work to be done." He stood and offered Breeze his hand.

"Well, tell me what needs done. I'm right here beside you."

Alain couldn't look at him as they made their way down the hill. "That's good, because we have plenty of manure to spread."

THAT NIGHT after dinner, Alain remembered Breeze's gift. He excused himself and slipped out of the kitchen while Breeze and Courtenay washed the dishes and Fenn swept out the hearth. They'd finished by the time he returned with his cloth-covered bundle, and Courtenay sat reading by the fire while Fenn drew in the hearth's ashes with a stick and Breeze sat with a glass of wine.

"What's this?"

Breeze looked as curious and excited as the children as two sets of wide blue eyes and one pair of rich, golden brown ones flecked with liquid gold focused on Alain. He felt foolish. What he'd purchased wouldn't be good enough, but he couldn't go back now, so he sat down at the table and passed it over to Breeze.

As he unwrapped it, Breeze whistled through his teeth. "Can't remember the last time someone gave me a gift."

Just before he lifted the final layer of cloth, Alain caught his wrist and looked hard into his eyes. "It isn't much. I don't want you to be disappointed."

"Alain, how can I be? You saw something and wanted me to have it. It's enough that you thought of me—Bleeding Shades!" He lifted the sword and held it out in front of him while Fenn jumped up and down and clapped. After looking down the blade from various angles, inspecting the hilt, and running his fingertip gingerly along the edge, he laid it across his lap and looked up at Alain again.

Alain's face fell along with Breeze's. Breeze was disappointed. Alain knew he should have bought the sword with the fancier hilt and etchings on the blade, but it had been so expensive. Again, he had failed to provide the best to his family. *Remember, he isn't your family. He never will be.*

"Alain…. Goddesses. This is a really good sword. It's too expensive. I wish you hadn't done this."

"There was a fancier one, but the swordsmith said in actual battle, this one won't let you down. He said it's very similar to swords he makes for the knights of Lockhaven and Windwake, and just as high quality."

"I can see that," Breeze said. "It's better than my old one. I can't believe you did this for me."

Alain grinned so hard his cheeks cramped. He loved watching Breeze marvel over his weapon like a boy. Even Fenn didn't look as fascinated and awestruck. "You said you didn't feel like yourself without one." Alain recalled he'd said *naked*, and he smiled even harder. "I want you to feel like yourself."

"Well, you've done me a real favor. To get back to Rosecairn, I'll have to travel alone through some hostile territory, and I'll be much safer if I'm armed." As Breeze looked across the table, his eyes told Alain everything he couldn't say with his words or his body. Alain could practically feel the kiss of gratitude.

"Can I hold it?" Fenn asked.

"It's very sharp," Alain cautioned gently.

"At least show us what you can do with it!" the boy pressed.

Breeze chuckled. "In the morning, lad. After all, we're still planning to meet by the garden for an archery lesson, right? I had an idea. We can scare up some old grain sacks and a piece of chalk. Draw some enemies on them for you to shoot."

Fenn hooted. "Oh, good idea! Breeze, you have the best ideas! I'll get started first thing. I'll draw a bandit, and a marlcat, and a Cast-Down assassin—"

"No," Breeze said. "Not that, son. That's not a wise thing to mention, let alone make into something real. You should not even think of such things. Nothing that could risk drawing them."

Alain thought that was maybe a little superstitious, but Breeze knew far more about such things, and he had to admit, every story he'd ever heard about...that... had chilled him to the core. He was glad when Fenn changed the subject.

"A mage, then!"

"Aye, a mage," Breeze said with a wink at the boy. "There are tricks to fighting mages, and I know them all. They like to come across like they're all powerful, but if you know what to do, you can take them down."

"I'll shoot his eye out!"

Courtenay blew out an exaggerated sigh. "You're ridiculous! Why do you have to be so loud?"

"Courtenay," Alain scolded, surprised. Shame followed shortly as he realized she hadn't said much during or after dinner, and he'd ignored her reticence in favor of Breeze's present.

"Leave me alone, Alain." She stood, threw the napkin that had been on her lap down so hard it toppled an empty cup, and turned theatrically on her heel. "Just leave me alone. I'm going to bed."

After a few moments of stunned silence, Alain tousled Fenn's hair. "You too. You have big plans for tomorrow, remember?"

With a few more longing glances at Breeze's sword, Fenn turned and went up the narrow staircase. Breeze continued to admire his new weapon as Alain moved to sit next to him on the bench and refill their clay goblets. He rested his shoulder lightly against Breeze, comforted by his solid warmth. "I wonder if I should be worried about Courtenay. She's always kept to herself, but lately she's been even more aloof. She barely speaks all day, and then she does something like that. I wish I knew what to do for her. What could be troubling her?"

Breeze rested his sword against the edge of the table, turned, and straddled the bench so he could knead Alain's tight neck and shoulders with his strong hands. His sigh ruffled Alain's hair and made gooseflesh bloom all over Alain's arms. "I think I know what's troubling her. She's been through a lot, losing her father, but it might be more than that."

"You're worrying me more," Alain said. "What?"

"Nothing as serious as I'm sure you're thinking." Breeze scratched lightly at the back of Alain's neck and into his hair. "Girls—young women—they go through things. I had sisters. They get... breasts. Bleeding. Weird moods. Can't say I can explain it. She just needs somebody who can. Another woman. Maybe Marion could sit down with her. She seems a nice lass."

Breathing a sigh of relief, Alain curled back against him and leaned his head on Breeze's shoulder. "What would I do without you? You figure everything out. You see what I don't. What am I going to do...?"

Breezed wrapped his arms around Alain's waist and laughed as if he didn't know what Alain had almost let slip, so Alain let himself believe Breeze didn't know. "Don't worry. It'll pass. In a few years, she'll be your sweet daughter again. That's what happened with my sisters. Went bleeding mad for a while, and then back to normal. Not that they were ever sweet. Vain, power-hungry, scheming, pampered harridans. Mother taught them well." Alain detected the bitter note beneath his affected humor, like a rancorous finish on a wine, just on the back of the tongue after swallowing.

"Goddesses." Alain tried to mirror the false comedy. "A few years?"

Breeze brushed his hair aside to kiss up and down the side of Alain's neck. Alain let out a fragmented breath. He closed his eyes and soon everything faded away except Breeze's lips on his skin, his finger circling Alain's nipple through the thin fabric of his shirt. Breeze whispered something near his ear, and the sound moved down Alain's neck and chest, straight to his tightening root. "Breeze? What did you say? What were we talking about?"

His chuckle, damp against Alain's face, reverberated through Alain's belly, making his insides quiver and clench. "I was suggesting we finish cleaning up here and go to bed. What you did—everything you've done for me—has meant more than I can tell you. I might have better luck showing you instead."

HIS THIGHS and belly trembling with exertion, Alain dropped his head between Breeze's shoulder blades and clutched tight to his waist, distantly aware of the smooth skin on one side and the spongy, tangled scar tissue on the other. He immersed himself in Breeze: the tight heat of his body, the scent of his skin, the sound of his hitched breaths and the swish of his blood. As he pressed deep into Breeze, eliciting a grateful groan from him with every thrust, he let himself sink, let himself drown in Breeze until the waters were still, with no ripples on the surface and no sunken rocks and locked boxes beneath. There was just Breeze and the way his inner muscles hugged Alain's cock until Alain could feel the heartbeat within him, and still he wanted to get closer, deeper, lodge himself in Breeze until they couldn't separate themselves any more than a vine could tear its roots from the nurturing soil.

Breeze shook with the strain of holding himself up on his weak arm, and Alain held tight to his chest as he lowered him against the bed so he lay flat on his belly. The new position increased the pressure around Alain's cock, and even though he couldn't go as deep into Breeze, it let him angle himself to pump against Breeze's honey spot with every shallow plunge. Breeze buried his face in the pillows to muffle his rhythmic cries. More than anything, Breeze's pleasure and complete abandon, his total and unconditional offering of himself to Alain, drove Alain over the edge. Beneath him, Breeze stiffened, jerked his hips, and shook.

"Oh, goddesses." Alain hadn't even touched his dick, but Breeze thrashed his head from side to side, sweaty dark hair flailing around, eyes rolled back in his head. "You... are... so beautiful. Breeze, I...." Alain closed his lips around Breeze's neck and sucked at his skin as his entire being coiled, tightened, and then broke apart like a sudden storm from a summer sky. He didn't even know he was crying out, almost wailing, until Breeze twisted around to catch his mouth and swallow the sound.

They lay together, still joined, caressing each other and catching their breath as they floated down from the heights of their pleasure. It had left Alain feeling raw and vulnerable, his emotions exposed like a root after a hard storm as he rolled off Breeze and onto his back. Breeze seemed to sense it, and he guided Alain over so they could wind their arms around each other and press their foreheads together.

Stroking Alain's cheek with his knuckles, Breeze asked, "What?"

Alain hesitated, wondering what and how much to say. After a few minutes in Breeze's arms, he settled down and felt content and drowsy. "I've never done that before."

Breeze traced his finger along the shell of Alain's ear. "You'd never know it after that performance."

"It was all right for you?"

With an incredulous chuckle, Breeze said, "Friend, I blacked out so hard when I came I thought sure I was dead, and I didn't care. And when I came to, I swore I was with the goddesses. Still not sure I'm not. You can do that to me again anytime."

"With," Alain said.

"Hmm?"

"Not to you. With you. I know the difference between having it done to me and someone doing it with me. That was *with*, wasn't it, Breeze?"

"Aye." The sweet gentleness of Breeze's kiss said more than his single word. "Then with—me and you—anytime you like. Any way you like."

"I'm going to do it," Alain said suddenly.

"What, already?"

Alain chuckled and kissed the tip of Breeze's nose. "No. I'm going take your advice about the ice wine. I'm going to take a chance for once. The majority of the grapes we have left are the best ones to make it—the breumaurinier and the l'oeil d'Estrelle."

"What are those?" Breeze asked, leaning up on his elbow to look down at Alain.

"'The Eyes of the Goddess Estrella.' They're amazing grapes: tiny, almost completely white. At night, they almost seem to glow. In a moon or so, we can stand at the crest of the hill and look down at them. It's like looking at a field of stars. And they're delicious, with a delicate bouquet like wild lavender, tart apples, and violets. Mix the two grapes, and the result is amazing. From the two intact fields at the southeast corner of the vineyard, we can get at least two thousand bottles of ice wine. If we can… oh, goddesses, I'm sorry. This isn't your problem. You must be ready to fall asleep, listening to me prattle on." Alain flopped onto his back.

"No." Breeze circled his sensitive, slightly tender nipple. "It's actually fascinating. All the wine I drank over the years, and I never realized how much went into it. It's an art. Something way beyond a man like me, but I'll help all I can while I'm here. I'm at least good for spreading shit, right?"

Alain didn't find it funny when Breeze put himself down. In fact, he hated it. "No. No, it isn't beyond you. You've learned it all so fast, learned what it usually takes me years to teach the apprentice vintners. You're hardly some barbarian oaf swinging a club, and I don't like it when you talk about yourself as if you are."

Breeze's fingers wandered to the meandering trail of hair below Alain's belly button. "It was just a joke, but you don't like jokes, so I'm sorry."

"I'm sorry too, for taking things so seriously. I just don't like jokes when they hurt people. It hurts me to think you might actually believe that about yourself."

"Well, you hear it long enough, it's hard not to believe it a little. Fuck, now I'm whining."

"That's hardly whining," Alain said.

"Can we get back to your ice wine? I take it you'll make a lot of gold if you can make your two thousand bottles. But what if it doesn't get cold in time? Then you'll lose two thousand bottles."

"This was your idea, wasn't it?" Alain reminded him.

"It was, and it's what I would do if I were you, but I'm impetuous and not terribly clever."

"You're doing it again."

Breeze laughed. "Yeah, sorry."

"My turn, then," Alain said. "I'm frightened of failing, of the future, of being alone, left with nothing but memories and dead dreams. And I'm tired of it. The ice wine will either be a brilliant success or it will go down in flames. Oh, bad choice of words."

"Very bad," Breeze agreed with a lopsided grin. "For what it's worth, I think you'll do it. I think you'll make three thousand bottles of the best wine Selindria has ever tasted."

Alain raked his nails through the soft, dark hair on Breeze's belly, even thinner than his own, just a dusting to accentuate the groove between his muscles. "Hmm. You may be biased."

"Fucking right I am," Breeze said. "I think you're brilliant, and beautiful, and amazing with making things grow, and, fuck, Alain, I... I know you can do it."

"I could save you a few bottles," Alain dared, drunk on the hope blooming in him for the first time since the fire. "Put them in the cellar, in case you ever find your way back here."

Breeze's silence, the way he turned his face from Alain's on the pillow, shattered that hope like a bottle dropped on cold stone.

"I should go," Alain said, sitting up. "I can't fall asleep here."

To his surprise, Breeze pulled him down when he tried to leave the bed. He held Alain against his chest and crossed his arms over Alain's back. From the way he breathed into Alain's hair, Alain expected some profound declaration, but Breeze said, "I should throw you over my shoulder like a maiden and carry you off to Rosecairn with me. No one would care if we shared a bed. And then, then I could finally introduce you to the sweetest pleasure in the goddesses' world."

"Oh, and what's that?"

Breeze pushed his hardening cock against Alain's belly and reached down to slip a finger between Alain's cheeks. "Sleeping until after the midday meal. Waking up to cold ham, flat ale, and a slow, sleepy fuck that lasts an hour or so. Then a little more sleep. Bread, cheese, more ale. More fucking. More sleep. And then again. See?"

Alain chuckled against Breeze's neck as he circled his hips. He decided he might really like straddling Breeze and riding his cock. He sat up, arching his body forward, pushing his nipple right into Breeze's insatiable mouth. "Oh, goddesses, Breeze. Stop it. Stop. That's sore. Goddesses, that one too."

"Sorry. I wish I could take you with me, though. Wish you weren't so trapped here."

"You still don't understand me," Alain panted into the part of Breeze's hair as he reached behind him for the salve. "I don't want to leave here. I love this place. And I... I don't want to trap you. I wish we had longer."

"We have tonight," Breeze said, closing his hands over Alain's thighs to move him into place.

"We do." Alain eased himself down and took full advantage of the few hours until daybreak.

Chapter Fourteen

POSTS HAD to be put up to support Alain's suckling vines, and thick ropes strung between them to cradle the tendrils, which meant a few hard days of digging, setting poles, and filling in the pits around them. By the fifth day, Breeze's muscles ached, though it satisfied him to look down the rows and see the sturdy, even supports they'd set. They only had a few more rows to go to complete the trellises for the northwestern field of sienscerre, and then Alain had promised him a bath and a massage—one he intended to return. As soon as they finished, he could get his hands back on that ivory skin. The visions in his head motivated Breeze to dig even though his injured muscles began to protest.

Breeze dug the holes, the burly fellow called Denis placed the rails, and two lanky youths Breeze didn't know replaced the dirt around them. Following far behind, Alain fastidiously strung rope between the posts and guided the emerging tendrils to wrap around the supports, while stopping to clip any extraneous growth.

When he'd finally finished his row, Breeze stumbled a few steps, dropped his spade, and collapsed in the soft grass beneath a nearby tree. He took the water skin from his belt and drank deeply. Looking out over the field and the rows and rows of posts, little speckles of green dotting the ground, gave him hope the winery would recover. Continue. It pleased him to have had a small part in its healing, and being pleased surprised him. He'd found the work so crucial, he'd even forgotten to get bored.

Alain sat down next to him, smelling of sweat, soil, and verdant growth. Cheeks and nose burned. The most beautiful damn thing

Breeze had ever seen. He fought to keep his hands to himself when Alain sprawled on his back, reached his arms over his head, and stretched his elegant, pale neck. His pert nipples peaked the worn summer shirt he wore, and Breeze remembered torturing them playfully and wondered if they remained sensitive and red. With all his chastisements about fighting for money and foul language, Breeze had worried Alain might be a bit of a prude, but he'd proved enthusiastic and very willing to try new things. Alain had a good imagination, and plenty of ideas of his own.

Breeze was just about to remind Alain of his promise when Marion came running through the field, holding her skirts. "Alain, you have to come," she panted out.

He got to his feet and took her hands. "What is it? What's wrong?"

"Courtenay is missing." She turned and started jogging down the hill, and Breeze got to his feet to follow them. After a mile or so, the poor woman just couldn't keep running. She slowed to a brisk walk. "There is a large patch of owl-berries growing across the road from the main gate. I thought I'd take Courtenay to pick some, and then we could make jam. Maybe a pie. I thought it would give us a chance to talk, like you wanted. Courtenay seemed excited about it, so we left Fenn a ways inside the gate, playing with some of the other boys. Well, after a few hours, a fight broke out. You know how they are at that age.

"I didn't think anything of leaving Courtenay to go break up the boys. She's a good girl, and she knows the land for miles around like the back of her hand. Oh, Alain, I'm so sorry. I can't imagine what could have happened. I was only gone a little while, but Lou Hurron had a fat lip...."

"Just tell us what happened," Breeze urged.

Marion wiped her red, sweaty face on her apron. "By the time I got back to the berry patch, Courtenay was gone. All I found was a half a basket of berries. I checked by the wells in case she'd gotten thirsty, and then I looked all around in your house and the gardens. I can't find her anywhere, and no one's seen her."

"Please calm down," Alain told Marion. It was miles from where they'd been working to the front gate, and they'd made it about halfway by alternating between walking and running. Breeze hadn't realized how much damage the smoke had done to his chest until he found himself out of breath after a few miles of running. This time last year, he'd been able to run for hours. "Courtenay has been going off by herself lately, since Boyce died. I'm sure we'll find her hiding somewhere, probably with a book. And then I'll give her a good scolding for scaring the life out of you. Please try not to worry until then. There's really nowhere on or around the vineyard where she could get hurt."

"I know that," the woman said. "I'll just feel better when we find her."

They reached the gate, and Marion led them to the patch of owl-berries, apologizing over and over. Alain rested a hand on her shoulder when they reached the abandoned basket full of round orange berries with black dots that made them resemble an owl's eye. Breeze crouched down to take a closer look at the trampled grass. He could see where the girl's feet had made little indents as she'd wandered from bush to bush, but he also found deep ruts where the grass had been uprooted in a regular path leading toward the road.

"I'm sure she just wandered off," Alain said to Marion. "Probably chasing a butterfly or something."

Breeze stood, a cold dread in his belly he'd never felt in regards to his own safety, and a fire pumping through his veins, making his hands tremble with rage. "No. No, Alain, she didn't. Look at these marks on the ground. Horses. At least three or four." He took Alain's wrist and pointed. "They turned around here, and then they made their way toward the road. See how the prints get farther apart? The horses picked up speed when they reached the gravel. They're heading southeast. What's in that direction?"

"Nothing," Alain said, the color draining from his face. "Fields. Some forest. A few villages, but not for half a day's ride. Why would anyone take Courtenay? Goddesses, that oily merchant from Y'Airns! Could he have.... Breeze, what should we do? Go to the castle? Tell the valen and his knights? What?"

"It's hours to the castle. We should go while the trail is fresh, so we don't lose them. Send one of your people to tell the valen if you want, but we should go after her. Now. I swear to you, Alain, I'll find whoever took Courtenay, and if they've so much as put her in a foul mood, I'll kill them. Go saddle your two fastest horses. I'm going to get my sword."

Whoever had taken Courtenay had a few hours' head start, but Breeze had little trouble following their trail through the rocky, mountainous terrain, past a few farms and fields of goats and sheep grazing on the windswept grass. They pushed their horses hard to try to bridge the gap, through a little evergreen forest and into the deeper woods, where the trees grew thick enough to block the sun and cast them in a greenish gloom. So far, the riders had stayed to the road, and when it branched off, Breeze didn't think he'd have trouble discerning which path they'd taken. Problem was, from the hoof marks on the ground, it looked like they'd split up—two horses continuing southeast and three, maybe four, turning dead south. Breeze reined his animal to a stop and dismounted, swearing.

"WHAT IS it?" Alain asked, pulling his bay gelding to a halt.

"They split off here." Breeze knelt down to examine the tracks. He had no trouble seeing which way they went by the gouges they'd left in the dark soil and the bent bracken alongside the trail, but he had no way to know which party included Courtenay.

"Maybe we should do the same," Alain suggested. "You can take one road, and I'll take the other."

"No." He had no intention of letting Alain out of his sight, where he couldn't protect him. "You're not going off to face three or four armed men, and maybe others they're meeting, without me."

"She's my daughter, Breeze. I'm not a warrior like you, but dammit to the goddesses, I'm not useless. We're wasting time. They could be hurting Courtenay. Somehow I have to find them and stop them. I'm going south. You take the other trail. Breeze, please. Every moment we stand here…." Alain screwed his eyes shut tight, and Breeze couldn't bear to imagine the words he hadn't been able to say.

He had a point, and if Breeze had been with another one of the Roses, he'd have agreed. But Alain couldn't fight. He was brave and strong, and Breeze knew he'd fight fiercely to his last breath for his family, but he had never been trained to use a weapon. He didn't even have one. "I'm going where you go. We'll ride south, try to catch up to those men. If we find them and they don't have Courtenay, we'll make them tell us where the others are taking her."

"And give them goddesses know how much more time to do whatever they're planning to do!" Alain shouted. Breeze had never heard him raise his voice, but his terror was tearing him apart. "Breeze, take the other trail. I'm begging you. If you never do anything else for me, do this. Please!"

He couldn't agree. If Alain rode into a camp of mercenaries alone, unarmed, he wouldn't be riding out. But how could he deny Alain the only thing he'd ever asked of him. Fuck! They should have taken the time to round up a few more men, but Alain had been so frantic—

"Breeze, let's go!"

Breeze held up his hand. Amidst the muted browns, grays, and greens of the dark forest, something sparkled down the southern path. Breeze sprinted toward it, knelt down, and pushed the leaf litter away to reveal a soiled blue satin bow. "Oh, good girl. Clever girl." He ran back to retrieve his horse.

As they rode, Alain informed Breeze the forest was home to woodsmen, hunters, charcoal-burners, and many others. The narrow, twisting paths branched off, circled back, and split several times, but each time, Breeze found one of the clues Courtenay had left: a button, a scrap of fabric from her dress, a lace from her boot. When she'd run out of things she could drop without alerting her captors, she'd resorted to pulling out clumps of her pale yellow hair and leaving them caught on bracken and low-hanging branches. By sunset, they'd reached a part of the woods that would abut the mountains in a few miles. These bastards had nowhere left to go.

"We're going to find these sons of whores," Breeze said. "And then I'm going to make them wish they'd never seen the light of day."

COURTENAY HAD never been so scared. The three men in the dirty armor and patchy furs who smelled like onions and stale wine stopped their horses in front of a rickety little shack with moss on the roof. The one she'd been riding with, a fat man with a swollen red nose, lifted her from the saddle in front of him and set her on her feet. She ran, but she didn't get far before the one with the white beard, stained yellow around his lips from his stinky pipe, caught her around the waist and clapped his hand over her mouth. She squirmed and tried to scream, but he carried her into the shack with the other two following.

The third man was young and reminded Courtenay of someone who might work with Alain on the vineyard. His eyes didn't seem as hard as the others, and he didn't laugh when the man with the white beard tossed her on her hip. She scuttled to the corner of the windowless little room and drew her knees to her chest.

The man with the red nose drew his sword and pointed it at her. "You sit right there and be a good girl, and we won't have any problems. And when Tam Almes gets here to take you, you be a good girl for him too. You're to be his wife, and you'd better act like it." Everyone but the young mercenary chuckled. Then they left and locked the door.

Courtenay scanned the room for something she could use to defend herself. She'd been watching and listening as Breeze taught Fenn to use his sword and his bow, and Breeze hadn't played at it, hadn't given her brother the child's version. From observing, she knew a few tricks: to hit them in the groin, to go for the eyes, how little it took to break the bone between a man's neck and his shoulder. Of course, the men who grabbed her while she'd been picking berries hadn't left her with so much as a twig. The room didn't even contain a chamber pot she could use to hit them in the nose. She tugged on the door handle, but it didn't budge. She wanted to scream and cry, but she didn't want the men coming back. Moving along the walls, she checked the boards for anything loose, anything rotten she could kick in to make a hole big enough to crawl out. She found nothing. One way or another, she had to get out of this room before that greasy man from Y'Airns Market showed up to make her his wife.

From stories, from sneaking books Alain said she couldn't read until she was older, she had some idea what being a wife meant. She didn't understand exactly how it all worked, and she didn't want to find out—not with flabby old Wagonnier Almes. She just wanted to go home.

She sat down on the floor and cried. A man was on his way to hurt her and take her away from her family. Alain and Breeze hadn't found the clues she'd left along the trail; it hadn't worked like it had in the story. What if they weren't on their way? What if they didn't make it in time? She felt bad because she'd called Fenn a grubby little piglet that morning, and now she might never see him again.

And that made her angry. What right did these bastards have to decide who she married? To take her away from her life and her family? Rage formed a hot ball in her belly, so hot it hurt her chest. It moved down her arms and legs, making her skin tingle. Her fingertips felt numb, hot and cold at the same time, and her teeth wiggled in her mouth.

UP AHEAD, sheltered by an outcropping of rock that cast it in shadow as the sun fell, stood a run-down shack with three horses tied in front. Though it looked tiny from this distance, they'd reach it in less than half an hour. Alain dug his heels into his horse's ribs, ignoring Breeze's pleas that he wait. The animal cantered hard for a few moments, nostrils flaring, but then the steady and reliable gelding reared and whinnied. To keep from being thrown, Alain grasped a handful of mane, and then the reins with his other hand. The horse spun in circles, his nose almost touching his flank, as Alain tried to guide him back onto the path and toward the cabin. A look over his shoulder showed Breeze struggling with his chestnut mare.

Everything went quiet, and all sound—the wind in the leaves, birds, and insects—died. A shiver moved up Alain's spine, and cold quills brushed over his skin, raising gooseflesh, making him feel like his teeth wanted to escape his mouth. He recognized the feeling, though he couldn't remember from where or when.

"Bloody Shades," Breeze shouted, the volume of his voice feeling like sacrilege, like he'd shouted in a temple. "Alain, it's a spell. Someone's doing magic!"

"What do I—" Before Alain could finish his question, the tiny shack in the distance burst into flames. The horses snapped their reins and ran from the building engulfed in a ball of fire. Acting on pure instinct, Alain leapt from the saddle and ran, praying Courtenay wasn't inside, ignoring the warnings Breeze shouted at him as he struggled to keep up. Alain had no idea what he'd do when he reached the burning building, collapsing now, sending mushrooms of smoke and streams of sparks into the darkening sky, but he had to get there. Goddesses, whoever had taken Courtenay had a mage!

The smell of the smoke made Alain's stomach lurch as it summoned all his memories of the last fire he'd endured, and what it had cost him. No. Not this time. No more burnt flesh and dead dreams. How much more could the goddesses take from him?

Still, he faltered when he reached the blaze, all of it rushing back as he felt the heat on his face. He wanted to curl in a ball and cover his head. Even Breeze, when he caught up, swore and pressed his fist against his teeth. He found his fortitude faster than Alain, ran to the shack, and kicked the door open. A gust of smoke obscured him for a moment, and Alain scrubbed at his watering eyes. When his vision cleared, Breeze carried Courtenay in his arms. She sobbed and wailed as she held on to his neck, her dress torn, her hair a mess, soot streaking her red face, but whole and alive. Alain ran to them and threw his arms around both of them, pressing his face to Courtenay's and shedding a few tears of his own. "Oh, goddesses. I thought I'd lost you too."

The three of them held each other, crying and uttering prayers of thanks, while behind them, the shack fell in on itself. Finally, Alain lifted his head and met Courtenay's red, swollen eyes.

"What happened?"

"Can we sit down?" Breeze asked. "This has taken it out of me. I'm sorry, but if I don't sit, I'm going to fall over."

Alain felt the same, though he hadn't realized it until Breeze said something. They walked a little way into the woods and collapsed on the ground. Courtenay moved from Breeze's lap to Alain's, and he held her tight. He never wanted her out of his arms again. "Love, what happened?"

"It was that oily merchant from Y'Airns," she choked out. "He still wants to marry me. He paid those men to bring me here. He was coming to… to get me."

Breeze lifted his head from where he'd rested it on his knee. "That slimy son of a bitch is coming here? I say we wait for him."

"No!" Courtenay shrieked. "No, Breeze! Please no. I don't want to see him. Not ever. I just want to go home."

"Take her home, Alain. Let me wait for that dog-fucking piece of shit. I'll see he never leaves this wood."

"No, Breeze," Courtenay pleaded. "Please. Please come home, so I don't have to worry anymore. I just want everyone I love home and safe. I want to get away from this place."

"Courtenay, how did the fire start?" Alain asked.

"I did it," she said.

"With what?"

"With nothing," she answered, looking down at her tiny fists. "I was so angry and so scared, and it just... came out of me. Out of my hands. Out of the wood. The walls. Everywhere. It burned a hole in the wall between me and the soldiers. They took their weapons out, but it was still coming. I don't know how it happened, but it hit the men who wanted to hurt me and killed them, and it let me get out of there. Maybe the goddesses sent it."

"No, they didn't," Breeze said. "Princess, my love, you made that fire. Courtenay, you're a mage."

IT TOOK some time to find where the horses had wandered, but when they did, they made their way toward the main road and home. Soon, Courtenay slumbered in the saddle in front of Alain. They let the horses take their time, and the moon rode high above them by the time they cleared the woods. So many questions swooped and swam through Alain's head that he couldn't catch a single one long enough to put it into words. Like Courtenay, he wanted the safety of his gate and his stone walls, the familiarity of his land and his grapes. He wanted to talk, but he couldn't express the new fears and doubts piled on top of the old.

Breeze guided his mare alongside Alain's horse as soon as the trail widened out. He reached over and rubbed Alain's shoulder. "Friend, I want you to know the men in my company aren't like the ones back there."

"I know."

"Octavian wouldn't take a job like that, no matter the pay. No one in the Roses would."

"You don't have to convince me you aren't like those men," Alain said. "I'm just glad it's over."

For a few moments, nothing broke the night's silence but the clomp of their horses' hooves. When Breeze spoke, Alain barely heard him. "Perhaps, perhaps not."

"What do you mean?"

"The hirelings were killed in Courtenay's fire, but Almes wasn't. He seems determined. He could hire more men and try again."

"Goddesses." Alain's thoughts rippled and churned. "I should go to the valen. What Almes is doing can't be allowed under the law."

"Alain," Breeze said cautiously, looking over, probably to make sure he hadn't woken Courtenay. "A wealthy man carrying off a country girl for his bride? I wish I could say otherwise, but it happens all the time. What do you think the valen will do? Send knights to guard your daughter? Send them to apprehend this man and drag him to a trial before the priestesses?"

"I guess that does sound silly," Alain said, despairing. "What do I do?"

"You aren't alone in this," Breeze said. "I'll figure out a way to put a stop to it, and until I do, I'm right here, protecting you and our... and your family. I swear. Besides, your girl can take care of herself now. She's powerful."

"How can any of this be true?" Alain asked the stars and the jagged fringe of ironstone mountains far to the north. "How can Courtenay be a mage? There's no magic in our line."

"What about in Boyce's line?" Breeze asked.

"I honestly don't know. I don't know much about his family. He met my sister at a small country fair, and they were married by the end of the summer. It goes against tradition, but he came to live on the vineyard instead of Sabine leaving to live with him. She told him she couldn't live doing anything other than growing grapes, and they were very much in love."

"And what did he do before?" Breeze asked.

"He was a healer's apprentice."

"A mage?"

Alain shook his head. "He knew how to make poultices and tinctures, how to work with herbs and minerals. He could set bones and bring fevers down, but he didn't have the gift."

"It doesn't matter where it came from," Breeze said. "She has the gift, and it's strong."

Alain felt like he'd plummeted into a bizarre dream, suspended in dark water and unable to find the surface. "Something else must have happened. She knocked over an oil lamp or something. It has to be something like that."

"Alain, denying it won't make it go away."

"What do you think I should do next?"

"She clearly has a lot of magic she can't control. She'll need training. You might find a local mage, but the best place is Espero. In Espero, there's nothing unusual about being a mage. She'd never be made to feel different or alone."

Alain gathered Courtenay tighter. He couldn't bear the idea of sending her away—of losing her years before he would have under normal circumstances. "You dislike mages," he muttered into her hair. "Does that mean—"

"That I dislike Courtenay?" Breeze snorted. "Don't you know me better than that by now? I love her. Of course I do. It's no more her fault that she has the gift than it was mine that I didn't."

Thankfully, a few young men were still working in the stable when they reached it, and they offered to take the horses. Alain accepted gratefully and thanked them. Despite having been in the fields since before dawn, he carried Courtenay up the hill to the house. He couldn't stand the thought of her out of the safety of his arms. With Breeze following, he trudged up the stairs to her book-lined room and laid her gently on her bed. He sat on the edge to remove her boots. Her feet were so small and perfect, her toes like little pink beans. Alain remembered marveling over her tiny feet when she was a baby, and looking at them now, he thought she was still so young—too young to leave home for an island halfway across the world. He leaned in, kissed her, and whispered into her hair, "Everything's going to be all right. You're back where you belong."

"Alain, will you sleep here with me tonight? I don't want to be alone," Courtenay mumbled.

"Of course." He stretched out and pulled the worn blue quilt over them. Courtenay put her head on his chest, just as she had when he'd rocked her to sleep as an infant.

"Well, good night, then," Breeze said, smiling as he turned toward the door.

"Breeze," Courtenay muttered, already drowsy, "can't you stay too? I feel safe when you're here."

After the day they'd endured, Breeze had to be stiff and hurting. A night on the padded bench beside Courtenay's bay window would make for a miserable morning for him. "He'll be right downstairs in his bed," Alain said. "He should be comfortable. He's still wounded."

"I understand," she whispered.

"Nonsense," Breeze said, fluffing one of the pillows on the bench. "Compared to some of the places I've slept, this is the bosom of the goddesses." He lay down and let his feet dangle over the edge of the couch. In moments, his breath grew deep, slow, and even. Alain doubted Breeze intended anyone to hear when he spoke; he might have been talking in his sleep. "This is where I belong, protecting the people I love."

Chapter Fifteen

THREE DAYS later, while Alain and Breeze worked in the southeastern corner of the vineyard, tending to the l'oeil d'Estrelle upon which Alain had placed the winery's fate, a carriage flanked by six riders pulled to a stop in front of the main gate. Though Alain had a good idea who they belonged to, he looked to Breeze for confirmation. The mercenary stood with his fists clenched tight and a muscle twitching at the corner of his jaw. "Come on, Alain. I've been waiting for a chance to have a word with this son of a bitch."

Alain didn't know whether to thank Breeze or to beg him not to make trouble for the vineyard, so he just jogged along behind him, chewing on his lower lip. By the time they reached the gate, dozens of people had gathered, leaning on their rakes and spades and shielding their eyes from the strong sun as they stared at the carriage and the armed men guarding it. Breeze, with Alain in tow, shouldered his way through the throng until he stood just inside the iron bars. Though he sweated and shook, Alain lifted his chin and stood shoulder to shoulder with Breeze. He even found the courage to speak in a clear voice that belied none of his nerves. "If you are here to patronize our winery, we will be happy to serve you. If not, we'll have to ask you to be on your way. At least show us the courtesy of telling us who has come to call."

Behind Alain, his workers and friends grumbled their assent as the carriage door groaned open, and predictably, Tam Wagonnier Almes waddled out. Breeze lunged, but Alain reached out an arm to halt him and said, "We have no interest in your patronage, I'm afraid. You're not welcome here. Leave."

"You know as well as I do I have no interest in your wines. There are plenty of other vineyards. You know very well what I want. Give me what I came for, and I won't demand recompense for the men of mine your daughter killed and the damage she did to my property. Turn her over to me, and I'll teach that little wench some respect for her betters."

Alain could no longer hold Breeze back. "You son of a donkey-fucked whore! Tell you what, get the fuck out of here and I won't come over there, tear off your balls, and shove them down your throat!"

Many of the people assembled cheered openly. Word of what had transpired at Y'Airns Market had spread, and on the vineyard, nearly everyone looked at Courtenay as a daughter, just as they did all the other children. They were a family, and no one threatened one of their own without facing the whole clan. By now, the men, and even some of the women, brandished their farming tools like weapons.

Almes just chuckled, making the wattle of skin on his neck flap back and forth. "Yes, I remember you. The mercenary, and quite a skilled one. Tell me, how does a simple winemaker afford to hire a man of your caliber? I asked myself that question, and the answer seemed simple enough. Clearly, this handsome young vintner is offering you something other than coin. I won't sink so low as to naming what we all know that is, but if you don't do as I demand, I'll make sure everyone knows it. See who'll want to buy your wine then. Who will want to buy wine from an unnatural deviant? I'm a very successful merchant, and I can ruin you."

"Not if I ruin you first!" Breeze grabbed the bars and shook the gate. One of the men on horseback drew a sword, but before he could swing, a tiny arrow flew through the air with a hummingbird buzz, and pierced his palm. The man howled, and his weapon fell with a clang to the ground.

"My Uncle Alain said get out of here." Even with his high-pitched, young voice, Fenn sounded fierce. His next arrow found a mark in another mercenary's thigh. Though the man screamed, cursed, and threatened to tear Fenn in half, Alain couldn't help feeling proud. He'd never wanted his nephew—son, now—to be a warrior, but Fenn's bravery and skill impressed everyone. The other farmers hooted and volleyed taunts back at Almes and his hirelings.

Almes shouted above everyone. "Give me what I have come for! One worthless, stupid little girl! Give her to me, or compensate me for the damage to my people and property."

"They got what they deserved for agreeing to kidnap a child!" Breeze threatened to tear the gate from its hinges. "Open it, Alain!"

Almes took a step back, the coward. Part of Alain wanted to let Breeze have a go at him, though he'd never been one to believe anything could be solved through beating someone to a bloody smear. In Almes's case, he might make an exception. But he never got a chance to express an opinion, one way or the other, because a stone sailed over the top prongs on the gate and struck Almes in the cheek, opening a gash. He cried out, but the stones kept coming until he retreated into his carriage. His men backed their horses away as they tried to shield their faces with their arms. The farmers grew rowdy and waved their tools in the air, shouting for the men to leave in no uncertain—and in some cases, very vulgar—terms. Stones continued to arc over the gate until Almes and his party had no choice but to retreat. As they whipped their horses to hurry away, Almes shouted something out his carriage window, but over the other voices, Alain couldn't make out his words. Goddesses forgive him, he held up his hands and made that rude gesture he'd learned from Breeze at the men's backs.

Grinning wide, Alain turned to Breeze, surprised when his victory didn't reflect back at him from the other man. Breeze kicked some dirt and gravel against the gate and scowled. Alain supposed he just regretted losing his chance to give Almes and his mercenaries a good thrashing. Part of Alain lamented missing the opportunity to see it— Breeze fighting, moving so fast with such fluid grace—allured him and stoked his lust. The first time he'd seen it, he'd been left tingling with his mouth hanging open. But Breeze would get past it, and so would he. At least they'd driven the bastard off. Alain clapped Breeze on the shoulder. "I think we've seen the last of him now! He knows what to expect if he comes round here again!"

"'Course, Alain," Breeze mumbled, staring down at the dust coating his boot. "I'm sure that's done it. Go on, then. I want to check on Courtenay, make sure all of this hasn't upset her."

"Thank you." Alain wanted to kiss him, hard, victoriously, but he contented himself with a smile that promised proper gratitude later.

Then he found Fenn, scooped him up to sit on his shoulder, and addressed his gathered friends. "Let's all gather for dinner at the main house tonight. It's been too long since we got together to celebrate this vineyard and the people who make it what it is. Bring anything you like, or nothing at all. We'll roast meat over the fire, and I'll provide the wine."

COURTENAY WORE the pretty dress Alain had just finished, the one made from the fabric Breeze had chosen, with the embroidered roses, to the informal feast. Alain let Fenn carry his bow, but not his arrows, and brag to his little heart's content about how he'd shot two mercenaries threatening the vineyard. Even boys twice his age were suitably impressed. Fenn deserved the accolades. Everyone seemed to have a wonderful time, though Breeze kept his distance and spoke little to Alain until the children were in bed, everyone had gone home, and the fat, rosy summer moon made leisurely progress toward setting.

Together, they gathered the few errant plates left behind on the porch or the grass and piled them in the sink. They doused the fire and blew out the candles and lanterns, and then they went inside to the sitting room. After they sat a few moments in silence, Breeze said, "I'm leaving in the morning."

Alain felt like someone had reached inside him, pulled out his belly and his heart, thrown them on the floor, and stomped on them. "What do you mean?"

Breeze turned to face him on the bench, met his gaze, and took both his hands. "It's time I'm off. Back to Rosecairn. I'm well enough to fight again, and I can't keep hiding here and avoiding my life and my destiny. I should get back while the season is still fair. Tomorrow's as good a time as any."

"Yes," Alain said through a swollen throat. "Yes, why not?"

"Good. That's settled, then. I can't tell you enough how much I appreciate everything, how much I've enjoyed my time here. At first I thought it would be frightfully dull, but damn if you don't have something special here. I have to thank you for letting me be part of it for a little while."

"Stop," Alain croaked, a pitiful sound even to his own ears. "Please stop. I can't hear this."

"Why?"

"I... I don't know. I don't know the words to show you what's inside. You have to go. I understand that. You have chosen your path as I've chosen mine, but.... Breeze, it hurts. It hurts me to lose you. I know I shouldn't say so, but I cannot help it. I am going to miss you."

"I'm going to miss you too," Breeze said, reaching up to cup Alain's chin. "But we both knew this day would come. Your place is here. Mine... isn't."

"No. I suppose not."

"If you want to be alone tonight, I'll understand. I can be gone even before you rise in the morning."

"Breeze, no. Go to your room. Undress and wait for me. I have something to share with you: the last bottle of the pure fierrine my grandfather made, long before I was born. It was a remarkable year, the finest vintage in generations. I have been saving it for something special."

"You should keep saving it," Breeze said, holding on to Alain's waist. "I'm not worth that."

"No, stop." Alain bent at the waist to press his lips against Breeze's forehead until he could feel Breeze's bones against his teeth through his lips. "You're worth it to me. Please don't doubt that. Nothing more special than this is likely to happen to me, and I want to share the best of what I have with you." He kissed Breeze's full, dark red lips. "Go and wait for me, unless you don't want to."

"Bleeding Shades, Alain! I want to. I want to more than I want to see morning, but I worry it'll make it harder for you. I don't want to hurt you more."

"Pain is better than feeling nothing," Alain said. "Better than just being empty. Only a coward would pass up something wonderful to spare himself future pain. No. I'll be happy tonight, and if it hurts later, it'll be a fair trade. Unless you don't want that."

Breeze got to his feet and kissed Alain. Though his lips and tongue moved gently against Alain's, his need, his raw and vulnerable desire bled down Alain's throat—sweet, bold, and full of body at first, but bitter on the finish.

"DO YOU want to see me off, then, or should I just kiss you one last time and go?"

Breeze's words cut like a scythe through the thick fog surrounding Alain's sleeping mind. Blinking, he realized he'd spent the night in Breeze's bed after they could no longer coerce their bodies into acting on the passion they felt; he might have even consciously chosen to do so before surrendering to slumber. "See you off."

"All right. If you're sure." Breeze stood at the foot of the bed, dressed in a shirt and trousers formerly belonging to Boyce, with his chain-mail shirt, breastplate, pauldrons, gorget, and gauntlets over top. The sword Alain had bought in place of the fancier one he felt Breeze deserved hung from his hip by a leather strap. Somehow, he didn't look right to Alain; he should be wearing a simple set of clothes and ready to go out pruning the vines. But, Alain realized as he woke and sat up, that was the Breeze he wanted, and not the true Breeze, the mercenary fighter, not the grape grower. Breeze had no desire to live the simple, predictable life of a farmer, and Alain had no right to dictate his life. He stood, stretched, felt the bones along his spine clicking and popping, and found the clothes he'd discarded so haphazardly the night before.

"Wait a moment," he implored Breeze, and when he nodded, Alain hurried to the sitting room to retrieve what he'd placed on the bookshelf by the hearth.

Hand in hand, sheltered by the pastel shadows preceding the dawn, they walked slowly to the main gate. Alain unlocked it and swung it open. The creak of the iron resounded in the stillness of the morning, and Alain stood with his hand wrapping the rough iron of one of the bars as he watched Breeze step past him and onto the road, the road that would lead him back to Rosecairn, and out of Alain's life forever.

"Wait."

When Breeze turned back, Alain imagined his lopsided smile held hope. Would Breeze stay if he asked? Did Breeze want him to ask? Goddesses, did he have any right to ask Breeze to abandon everything he'd built for himself? If their places were reversed, Alain wouldn't—couldn't—give up Mountain Shadow Winery to be with Breeze. He couldn't expect Breeze to sacrifice more. "I have something for you."

"What? Something else?" Breeze asked.

Alain reached between his tatty summer doublet and his shirt. "It's stupid." He pressed the small glass vial into Breeze's accepting, open palm.

"Alain...." Breeze's eyes sparkled with unshed tears as he looked at the vine cuttings in the vial. One vine had twined its tendrils around a piece of older stock, wrapping it so tightly they couldn't be separated without destroying both vines. The vines had practically melded into a single plant, and it was hard to tell where one began and the other ended.

"I want you to have a part of this place to take with you," Alain said, curling Breeze's fingers over the glass containing the vines. "Something of me—us—you can keep."

"Thank you," Breeze said, dropping his forehead to Alain's shoulder and winding Alain in his arms. "I wish I had something to give you in return."

"I have my memories," Alain whispered against the unforgiving steel covering Breeze's chest.

"I hope they're good ones?"

"They... they are. Take care of yourself, Breeze. Don't die too young, all right?"

Breeze chuckled into the hair above Alain's ear. "No promises."

"All right. I... oh, to the Shades with it. I love you, Breeze."

"Alain.... If you ever need me, find me at Rosecairn. I'll do anything I can for you, no matter what. Thank you, again, for everything, Good-bye, my friend."

They pressed their lips together one last time, though the imminent cutting away prevented Alain taking much pleasure in it. According to the tradition of the vine, this wasn't necessary to his existence and should be culled. But, goddesses, it hurt. Maybe it would make him stronger, but it wasn't worth it. He had struggled and lost and endured enough. Nothing pleasant tasting could come of more cutting, but the vine had no say in the matter. With a brush of his hand over Alain's hair and down his cheek, and a crooked grin and another soft, sweet sweep of lips, Breeze turned, shouldered his pack, and started down the road.

After a while, Breeze turned back and waved. Alain lifted his hand and then let it fall against his hip. He stood watching until Breeze's silhouette grew tiny and then disappeared over the crest of a hill, and then he considered going back to bed, sleeping on Breeze's pillow and surrounding himself in Breeze's scent before it faded. But he couldn't bear being alone in the room he'd always think of as Breeze's, and after the hot, dry week they'd had, the l'oeil d'Estrelle and the breumaurinier needed water. Alain scrubbed at his eyes and made his way toward the well. Everyone on the vineyard needed those grapes to thrive. Breeze might be gone, and the hole inside Alain might have expanded until he felt he'd be torn in half, but his grapes needed water, so he went to fetch the pail.

Chapter Sixteen

THANKS TO a merchant caravan in need of a guard, and the ride on a cart Breeze earned in exchange for his protection, he reached Rosecairn in only half a moon. Soon he saw the houses built on the outskirts of their camp, and beyond them, the thick trees, sharpened to spikes at the top, that enclosed it. Above the fence, the red banners bearing the Roses' livery—the crossed halberds entwined with a thorny vine and a single white rose—flapped in the summer wind coming down from the northern mountains.

"Stop there," a familiar voice called from one of the watchtowers near the compound's main gate. "Announce yourself."

With a smile, Breeze opened his hands and held them out to his sides. "Fabrezio Orvina d'Caelus. Not that you can pronounce it, you old bastard! Get your ass down here and let me in!"

A few moments later, the gate swung open, and a man about Breeze's age, with rich chestnut brown hair, sharp brown eyes, and a neatly trimmed beard held his arms open. Breeze embraced him, and the other man chuckled against his neck. "Breeze, you slippery son of a bitch! We all thought you perished in the Battle of the Starlight Bridge. I'm glad to see we jumped to a premature conclusion. I should have known it would take more than a mad mage and the heavens raining fire to finish *Fabrezio Orvina d'Caelus.*"

Breeze rolled his eyes at Octavian's perfect pronunciation of his name; there wasn't much Octavian didn't do perfectly. Together, they walked into the camp, and two soldiers closed the gate behind them. As they passed the homes and shops, Breeze noticed quite a few new, young faces around Rosecairn. Apparently Octavian had been recruiting. Curious. Breeze would have to remember to ask him about it when they reached his house.

Octavian opened the door to his simple dwelling, and Breeze followed him into the kitchen, where they sat facing each other at a table beside an open bay window.

"Tell me what happened to you," Octavian urged. "Were you hurt?"

Breeze nodded. "I was badly burned. I would have died if not for the charity of the man who found me and spent moons caring for me with no expectation of payment. His name is Alain Lamont—" Breeze coughed into his fist to clear his throat. "A farmer. A vintner who makes the most beautiful wines. He tended to my injuries and made me feel welcome at Mountain Shadow Vineyard. I would have died without him."

Octavian stood, just as Breeze predicted he would. "Let me see your injuries."

Breeze worked open the straps of his armor, removed his mail tunic, and pulled the soft shirt Alain had given him over his head. Octavian bent, squinted, and examined the gnarled flesh over Breeze's ribs, even tugging Breeze's trousers down to inspect the wounds over his hip and thigh. It was nothing he hadn't seen before, so Breeze stood with his arm stretched over his head, wondering at the way Octavian's touch didn't incense his lust as it once had.

"The man who treated these burns was surprisingly competent," Octavian said. "It couldn't have been pleasant for you. Are you experiencing any lingering pain?"

"Not pain. The muscles cramp. In my arm, my leg, along my waist. It's hard to describe. It's almost like they're shorter, bunched up."

Octavian nodded. "Some of the muscle was destroyed, and now it's missing. In essence, your arm and leg *are* shorter. Flesh burned as yours was cannot simply grow back. Let me see what I can do."

A soft blue glow, accompanied by the scent of lilies and burnt minerals, haloed Octavian's hands. He closed his eyes to concentrate, a little crease between his brows and a line of sweat above his lip. Pleasant shivers moved from his fingertips and up and down Breeze's body, making his muscles quiver and ache as if he'd overexerted them. As Octavian skimmed his hands over Breeze's ribs, down the gouged and gnarled outside of his thigh, and back up to his bicep and the inside of his elbow, where the stiffness was worst, Breeze's flesh tingled and felt numb, hot and cold at the same time. Gradually, his muscles felt soothed, loose and relaxed as though they'd been massaged by a lover.

Octavian, pale, collapsed onto the bench by the table and reached for a pitcher of water with a shaking hand. As he had before when Octavian had healed him, Breeze felt disoriented, slightly numb, and a little giddy. He plunked down next to his old friend and stretched his arm out in front of him to test its range. Octavian had succeeded in restoring his full range of motion; when he stretched, the muscles didn't tremble or cramp. "Thank you, Octavian. Are you all right?"

He nodded. "Just give me a minute. Magic is like anything else: an expenditure of energy. Energy expended must be recovered. In this case, a few moments of sitting down and a cup of water should do. As I said, the man who attended to you did his job well. He did all he could without healing enchantment. He must have been quite dedicated and fastidious."

"Yes. He was."

Octavian rubbed his temples with his thumb and finger. "I'm sorry I can't do anything about the scars. If I had been able to heal you as the skin regrew, I might have been able to help it along. Though maybe not. It's an unpredictable process."

"I don't mind them so much," Breeze said. At first, he'd worried he looked horrifying, but Alain had thought nothing of it. Absently, Breeze rubbed his thumb over the patch on his jaw where his whiskers would no longer grow and down his neck. Alain had neither avoided the mottled skin nor gone out of his way to touch it, which let Breeze know his comfort with it had been genuine.

"Well, you should be fine to fight again," Octavian said. He took a small green apple from the wooden bowl on his table and bit into it with a crack.

"Is there fighting to do?" Breeze asked. "You're bolstering your ranks."

Octavian swallowed and smiled, color already returning to his cheeks. "Yes, though in reserve only at this point. We completed a campaign a few days ago, and most of the men are recuperating or spending time with their families. Or drinking and spending time with the unattached men and women of the 'Cairn. You can't have forgotten everything."

Breeze chuckled and selected an apple for himself. "No. I've missed it too."

Octavian looked at Breeze through his lashes, his dagger-sharp gaze cutting to Breeze's core, but his smile blunting the points. "And were there no such diversions on your vineyard?"

"There might have been." Breeze remembered the last night Alain had spent in his bed, how they'd made love again and again until both of them panted and trembled, their muscles like jelly, their skin coated with sweat and seed. Drained, but wanting. Filled, but still hungry.

"Ooh. Look at your face. More than a diversion, then. Do tell."

"I'll tell you, you perverse son of a bitch. But first, tell me. Why the new recruits?"

Octavian scowled and shook his head. "This new monarch, King Garith, is something of an upstart. He's determined to claim all the disputed territory on both banks of the Kanda River for the throne. I need not tell you we have no rightful claim to this land. I've heard rumors that he plans to drive us out."

"The little blackguard whoreson," Breeze hissed through his teeth. "Let him try."

"Exactly. He's in for quite a fight. Our position is defensible, the locals for miles and miles are grateful for our presence and will offer him no aid, and our men are skilled and loyal, probably more so than his knights. I—we—toiled and bled to build this place. I have put people I loved—good men—in the ground to make Rosecairn what it is. No one is taking it from us. You know, Breeze. You have been with me from nearly the beginning. Surely you remember when this place was little more that shoddy tents and men sleeping on the ground. Now we have entire families depending on us."

Goddesses, he sounded like Alain, showed the same strain of bearing the world on his shoulders as Alain had. Breeze patted the back of his hand. "I know. I remember. I was with you then, and I'm with you now. Until the goddesses won't let me stand by your side."

"I don't doubt it," Octavian said, brown eyes twinkling. "I have never doubted you, Breeze. Not even when you could barely lift a sword with both hands."

Breeze jabbed his elbow into Octavian's arm. "Like you were any better. You didn't even have a sword, just that ridiculous great dagger you'd never tell anyone where you got."

"I still have that dagger, and I'm still not telling you where I got it."

Breeze snorted. "From somewhere that makes your eyes glaze over and your cheeks as red as a spanked ass anytime someone mentions it. He couldn't have been *that* good."

"He who?" Octavian arched a brow. "I'm still not going to fall for it, Breeze. Talk of something else."

"All right. I have a favor to ask, actually. The man who saved me, Alain, took care of me for moons and moons and asked nothing in return. He's… a good man. A man with a lovely family. But he's been having some trouble with a merchant out of Felgard. Alain thinks it's over, but I know better. This hog-fucking piece of filth is only getting started, and Alain and his family don't deserve it. I was thinking maybe we could help them a little, pay back some of what he did for me."

"Who is this man who's threatening your friend?"

"Greasy pig name of Wagonnier Almes."

Octavian looked like he wanted to spit out something sour. "I know the man. He has tried to hire us on a few occasions, and I declined every time."

"Why? What jobs?"

"Mostly eliminating his competition—other merchants, and most of them honest. That's not the reputation I want for the Roses. I told him we're not assassins. That's not what you're asking me to do, is it, Breeze?"

"Pherara, Octavian. If that's what I wanted to do, I could do it myself. But no. Alain wouldn't want him killed. He'd be… disappointed. I only just convinced him we're not the same as the Cast-Down. No, I just want to pay him a visit, and I want you to come with me."

"Why?"

"Because you're Octavian Rose! If you tell him to keep away from Alain, he'll do it. I mean, if you want to threaten him a little…."

A wicked smile spread over Octavian's handsome face. "I see. I owe your friend Alain a debt for looking after you and getting you back to me mostly whole, and besides, what you propose sounds like a great deal of fun. This man thinks too highly of himself. Someone should show him his gold doesn't make him untouchable, and it might as well be me. We'll ride for Felgard in two days, and we'll take a dozen of the men along."

"Octavian, this means a lot to me."

"It's good to have you back, Breeze. Just see I don't lose you for so long again."

THE SPECTACLE they presented as they rode into Felgard exceeded Breeze's wildest expectations. Upon a sleek, black mare, he rode next to Octavian, mounted on a beautiful bay stallion. A dozen men followed each of them, and the residents of the city left their homes and shops to gather by the sides of the street and watch the procession. All of them had polished their armor until it gleamed in the summer sun. They wore red capes and sashes emblazoned with the Roses' symbol across their chests. Breeze had argued it would be a hindrance in battle.

Octavian had said, "There won't be a battle. This man, this Almes, is a superficial fool. Extravagance and illusion are easier for him to understand than substance. We could show up in our battered plate and leathers, but this will mean more to him. Artifice is his entire existence. Trust me, Breeze."

Breeze trusted him, because Octavian was the cleverest man he'd ever known. He could watch a man for a few moments and see all the contents of his heart, everything that frightened him most, everything he desired. In the case of Wagonnier Almes, a man with greater influence than his own scared the shit out of him. He wanted his ass kissed; even Breeze saw that.

Their retinue stopped on the cobbled street in front of a grand three-story house. Instead of announcing himself or demanding audience, Octavian just waited to be noticed. It didn't take long, not with half the city gathered to gawk at them. A young man, a servant, opened the heavy double doors and asked their business.

"Fetch your master, Wagonnier Almes," Octavian said.

The boy went into the manor and reappeared several moments later. "Tam Almes isn't at home."

"Fine," Octavian said. "We will wait until he arrives. No matter how long it takes. However, waiting wears upon my patience, and I may be much less cordial if I'm delayed."

Predictably, Almes appeared not long after, flanked by two armed men. "What can I do for you... people?"

"My name is Octavian Rose, of Rosecairn. Perhaps you have heard of me and my company, the Thorns of Rosecairn, or the Roses. It makes little difference. We have come to deliver a message. My valued comrade Fabrezio Orvina d'Caelus will relay it. Be polite and don't interrupt him, if you please."

Octavian had advised Breeze calm and indifference would alarm Almes more than anger, but Breeze struggled. When he thought of Courtenay's tear-streaked face and Alain blanching under the merchant's threats, he just wanted to leap from his saddle and pummel the oily fuck into a smear on his doorstep. He took a deep breath and tried to speak as Octavian would. "We've come on behalf of the Lamont family, of Lockhaven, of Mountain Shadow Vineyard and Winery, specifically. We demand you do not bother them again, you filthy, fat, fu—"

Octavian cut him off. "We must further insist you do not slander these good people. We'll take offense to it. The Thorns of Rosecairn will return to speak with you if word reaches us that you have spoken ill of these simple people. Look around you, Tam Almes. The people of your own city bear witness to my words. Likely, they know you are a tyrant, and likely, you have exploited them as well." Octavian addressed the gathered crowd. "The Roses will offer a substantial reward to anyone with news of this man going anywhere near Mountain Shadow Winery, or gossiping about the good people there. People just like you. Farmers, struggling to make a living and resist the manipulations of the bloated privileged. If this man does anything to hurt anyone, get word to us at Rosecairn, and I swear by the goddesses, we'll not only compensate you, but we'll make it right. The Roses are happy to defend the common man. We are common men ourselves. If the cause is just, we'll ask no coin."

Almes balked as the throng cheered. A few people threw trash and bottles he had to dodge, and one of his hirelings took the opportunity to slink off and disappear. In his defense, Almes pointed a chubby finger at Breeze. "That man is unnatural. I know for a fact he has committed vile sins against the goddesses with the very farmer these *mercenaries* swear to defend!"

"So says the man who tried to kidnap and rape an eleven-year-old girl!" Breeze shouted. "I ought to tear your shriveled old cock off and shove it down your gullet!"

Almes ignored him and appealed to Octavian. "Octavian Rose, you are known as an honorable and just man. I implore you, tam, see reason. The Esperon serpent you keep in your company is a foul deviant. I can swear he has had unnatural relations with another man. What do you have to say to that?"

Octavian guided his horse to the foot of the steps, dismounted, and in a single smooth motion, he scaled the stairs, grasped Almes by the back of the head, and pressed that odd dagger he seemed to love so much to his throat. Breeze heard what he said, but he doubted many others did. "I have this to say. Breeze is very important to me. He wants you to leave the vintner alone. You would be wise to do it, although, at this point, I'm almost hoping you ignore my wishes. I would be more than happy to come back here, or to find you wherever you decide to go. Now, do we understand one another?"

Almes nodded as best he could with Octavian gripping his hair.

"I'm sorry, I don't think I heard you, Tam Almes."

"Yes."

Octavian wrenched his head back further, making him gurgle and choke. "Yes what? Your audience is dying of anticipation."

"I will have nothing more to do with the vintner Alain Lamont. I will not even speak of him."

"Or go near our… his family!" Breeze interjected.

"Or go near his family."

Octavian released the man, and he fell facedown, covering the back of his head with his hands.

Without paying Almes the favor of looking back, Octavian walked away and mounted his horse. He turned the animal around, and Breeze followed, despite his desire to rail at and insult Wagonnier Almes. He understood how much more of a slight just leaving him on his hands and knees without a word was in the eyes of everyone who watched.

The Roses rode out of Felgard followed by a significant crowd, including maidens offering flowers to the men. Now and then, Octavian paused and gave a copper piece or two to beggars. Almes's mercenary followed near the back of the throng, and Breeze had no doubt he'd request to join the Roses.

"Satisfied?" Octavian asked Breeze.

"Yes, thank you."

"Good. I can't have you distracted. You're one of my best fighters, and we have work to do. Are you beside me, Breeze?"

"Always. To the end, Octavian."

Chapтer
Sevenтeen

FOR WEEKS after Breeze left, all Alain could find to thank the goddesses for was his work. Grapes grew fat and ripe on the vine as late summer proved hot and dry, but Fenn had been cranky and surly since Breeze's departure, and Courtenay barely spoke to anyone, spending most of her time in the library. Alain didn't know what to do or say to ease his children's pain; probably they thought everyone they loved would one day leave, one way or another, and Alain couldn't bring himself to tell them otherwise, not when he felt like he was lying to them. Sabine and Boyce would have known what say. Even Breeze would have known, but Alain didn't, so he picked grapes from sunrise till sunset, day after day. When the workers he'd selected to harvest only grapes ripened to absolute perfection retired for the evening, Alain joined the group who helped him press the fruit and seal the juice into barrels. Only after they finished, well into the night or the early morning, did Alain retire to a long-vacant room he'd claimed. He could no longer bear to sleep in the room that had belonged to Boyce, or the one they had shared, or the one that had belonged to Breeze. Most nights, he barely slept a few hours.

Tonight, after pressing a meager crop of fierrine, barely enough to fill a dozen barrels, Alain didn't go back to the house, not even to drink until he stilled the thoughts and fears that darted to the surface of his mind as soon as he closed his eyes. Instead, he wandered to a gentle knoll and sat down in the high, sweet grass, hugging his knees to his chest. A summer wind pushed the clouds from in front of the moon, and its silvery rays fell on the field of l'oeil d'Estrelle stretched out below him. It looked like every star in the firmaments had fallen into the valley, all of heaven gathered in that little corner of his little vineyard. The beauty made Alain smile, but he longed for someone to share it with him. He had intended to show Breeze, but Breeze had left before the grapes grew mature enough to develop the fine powder on their skins that made them glow.

The grass swished softly behind him, and Alain, almost deliriously exhausted, expected Breeze to sit down next to him. Instead, Courtenay sat on her heels, the billowy, white fabric of her nightdress fanning out around her. Alain smiled and reached over to take her hand, glad of the company. "Isn't it beautiful?"

She nodded, and for a long time they sat in silence before she spoke again. "Do you think they'll freeze in time?"

He shrugged. "It will still be a moon or so before they're ripe. They're native to the north, and they ripen slower than the fierrine and the verlaut. Then we only need one cold night. Just one perfect night. If everyone on the vineyard works together, we can pick them and press them before they thaw. If the goddesses don't look kindly on us... I don't know. I don't have many answers anymore, I'm afraid."

"No one does," she said. "Life can be so uncertain and scary. A few moons ago, I thought you and Papa would pick grapes and make wine and we'd all be happy forever. I never imagined he could die, or the vineyard could burn, or I could end up being a mage. All those things seemed like things that happened to other people, people far away or in books. I didn't think they could happen to us. To me."

"Does being a mage upset you?"

She nodded and chewed her lower lip. "I'm scared. It just—the magic just came out of me. I didn't want it, and I couldn't stop it. What if I hurt you or Fenn?"

Alain didn't have an answer, so he repeated the words of someone who did. "Breeze said you should probably get training. He said your gift is stronger than usual."

"He knows about things like that, I suppose." Courtenay nestled against Alain's chest, and he straightened his legs so he could pull her into his lap and wrap his arms around her. She was still so small, but not much of a child anymore. Boyce had wanted her to be a little girl, to have that golden season of innocence and freedom from worry, but Alain had failed to protect her.

"Do you want to go to Espero?"

"Is it very far?" she asked.

"Mmm," he said into her soft, fragrant hair. "We'd have to travel to the Barrier Bay in Windwake and take a ship. After that, I think it takes a moon by sea. Maybe two. I'm not sure. I've really never had to think about it before."

"So far," she said to herself. "Farther than I thought possible. And so strange. Do you think the people there are as kind and brave as Breeze?"

Alain didn't think anyone, anywhere, was quite like Breeze. "Maybe."

"I could be an important person there," Courtenay mused. "Important because of my mind and my skills. I wouldn't be limited to woman things. All women here are allowed to do is have babies. But… but I'm afraid to leave home."

"You could always come back," Alain said. "This vineyard will always be your home. And if you don't want to go to Espero but you don't want to marry and have children, you'll still have a place here. But if you do, if you want to go, well, Breeze once told me destiny favors the brave and ignores the timid, or something like that. I'm afraid it's a decision only you can make."

"I wish you had a wife and children," she said.

"What? Why?"

Courtenay tilted her head to kiss his cheek. "Because you're so lonely. And if I leave and go to Espero, you'll be even more alone."

"No," he lied. "No, I'm happy here on the land with my grapes. It's all I ever wanted, all I want. Besides, I am a grown man. You have to live the life you want. You cannot let me come between you and your path."

"Is that what you said to Breeze?" she asked. "Alain, why didn't you ask him to stay?"

"Why would I do that?"

"Because he made you happy," she said. "He would have stayed if you had asked him to. I know it. You should have asked him, Alain. You made him happy too."

"My love, I know you mean well, but you don't know what you're talking about. There are… things between adults you do not understand—"

"I understand some of it," she said. "Besides, if he made you happy and you made him happy, what else is there? What else is important?"

"Many things, Courtenay. Life is more complicated than that. Breeze and I are very different people, who want very different things from life. I couldn't stand in the way of his dreams any more than I can stand in the ways of yours."

"So you think I should go?"

"It depends what you want," he said, stroking her springy curls. "Do you want to be an important mage, or do you want to be a vintner with some magical ability? Some magic might be useful around here. You could heal the animals if they got sick or hurt."

"I don't think I have an aptitude for healing," she said.

"Fancy words." He chuckled. "Did you learn that from those books we bought at Y'Airns?"

"I learned enough about magic that I think I want to know more," she said. "Did you know there are fewer children born with the gift every generation?"

"No."

"I'm afraid to leave you, Alain."

"You mustn't be. I promise I'll be fine."

She blew air out her nose. "I know you. You tell everyone you're fine, and then you cry when no one's looking. I know because I do the same thing. I don't want to leave until you have someone to hold you while you cry, because I know that's what you really want."

His eyes stinging, he squeezed her as tight as he dared. "Goddesses, you are so like your mother. Just as beautiful, and you can read my mind like she always could, from the time we were barely walking. When I was hungry, Sabine would go to Mum and say, 'Alain wants a biscuit.' And when I was sad or frustrated and couldn't put the why of it into words, she spoke for me, and she always got it right. She could always express what I felt better than I could."

"I don't remember her much," Courtenay admitted. "Is it bad that I don't feel sad, don't miss her like I do Papa?"

"No, love. She wouldn't want you to be sad. She'd want you to be bold and live the life you chose. You know, when she fell in love with your father, it was quite scandalous that he came to live with her family instead of her leaving to go with him. But Sabine didn't care. She loved your papa, and she loved growing grapes, and nobody was going to tell her she had to pick one or the other. She was... amazing. She went after what she wanted in a way I always envied."

"It's because you put what you want behind what you think everyone else needs."

"Perhaps," he conceded. "But a great many people are depending on me."

"You should get to be happy, Alain."

He stood and brushed the grass of his legs and bum. "Oh, I'm happy enough. I have my land and my grapes, and I'm a part of this place. It's enough." It would have to be enough, because soon it would be all he had left.

THE GATE to the crude fence around the smugglers' compound was in sight. It wouldn't take much to batter it down once they fought their way through the ten or twelve men guarding it. From their position at the tree line, Breeze scanned the area. A couple of archers watched over the barrier. Beyond it, a few crude buildings: stone and wood, recently constructed. A few horses. Dogs barking. He drew the sword Alain had given him. The other mercenaries had been impressed by the quality of the blade, and it had served Breeze well in the small skirmishes he'd been involved in since he'd returned to Rosecairn.

Dammit, he wished he'd have left Alain something to remember him by. Something so Alain knew how much he'd meant to him. Alain would hate what he was about to do: roust out a group of smugglers who had infringed upon the territory claimed by the smugglers who'd hired the Roses. He would have a point. All they were really doing was defending a better-funded group of criminals against a smaller batch. Still, no one here was innocent, and Breeze had a job to do. He needed to concentrate on the task at hand.

Off to his left, Octavian nodded at a trio of archers, then jutted his chin in the direction of the men guarding the gate. The men drew their bowstrings, and each of their arrows found a mark in the legs, arms, or shoulders of the guards. Octavian didn't abide unnecessary killing, although he didn't cringe when there was no other option. The archers had taken three men out of the battle, and they would live, even if they might never fight again. It was a risk all warriors took. But by firing on their enemy, they'd given away their position. Breeze and the ten other men who accompanied him didn't hesitate. Weapons drawn, they ran to meet the warriors. Steel clanged against steel halfway between the smuggler's camp and the stunted trees where they'd been hiding.

Breeze raised his blade to block a blow from a big man with a red beard and a double-edged ax. As the stocky son of a bitch pressed down on him, Breeze drove the heel of his new armored boots into the bastard's balls. There was no such thing as a fair fight. The big fucker doubled over, and Breeze hit him in the side of the head with the pommel of his blade, knocking him out. He fought his way past a quick, wiry little whoreson with a pair of shortswords, leaving him dragging himself from the fray with a shattered knee and at least a couple of broken ribs. Their goal was the gate. Get inside the compound, drive out the rival smugglers, and secure it so their patrons could claim it. The Roses were entitled to any goods they found inside.

Maybe, if they found something good, something he could sell, he'd send some coin to Alain. Anonymously, because he didn't want gratitude. He just wanted good things for Alain. Didn't want Alain to worry so much over coin. Wanted to take some of the burden off his shoulders.

Breeze didn't see the man with the nasty serrated sword rushing him from the right until it was too late. With the jagged blade bearing down on him, he had no time to parry, doubted he could block. Fuck.

A mineral-scented stream of blue light shot past Breeze, so close it ruffled his hair, striking his adversary in the chest and knocking him to his back. A long dagger followed, sticking in the other warrior's shoulder and making him reveal a few rotten teeth as he howled. Octavian bounded past Breeze, knocked the man silly with a backhanded blow, and retrieved his outlandish, beloved knife. Still crouching, he looked over his shoulder and met Breeze's gaze. "Where in the Shades' is your head? You're going to get yourself killed!"

Breeze mumbled an apology, but neither of them had more chance to speak. Two men ran toward Octavian while Breeze hurried to aid one of his comrades who'd ended up on the ground with an arrow through his forearm. Breeze grasped the man beneath his arms, dragged him back to the safety of the woods, snapped the arrowhead off, and pulled out the wooden shaft. He tore a strip of cloth from the wounded man's tunic, wrapped the wound tight, and tied it off, just as he'd been taught. "Keep safe, friend. Octavian can mend this in two shakes of a whore's tits. Provided you don't die."

"Thanks, Breeze. Give that fucking archer a kick in the sac for me, will you?"

"Aye, that's a promise." Breeze turned and sprinted back toward the gate. Most of the Roses were gathering the wounded and unconscious enemies and tying them up, binding them together with coarse rope so they couldn't recover and surprise them. Octavian widened his stance, held his right arm at the elbow to brace it, and sent a blast of arcane energy at the shoddy gate. It broke to splinters, shards of wood flying in every direction. Breeze and the rest of the Roses regrouped behind their leader and prepared to take ownership of the camp.

Inside, they encountered much heavier resistance than they'd been told to expect. The enemy, twenty men or more, surrounded their group on a circle of wet, sandy ground at the center of a circle of buildings. The Roses stood shoulder to shoulder and back to back, pushing any man who sustained a wound to safety behind them. Well covered and at higher vantage points, the enemy archers had a definite advantage. Octavian did his best to conjure a shield around them to protect them from the arrows, but combat magic had never been his strength. He was a healer by nature, and in a kinder world, he could have eased much suffering. Breeze wondered how that had never occurred to him before, but he dismissed the thought as a man with a sword ran at him. He deflected the thrust meant to stab him through the belly and swung at his adversary's leg when the man lost his balance. The gash erupted blood, and when the man dropped to his knees, Breeze kicked him beneath his chin and sent him sprawling on his back.

An arrow struck the man fighting next to Breeze in the chest. His mail shirt took the worst of it, but blood oozed out between the links. Shoving the man behind him with one hand, Breeze raised his sword to deflect a blow with the other. Crouching and spinning, he kicked his enemy's legs out from beneath him and broke his nose almost before he hit the ground.

"Octavian!" Breeze shouted over the resounding clang of steel against steel and men screaming and cursing. "The last of the archers. On the roof of the shed. Your left!"

Octavian, white and waxen, his hair drenched with sweat, nodded and turned in the direction Breeze indicated. He raised a shaking arm and sent a spear of blue light toward the thatched roof. A man tumbled down, his bow bouncing away from him. Octavian staggered and dropped to one knee. Breeze caught his arm and hauled him back to his feet, stepping in front of him just in time to stop a warrior with a spiked club. Breeze drove the hilt of his sword into the man's diaphragm, and another of the Roses finished him with a strike to the face.

By the time they finished the fight, more of the Roses were wounded than weren't, and it would be a while before Octavian could attend to them. Their leader had suffered a blow to the waist, and likely at least a few cracked ribs. He draped an arm over Breeze's shoulder as they checked to make sure all their enemies were bound and none were lurking in any of the buildings.

As they waited for the smugglers who had hired them to come and take possession of the compound, Breeze inspected the goods the rival smugglers had assembled. Weapons, and lots of them. Well made, probably from eastern Gaeltheon. Jewels too. Mostly rough and uncut, but still worth a good bit. Some fine leather armor Breeze would probably sort through to find something for himself. Chain mail, a bit of plate. Some staves and crystals that looked magical. Some coin. An impressive batch of loot overall, and their employers didn't want any of it—they just wanted control of the little inlet southeast of the Starlight Bridge, where many of the mercenary groups and warlords came to procure goods. Breeze's share would be handsome—more than enough to send something to Alain. To send something to a man he'd never see again, let alone get to bed. What in the Shades' was he thinking?

Breeze sent one of their men to fetch the carts they'd left a few miles down the road. Then he went to check on Octavian and found him leaning against a fencepost and clutching his side, his handsome features contorted in pain. Breeze crouched down next to him. "All right?"

"Had worse," Octavian said.

"Nice haul," Breeze said.

"Good. I'd hate to think this was a waste of time. Breeze, what—"

Cutting him off, knowing he only delayed the inevitable lecture, Breeze said, "Heal yourself. Nobody of ours is dying. They'll be fine till we make it home and you have a meal and a bit of rest. Then you can see to them."

"Since—" Octavian coughed, winced, and held his ribs. "Since when are you such a mother hen?"

"I am not," Breeze protested. "It's only practical. You can't ride like this, and you're the only one who can heal the others. So heal yourself, ride back to Rosecairn, heal the others. Everybody's happy."

"Goddesses, for a stubborn ass, I guess you have a point." Octavian leaned his head back and closed his eyes. A sheath of crackling blue enveloped him, smelling like flowers and charcoal. The azure glow focused over his ribs until Breeze could see their broken rungs, dark against its brilliance. He squinted as the bones mended and Octavian dropped his hands to the ground at his sides and panted.

"Sleep," Breeze urged, cradling his friend's head against his chest. "The others are going to need you. Need every last drop of you."

With a nod, Octavian dropped off against him, and Breeze sat holding him as the others loaded their riches into the carts. A few hours later, the smugglers who had hired them arrived, and Octavian went into one of the buildings to speak with their leaders. Then they rode for home and divided up the spoils. Breeze carried his share to his single-room stone house near the northern edge of their camp, where it stayed relatively quiet when the men celebrated a victory. He had been pleased Octavian hadn't offered it to another, and not just because of the chest of coins he had hidden beneath the floorboards. It was the first place that had ever been his, and he liked sitting on the bench on his porch, watching the rest of the Roses frolicking around the fires down the hill.

He was sitting on his bench, holding the vine cutting in the glass vial, when Octavian found him. His oldest friend and trusted leader sat next to him and passed Breeze a bottle of wine. "Probably not as good as you're used to now."

Though Breeze drank deep, he found the stuff inside the bottle weak and bitter on the finish. A far cry from even Alain's poorest wine. Still, he muttered a few words of thanks to Octavian for sharing.

"Breeze, what in the Shades happened today?" Octavian asked.

"Seems like we won," Breeze said, taking another swig from the bottle. The more he drank, the less he minded the taste.

"Goddesses." Octavian drank. "We're friends. I have never seen you so distracted in battle before. I have never seen you as you've been these past few weeks. Do you think I don't see you, sitting out by the cairn all day, staring off into the sky and playing with whatever you keep in that little bottle? Breeze, you're pining."

Breeze prickled. "Oh, fuck you, Octavian. I am not pining. Are you calling me a lovesick maiden?"

"Lovesick, maybe. Tell me I'm wrong. Tell me I have you back, all of you, that you didn't leave your heart and spirit on that vineyard. That was where your head was in the fight today, wasn't it? With your vintner."

"It won't happen again," Breeze said.

"I think it will," Octavian said.

"If you don't want me in this company, Octavian, just say so. If I'm not worthy of the Roses, I'll leave."

"No, friend, you misunderstand. Alain Lamont. Tell me about him."

Breeze chugged a few healthy gulps of the cheap wine. "Alain... goddesses. Beautiful. Fucking amazingly beautiful. White skin, quick to blush. Hair like sunlight, eyes like the sky. He hates to be teased. Sensitive, you know? He's... good. Puts everyone ahead of himself. Suffers so others will be happy. Just like when he took care of me. What he did for me—I don't know if I could have done it. I thought he was soft, pampered, but he's stronger than I am."

"And what do you want?" Octavian coaxed.

"I want him to be happy. Not have to worry so much." Breeze swallowed more of the bitter wine, and then more, even when it stung his throat and belly. "I... I want him to get to dance. He should dance every day. He should have someone he can always rely on. In celebration, or to cry against. He should have someone to protect him, someone he knows won't flinch no matter how ugly it gets. I... goddesses. I want it to be me. I want him to know I'm the one who always has his back, who'll hold him up when he needs it. When he needs someone who'll never let him down, I want him to think my name. But I can't be that man."

"Why not?" Octavian asked.

"I'm not worthy of him, not good enough. Not for him and Courtenay and Fenn."

"Who says so, Breeze? Who says you're not good enough? Your Alain? I doubt it. It's the poison your parents planted in your head. I know it well."

"So what do I do? I'm a warrior. I don't know how to do anything else. This is home. Rosecairn is the first place I've ever felt useful."

"The first, but maybe not the only," Octavian said. "You are a fine fighter, and you'll always have a place by my side. But you're also my friend, and I love you, and if you'll be happier somewhere else, well, I'll be happy for you. Breeze, you do not seem happy here the way you once did."

He shook his head and rubbed his finger across his eyes. "It's just strange being back. I'll get over this." He forced a laugh. "What else? Can you honestly imagine me spending the rest of my life as a farmer?"

"I don't know. Can you?"

Goddesses. He almost could. "No. I'd be out of my mind with boredom in a week."

Octavian took the wine from Breeze, drank, and said nothing.

"I mean, how common. I didn't learn to fight and make a name for myself to prune grapevines. It would be a waste of my skill and all I've worked to achieve."

"If you say so," Octavian said.

"Alain had this analogy about trimming the vines. You'll like it. It's poetic nonsense, like most of what you say. He said you have to see the essence of the vine and then cut away everything else. Cut off everything but what's essential to it, and that makes it fight, makes it strong. Well, that's me as well. I'm a warrior. I just need to cull the rest."

"But surely you can cut too much," Octavian noted. "Take off all the leaves and the plant will surely die. It needs enough to soak up the warmth of the sun and drink in the rain. It must be a very fine line between strengthening the vine and removing its ability to absorb everything good it needs to thrive."

Breeze nodded, recalling the pleasant afternoons he'd spent next to Alain, working with shears, and the pride and satisfaction he'd felt after a job well done. "There's an art to it."

"Certainly. There's no beauty to a shriveled old vine with no green leaves. No sweet fruit can come from something like that, something dead."

Damn him. "I can't imagine losing what I've made here."

"There is always loss," Octavian said. "We both lost something when we left our families. But sometimes you need to cut away what's dead to make room for the new growth, just like with your burns. No good comes from holding on to something that's past its time. As you said, there's an art to knowing which is which."

"Well, I do know which is which," Breeze snapped, irritated for no reason he could make sense of. "I worked and bled to get where I am, and I'm happy with the life I've made. All of it. The gains as well as the losses. Now, did you come out here just to pester me and spout poetry?"

With a chuckle, Octavian stood and brushed his hand down the side of Breeze's hair. "Actually, I came to see if you might want me to warm your bed tonight, but I suspect the answer to that is no. You might want to ask yourself why that is." He leaned down and pressed a kiss to Breeze's forehead, and it ignited none of the desire it had in the past. "Good night, Breeze."

Whistling, Octavian wound his way around the simple homes and buildings in the direction of the central fire, the nearly empty bottle of wine dangling from his hand. He would find another man to entertain him. He could have his choice of the men interested in that. So could Breeze, but he found he'd rather sit by himself and look up at the stars.

Why indeed?

Chapter Eighteen

ALAIN CURSED the heat still rising from the ground as the sun slid slowly toward the western sea. He stayed in the field until the darkness prevented him from discerning the grapes starting to rot from the ones hanging in perfectly ripe clusters, bursting with juice, from the vines. For the last three days, his insides had been wound up with worry. Near the advent of Berris's Moon, they'd harvested all the red grapes and pressed them. The yield had been even worse than Alain had predicted—a mere five hundred barrels, not even enough to fill the orders from his regular patrons. The sweet white grapes in the southern fields would putrefy if they weren't picked. The new vines Alain had started wouldn't yield fruit for years. He needed gold for more mature vines. He needed gold in case Courtenay chose to go to Espero—he predicted she would—so he could hire guards to escort her and a ship to carry her to the island. He needed these bloody grapes to freeze, and he needed them to freeze yesterday.

He couldn't wait any longer. Tomorrow or the next day, they'd have to start harvesting. He could make something from these grapes, just nothing as valuable as the ice wine. For days, he'd vacillated between fear of losing the crop completely and holding out one more day and praying for frost. If he picked the grapes and the cold came the next night, he'd kick himself. But then, if they lost the entire fields, the winery was doomed. Most of all, he wanted someone to share his worries with, someone who could tell him what to do—Sabine, Boyce, or Breeze. But they were all gone, and none of them were coming back. He had to be strong and make the right choice on his own; everyone depended on him.

Tomorrow night, Alain decided. If the frost didn't come by tomorrow night, they'd pick the white grapes, and he'd make something of their juice. He looked up at the fat, rosy moon hovering just above the horizon, and then east, toward where he imagined Breeze was, in Rosecairn. *Please. Goddesses, please. Just a frost. One cold night. Is that so much to ask?*

After stumbling back to the house and up to the sparse room he'd claimed, Alain managed a few fitful hours of sleep before waking to find the morning cooler, but not cool enough. A strong wind coming down from the mountains to the north gave him a glimmer of cautious hope, and he muttered a few more prayers, but they'd never been answered before. He hated to be bitter and wallow in pity for himself, but all the goddesses had ever done was take away everything important to him. He spent the day working in the fields, carefully culling the rotten fruit away from the healthy so the foulness wouldn't spread.

Dinner that night was quiet, tension hanging so thick in the air even the children felt it. They finished their meal quickly, washed up, and went to bed, leaving Alain alone in the sitting room without even the energy to open a bottle of wine. He sat staring at the fire flickering low in the hearth, and eventually his eyes closed on their own and his head lolled back on the bench. Even in slumber, he worried, dreaming he woke to find his grapes rotted to slimy, brown clumps on the vine. He started awake and bolted up, still convinced he had to rush out to pick them. As he blinked off the deep slumber he'd fallen into, he realized he must have slept for hours; the fire and even the embers in the inglenook had gone out. He also realized a sound, something distant, had roused him from sleep. But now the house stood perfectly still, only the wind outside rattling the windows and making the nearby tree branches creak. Clearly, exhaustion was taking a toll on his mind until he couldn't separate his dreams from reality.

Goddesses, when—if—the grapes froze and they picked and pressed them, when that sweet, golden juice had been barreled and stored, he would curl beneath his blankets in his narrow new bed and stay there for three days.

Just as Alain nodded back off, a series of sharp thuds against his front door woke him. Terror turned Alain's blood to ice and transformed the stew he'd had for dinner to boiling acid in his belly. No one on the vineyard would come calling unless something was terribly wrong, and if it wasn't one of his people, who could it be in the middle of the night? Who could have made it past the stone walls and the iron gate protecting them? As he stood, he scanned the room for something to use to defend himself, and before he went to the door, he picked up the heavy iron fireplace poker with a shaking hand.

The rapping grew sharper and more insistent as Alain padded slowly down the hall, making as little sound as possible, avoiding the squeaky floorboards, hoping to catch whoever stood outside off guard. Goddesses, what if Almes had returned with more mercenaries? Ever since the last time, some of the men had agreed to take turns watching the front gate through the night. How could he have gotten past them? Unless—

Alain turned the brass knob and opened the door, raising the poker over his head to strike. The sight that met him almost convinced him he was still dreaming, trapped in a vivid vision his mind had sent to torment him, one crueler than the image of the putrid grapes. He dropped the poker. It clattered to the floor, and he grasped Breeze's cheeks in both hands, feeling warm, smooth skin and a spatter of stubble beneath his palms and fingers. Without thinking, he pulled Breeze forward and smashed their lips together, laughing and smiling so hard he couldn't kiss Breeze properly. He just grinned against his mouth and rubbed his cheek against Breeze's face. "Say something. Tell me you're not a dream."

Breeze chuckled, his breath hot and sweet against Alain's lips, moving his fingers into Alain's hair to grasp it and pull Alain back so he could look at him with sparkling eyes. "Tell me you're not. I've had nothing but you in my head since the day I left this place. I don't remember you being quite this beautiful."

Suddenly, Alain remembered his hair, mussed from sleeping, and how bitter his breath must be. He took a step back and took in the details of the man he loved, who had left a bottomless hole in his heart. His wavy dark hair hung to his chest, the ends brushing the old chest plate Alain had taken off him when he'd been burned, what felt like a lifetime ago. Beneath it, he wore a mail shirt, new leather leggings, and sturdy, armored boots. Over top, a thick wool cloak, maybe bearskin, covered his shoulders. He wore the sword Alain had given him strapped to his hip, and a heavy canvas pack hung from his back.

"My friend, can we decide if we're real inside, by the fire?" Breeze asked with his lopsided grin. "It's colder than Fayelle's frigid backside out here."

"Oh, yes, I'm sorry." Alain stood aside so Breeze could enter. How had he not noticed the red nipped across Breeze's sculpted cheeks and nose, or the ice crystals clinging to his hair, eyelashes, and cloak? "Wait... cold?"

In his bare feet, Alain ran out of the house, down the porch steps, and onto the road leading to the gate. His breath froze and misted while fine powdery snow swirled across the ground. A biting wind howled through the trees. The cutting, frozen mud against his soles was one of the best things Alain had ever felt—second only to touching Breeze's face, kissing him, when he never thought he'd have another chance. He jumped up, punched the air, and hooted, waking a dog who answered him with a series of yips.

At the top of the stairs, Breeze looked at Alain like he'd gone mad. Alain didn't care. It was cold, so damned cold his fingers and toes had already gone numb, and the powdery snow continued to fall, coating the fallen leaves and covering the ground. He bounded back up the steps and threw himself against Breeze. "You—you brought the cold!"

Breeze chuckled, warm against Alain's chilled neck. "Maybe I did. Damn storm's been at my back since I crossed the Starlight Bridge. Caught up to me a few hours ago. Conditions got right dreadful, but I didn't want to stop."

"Hours ago," Alain mused to himself. "If it's been cold for hours, the grapes will be frozen! We have to pick them and press them! We have to do it tonight, in case the morning is warm enough to thaw them. I have to wake everyone." He pulled away from Breeze and started for the steps, but Breeze caught his elbow and pulled him inside.

"You need boots," Breeze said around a smile. "And a cloak. And... I've been traveling hard, barely sleeping, and I need a few moments to speak with you. Can you keep your grapes waiting just a few moments for me?"

Alain nodded, watching the bow of Breeze's lips as he spoke. It was odd and frightening, after a lifetime of having everything he loved sliced away, to get everything he wanted handed to him in a single evening. His eyes stung, and he swiped at them, feeling like he daydreamed on a summer day by the lake even as the frigid wind battered the sides of the house. Again, he tossed himself at Breeze and held tight to him, as if he'd be cut away. "Anything for you."

"All right, then." Breeze nuzzled his nose into the side of Alain's hair and stiffened as if bracing himself. "I'm not a poet, not like Octavian. Not like you. So here it is. When I woke up here, I just wanted to get away, back to a life I thought was exciting and that made me important. But when I did, I realized all I want in this tired, goddess-forsaken world is you. To be there for you, to be someone who you know won't ever let you down. To be the one you look for when you need somebody. To make you fucking smile, 'cause your smile is better than anything I've ever felt. I don't know if you want me, not forever, and if you don't, I'll be on my way. But I had to say it, Alain. If you'll have me, I want to stay here with you, be a farmer. Goddesses, if you'll have me, I'll be the happiest fucking farmer who ever lived in this world. I'll do anything I can for this place. Anything to make you happy. 'Cause I know now, seeing you happy, being beside you, is all that's important to me."

So many words and thoughts filled Alain's head he thought his skull would explode, but for once, he threw a net around just the ones he wanted, hauled them to the surface, and presented them to Breeze. "I have loved you for a long time. I have loved you with a fierceness and fire I've never felt before, and nothing in this world would please me more than spending the rest of the days the goddesses grant me by your side. If… if you're sure. If you don't think farming and winemaking will be too dull for you. I don't want to take away the life you loved. I cannot ask you to give it up for me when I can't give up my life for you."

Breeze grinned wide, flashing straight white teeth between full, terra-cotta lips. He kissed Alain hard, sucking Alain's lips into his mouth, laving and nipping at them, thrusting his tongue in to twist around and bump against Alain's until both of them gasped for breath. "Oh, Alain. I'm just doing what you taught me. Just finding my essence and cutting the rest away. You, you're my sun and rain and rich soil. Ha! Octavian would be proud of that bit of verse. I love you. I need you, and oddly enough, I missed this place. Trimming the vines, mowing, even spreading shit. I always felt, at the end of each day, like I'd accomplished something, done something good. I want to help you make this place brilliant. I've thought about this, and I'm sure. If you're sure. I don't mean to assume I have a place here, or that you'll want me for the long haul—"

"Breeze, shut up." Alain kissed him hard, devouring his mouth and drowning in his taste as he tore at the unforgiving steel denying Breeze's body to his hands. He felt like his passion could compel his fragile fingers to tear the metal, break through everything until he got to the pure, essential core of Breeze. He felt it, smelled it in Breeze's hair and skin, the love and need leaking from his pores, and Alain wanted to gulp it down like the sweetest wine he'd ever tasted, because it was better. Wine, no matter how wonderful, was a fleeting pleasure, and this pleasure would last. He could scarcely imagine the character and complexity it would develop with age. What would it be like after twenty years, or forty? Only better, he knew, and he pressed his forehead against the bearskin covering Breeze's shoulder and made a sound between a laugh and a sob.

Breeze pulled him close and kissed the top of his head. "Alain. I'm a simple man. No poet, no scholar. I want it said simply. Me and you, then? For good? Forever?"

"Forever and then some, if it's up to me," Alain said.

Breeze made the same amused but tortured sound he had as he dragged his teeth up Alain's neck, nipped at his earlobe, and breathed into his ear. "For the love of the goddesses and all that's sacred, let me take you to bed."

Alain threw his head back, looked at the dark rafters against the white plaster ceiling through blurry eyes, and laughed. "Bed? No, you foolish man. Tonight, we pick grapes. Come on. You'll want to take off that armor, and I'll find you a pair of gloves. We'll be working at least until morning."

Breeze groaned but followed Alain into the room that had once been his.

EVERYONE ON Mountain Shadow Vineyard woke to harvest the grapes for the ice wine, right down to children barely old enough to pluck the fruit from the stems. Torches were lit and driven into the ground, and they burned pockets through the increasing snow and frigid mist for the people to work. They worked in an urgent silence, all of them knowing the winery depended on this harvest. Breeze felt it too as he hunched over the vines in his fur cloak, wearing the woolen gloves Alain had provided. Because getting these grapes picked felt so much more important to him than the battle against the smugglers, he knew he'd made the right choice by returning. As he squeezed the glowing white globes to test their firmness before plucking them and dropping them into the basket hanging by his hip, he swore—to himself, Alain, Courtenay, Fenn, and the vineyard itself—he wouldn't fail. If it bloody killed him, they'd get these grapes in and pressed before the morning thaw.

Hours later, Breeze had worn holes in the fingers of his gloves, and though he couldn't see it, he suspected his hands had cracked open and bled beneath them. But he couldn't complain when Courtenay and Fenn worked right alongside him, the girl's fingers wrapped in bandages and the boy on his knees because he could no longer stand. When Breeze thought his cramped fingers couldn't close around another cluster of grapes, fresh workers came to take their places. He helped Alain and some of the other men and women load the baskets into carts, and then he hopped aboard one and rode it to a long stone building. Inside, they worked together to dump the baskets into a massive tub. Breeze didn't know if the strain to his arms and back from hoisting the heavy baskets was worse than picking the frozen fruit, but he pushed his body harder than he had in any skirmish. With the drum filled, he helped three other men turn the huge wheel to bring the wooden disk down on the grapes and squeeze the juice out of them. Alain rushed back and forth, bringing empty barrels to the spout and dragging them away full when they'd filled with the honey-colored nectar. Then they jumped into the tub, shoveled out the spent skins for next spring's fertilizer, and returned to the fields to pick again.

Aside from those who had to attend to animals, every soul on the winery worked, repeating the process until every viable grape had been plucked and pressed. When they finished, sometime around midday, joyous hollers went up from the workers. After probably twelve straight hours of hard toil, Breeze couldn't even add his voice to the victory cheer. He dropped to his knees on the frozen, snowy ground, and let his face fall into his hands. He remained that way, curled over, every muscle in his body screaming, until someone shook his shoulder.

Looking up, he saw Alain, skin chapped bright pink, lips cracked, heavy black bags under his brilliant sapphire eyes. "Breeze, we did it. I can't believe it. Over a hundred barrels of ice wine."

He accepted the hand Alain offered to help him up, his mind and body collapsing fast. "Is that good?"

"It's brilliant. If we can sell it all, we'll have enough coin to sustain ourselves for probably two years, and some to spare for mature vines. I can't believe it. We... we're going to be all right."

With their arms draped over each other's shoulders, leaning on one another and not worried because so many of the workers did the same, they staggered back to the building where they'd pressed the grapes. It warmed Breeze's heart to see the dozens of rows of barrels lined up. He had done something good, been a part of something important, and it felt better than winning any battle. All of the people he saw helping each other to stand would have a home and food for a few more years, because he had helped. It felt damned good, and he wasn't ashamed.

They found Courtenay and Fenn curled together, asleep on a pile of straw with an old horse blanket for their pillow. Breeze realized they were his now, and thought if his heart swelled any more it would break his ribs and kill him. But no. To the Shades' with that. He wanted to live. Live with Alain until both of them grew old enough to totter about with canes and eat nothing but bread soaked in cream because their teeth had all fallen out. As Alain bent to scoop Courtenay into his arms, Breeze knew he'd love him, want and just fucking adore him, no matter how bald, sagging, and gray he became. As long as he could lift a sword, no one would fuck with Alain or his—their—family or their home. Breeze lifted Fenn's limp body into his arms, and together, they trudged back to the house and put their children in bed.

"I kept your room," Alain said when they reached the bottom of the stairs.

Breeze, more exhausted than he'd ever been, said, "Good" and then he pulled Alain past the threshold, where both of them collapsed on the bed without even removing their boots or gloves. They meshed their thighs together and wrapped their arms around each other, and the last thing Breeze remembered before unconsciousness dragged him under was: *This. This every night, forever. Bleeding Shades, this is what I've been looking for.*

"I fucking love you," he muttered against Alain's forehead. Alain mumbled something in response, but Breeze was too spent and drained to comprehend his words. He didn't have to; he felt all he needed to know from the way Alain twined around him and went slack as wet paper in his arms, the breath coming from his gaping lips warming and wetting Breeze's chin.

FEW PEOPLE on the vineyard were up before late afternoon. Breeze woke alone in bed, sat up, and stretched, his muscles tight and aching. With a groan, he reached back to rub his neck and shoulder before standing up. The house beyond his room was warm and filled with the scents of food cooking. Following the laughter and voices, Breeze went into the dining room the family so rarely used and found it full of people. Some platters of roasted meat, baskets of bread, trays of cheese, and bottles of wine had been spread out across the table.

Breeze recognized the shepherdess, Elle, Marion and Denis, Guy, the blacksmith, and several others he had worked beside but whose names he didn't remember. Denis stood from his bench and patted Breeze on the shoulder. "Alain says you're staying on at the vineyard. We're always glad to have another set of hands."

Alain looked up from where he sat, met Breeze's gaze, and smiled. "There's no reason for so many of the rooms in this old house to stand empty when someone can be using them."

Fenn ran across the room and launched himself into Breeze's arms. Breeze picked him up, and the boy wrapped his arms around Breeze's neck. "I'm so glad you came back! I missed you. If my sister goes to Espero, I'll need someone to play with, and that's you!"

Breeze laughed, feeling good, feeling as if he'd finally found a home, a place he belonged in a way he hadn't even at Rosecairn. "Aye, lad. But I'm going to be working, just like Alain. I'm not a guest here anymore."

"No," Alain said. "Now you're part of the vineyard. Part of the family." He'd smiled more since Breeze had walked into the dining room than he had in all the previous months Breeze had known him. It warmed and lit the room, despite the snow swirling beyond the windows.

Breeze sat and filled a plate. His travels and their exhausting night of work had left him famished. Throughout the day, dozens of people stopped by the main house with dishes to share. They sat eating, drinking, and talking; making plans for next season and welcoming Breeze to the family. He had worried initially, but no one seemed suspicious that he'd be living in Alain's house. The place did have plenty of room, and everyone clearly held Alain in too high of regard to think anything ill of him. Everyone seemed truly pleased to have Breeze on the winery, and though he knew he'd miss Octavian and some of his friends from the Roses, with every passing hour, he felt more secure in his decision.

It would be a good life. Comfortable. Meaningful. Full of friendship, camaraderie, family, and love. The coin and glory he'd traded for it seemed insignificant. He remembered how much gold he had in the pack by the bed in his room. Later, he'd talk to Alain about how best to invest it in the vineyard's future. For now, he had some other things in his pack he wanted to share. He excused himself to go fetch them.

When he returned and took a seat on a chair in the corner, he patted his knee. Courtenay and Fenn both crawled into his lap, eyeing the packages wrapped in brown paper he held. He handed the first one to Fenn. It contained a set of green leather gloves and bracers he could use when he practiced archery. They'd been made by the armorer at Rosecairn, and were hardly ornamental, though the leatherworker had embellished them with some cut-out ivy leaves.

"Oh, Breeze! These are excellent! Uncle Alain, can I go try them out?"

Alain smiled indulgently. "Go on, then. Put your warm cloak on, and don't be out there too long. It'll be dark soon."

With a hoot, the boy leaped from Breeze's thigh and thundered up the steps. "Letting him go out on his own now?" Breeze asked.

Alain sipped from his wine, and it left a purple sheen on his pretty, full lips. "He respects that bow. He's always very safe now. You taught him well."

"He's the envy of every boy on the vineyard with that thing," Elle said with a shake of her head and a small smile.

Breeze rolled his eyes. "So I'm to be accosted for archery lessons and war stories by every lad for miles?"

"Oh, certainly." Elle winked. "At least at first. But before long, the novelty will wear off you, and you'll be just another man working on the vineyard."

"I like the sound of that," Breeze said.

Elle looked surprised for a moment, but then she smiled and raised her cup to him.

Breeze turned to Courtenay. "Princess, I believe I made you a promise." He handed her the other package.

Courtenay carefully unwrapped it without ripping the paper and opened the small box she found inside. Then she lifted the pure white rose, with just a few streaks of red on its outer petals, up for everyone to see. "Breeze, it's beautiful."

"Waited all season for one with the red to bloom. This was the only one I saw all summer. My friend Octavian put a charm on it. He said it should stay fresh a long time. Maybe even for years."

She ran a fingertip delicately along the edge of one of the petals. "I think I can feel his magic in it," she said.

"He said you might, since you have the gift," Breeze told her.

"Can I take this with me to Espero?" Courtenay asked.

"It's yours, love. You can do anything you like with it. Sounds like you've made a decision. When are you planning to leave?"

"Alain says not till springtime. He says we'll need money for the ship, and we have to wait for a message back from the university. We'll need money to hire someone to protect me while I travel."

Breeze winked at her as she held the rose close to her heart. "Princess, I might just know some men who'd be willing to look after you for a discount. More than a couple of those dirty old bas-… men, owe me their lives. I'll talk to them after the winter. Give me an excuse to check up on Octavian." He looked back at the table to see Alain smiling at him, his cheeks colored with warmth, wine, and contentment. Breeze didn't think he'd ever get tired of seeing Alain happy and free from worry and loss. "You could come with me, you know?" he said to Alain. "Meet Octavian. Have a look at the place...." He left his vivid ideas about what they could do along the road and in the mercenary camp unsaid, but by the way the color darkened even more across Alain's cheeks and up his ears, Breeze thought he understood.

"Perhaps," Alain mumbled into his cup. "Spring is a long way off, and a busy time around the vineyard."

They sat talking, picking at their food and enjoying a day of doing very little. Breeze told Fenn cleaned-up stories of battles he'd fought in and told Courtenay all about the mage island where he'd been born. Finally it came time for everyone to go home and the children to go to bed. Breeze helped Alain gather and wash the dishes. They worked together as if they'd been doing it for years before putting out the lanterns in the kitchen and going back upstairs.

With the fire burning low in the sitting room, Alain reached for Breeze, leaned against his chest, kissed him softly, and spoke against his lips. "Do you want to keep your room? It's one of the nicest, but if you want to move into another...."

"Where's yours?" Breeze asked, rubbing the tip of his nose up and down the side of Alain's.

"Upstairs. I've changed rooms twice since you left. I didn't feel right in my old one, or yours, or the one I used to share with Boyce. And I just recently moved into another." He threaded his fingers into Breeze's and led Breeze to the foot of the stairs. "It's a large room with a bank of bay windows looking out over the gardens, two fireplaces, and a ridiculous huge bed. Maybe... maybe it can be ours."

"I'd like that," Breeze said, watching the way Alain's long golden hair brushed his back as he followed him up the steps, watching the sway of his hips and dying to get his hands on them.

As soon as Alain closed the door, Breeze took hold of his waist, twirled him around, and pressed his back against the wall. He sealed their open mouths together and swallowed the little whimpers and groans Alain made as their teeth bumped and their tongues met. Breeze curled his belly against Alain and ran his hands up the lean muscles of his back beneath his shirt. He dragged his nails lightly down the warm, soft skin as he circled Alain's lips with his tongue and ran the tip over the edge of his teeth. He could taste the vestiges of the sweet blended table wine he'd drunk on Alain's palate, smell it on the breath gusting out of him in heavy bursts. Even in the low light, he could see the color creeping up his neck and face, staining his small round ears a deep rose.

Alain let his head fall back against the wall, giving Breeze the opportunity to lick up the side of his neck. His sweat, his skin, tasted so good Breeze thought he could get drunk on the flavor. He pushed Alain's thick hair back to suck a little red oval from the skin above his collarbone. With his other hand, he moved around Alain's waist to his flat belly and scratched at the sparse trail of hair disappearing beneath his trousers. Beneath it, his erection pressed against the cloth, a little wet circle near the tip. Moaning with need, starved for Alain, Breeze grasped and squeezed him through the fabric as he nipped and suckled along his jawline and chin. Alain curved his hips and thrust into Breeze's hand.

"Breeze," he gasped, moving his hands down Breeze's neck, across his shoulders, down his back, as if trying to touch everywhere at once, "Breeze, let me light a fire…."

Breeze made a contradictory noise against Alain's skin. "I can't wait that long."

"It's freezing…."

"Don't care. You don't know what I've been through today, watching you. Watching you eat, moving your throat and your jaw. Licking your lips. Wine staining your mouth. Watching you smile and run your fingers through your hair. All that, and not being able to touch you. You're the most beautiful, most alluring fucking thing I've ever seen. Goddesses, Alain. Just watching you cross the room, watching your fingers while you gathered up the silverware…. I can't wait. I'll keep you warm."

As he spoke, he stroked Alain through his trousers, and soon Alain's eyes darkened and glazed. His lips, plump, tender, and deep mauve, hung open as Breeze pulled his shirt over his head and bent to kiss across his chest. He had to get his hands, his mouth, on all that silky, roses-and-cream skin, dusted with fine golden hair. He stroked down Alain's waist as he kissed the curve at the outside of his chest muscle. Beneath the crisp citrus soap he used, Breeze detected the faintest hint of Alain's unique scent, the sweat and arousal leaking from his pores. Breeze wanted to drown himself in it and never come up for air.

Alain twisted his fingers into Breeze's hair while Breeze circled his tiny, pale nipple with his tongue, flipped the tip over the end, grazed it with his teeth, and sucked the flesh into his mouth. When he released it with a pop, it looked red and swollen compared to the other. He latched on to it again, sucking hard, working it with his tongue, until Alain grasped his shoulders to try to push him off.

"That sore?" Breeze asked, giving the sensitive numb a little pinch and twist and earning a muffled squeal from Alain. "Sorry. I can't resist them. Never really paid much attention to a man's nipples before. Yours are… just wonderful." He gave it a last tiny squeeze before dropping down to his knees and kissing down the delightful gully at the center of his belly. He ran his lower lip over the golden hair to feel its texture against his mouth. Alain's seed had darkened a splotch at the front of his trousers, and the strong fragrance of it made Breeze salivate.

He freed the lacings so Alain's loose trousers could fall and pool around his feet. Breeze cupped Alain's full balls as he thumbed back his foreskin to lick away the clearish-white fluid gathered in his slit. It tasted amazing, and he wanted more of it. All of it. Wanted to feel the veins and ridges of Alain's pretty cock on his tongue, his velvety, defined head lodged in his throat. But not yet. Tonight, he wanted to cherish Alain, touch and taste every inch of his skin, explore his body until he'd know every pore and hair until his dying day. As he massaged Alain's balls, he kissed his way over the rungs of his ribs until he reached that neglected nipple and left it as red and distended as the other. By the time he let it go, Alain was mumbling nonsense, thrusting against and leaving wet trails on Breeze's chest, and trembling all over. Breeze knelt and chuckled against the heavy musk of Alain's golden curls, rubbing his cheek against Alain's length. "Cold?"

"Nn-uh."

"Good." Breeze gripped the base of Alain's shaft and ran his tongue along the underside from top to bottom, groaning as Alain's flavor exploded over his tongue. "Good. That's good."

He wrapped his lips around Alain's corona and teased at the slit with his tongue, drawing out more of Alain's nectar and making Alain's hips rock forward. Chuckling as he opened his throat to take Alain deeper, Breeze spread his fingers over the V of muscle above Alain's hip to still him. He didn't have a problem with letting Alain fuck his throat, but tonight he wanted to play, to tug at Alain's hood with his lips, graze the ridge beneath his head with his teeth, suck Alain's balls into his mouth one at a time and roll them over his tongue. Sucking hard, he swiped his mouth and lips up and down Alain's length a few times, just until he felt Alain's balls knotting up next to his body. Then he pulled back and turned his attention to kissing and licking up and down his creamy inner thighs, leaving faint bruises on his white skin. Again and again he brought Alain to the dagger's edge of release before leaving off. When he finally sucked Alain into his throat in earnest, it took Alain only moments to come so hard his knees buckled and Breeze had to grasp his waist to keep him from falling. He screamed Breeze's name in a ragged cry as what felt like a barrelful of seed erupted down Breeze's throat. He didn't let a single drop go to waste.

Alain thrashed his head from side to side and chewed his already puffy lower lip as he made sounds almost indistinguishable from sobs. Breeze steadied him as he got to his feet, and then he reached beneath Alain's knees, picked him up, and dumped him on the bed. *Their* bed. Goddesses, that excited Breeze. For the rest of his life, he'd end each day in this bed, with Alain sprawled out naked and compliant for his pleasure. *Their* pleasure. He hurried to pull off Alain's boots and trousers. He didn't want to wait any longer to sink into Alain, immerse himself in him, and he wanted to do it while Alain was still relaxed and open after his release. Fumbling beneath the bed, he found the vial of oil he hoped Alain kept there to pleasure himself. After tossing it onto the bed, he quickly kicked his boots away and pulled off his simple clothes.

He spread himself over Alain like a blanket. Goddesses, he'd never get tired of that first skin to skin contact, their flesh brushing together. He guided Alain's knees to his chest, uncorked the oil, and drizzled some over his cleft. He rubbed the rest over his cock and gripped the base to line it up with Alain's wrinkled opening. As they kissed, Alain opened to him, and Breeze pushed inside in a single smooth stroke.

Alain cried out, and Breeze petted his hair and kissed across his forehead to soothe him. Though buried in Alain's hot, tight flesh as deep as he could go, Breeze fought his body's instinct to thrust. Instead, he held still and kissed Alain. "Tell me when."

Alain, his face flushed and sparkling with sweat, nodded. He moved his hips a small increment before wincing and thinking better of it. For many moments, they just kissed and caressed each other with their bodies joined. Breeze no longer wanted to hurry, never wanted this amazing connection to Alain to end. Goddesses, he could feel Alain's heartbeat echoing inside him, vibrating against his cock and moving through his belly and chest until it seemed to set the rhythm of his own heart. Suddenly inspired, wanting nothing but to please probably the only man he had ever loved, certainly the one he loved most, Breeze carefully took hold of Alain's thighs and curled his spine slightly. He wiggled, and when Alain cried out this time, he knew he'd struck the honey spot inside him. He straightened his arm, propped himself up, and ran his fingertips over Alain's tender nipples. Alain flinched, but his spent cock started to fill, and he used his inner muscles to squeeze Breeze's cock in rhythmic bursts. Breeze had never felt anything like it, and he bit his lip until he almost drew blood to keep from exploding into Alain.

Alain kept at it, squeezing and stroking Breeze with his insides, pausing when he brought Breeze just to that ledge he wanted to jump off of and fly.

"Friend, if you keep that up, I'm never going to get a chance to fuck you."

"You're not fucking me," Alain said in a moist puff against Breeze's lips. "We're making love. Together."

"So sensitive."

Alain laughed breathlessly. "The word you're looking for is *sore*."

Goddesses, he'd made a joke. Teased. It made Breeze irrationally happy that Alain felt comfortable enough with him to poke fun at himself. "Sore? Not yet, you're not."

"Let's see what you've got." Alain spread his legs a little wider and thrust his ass against Breeze.

Breeze couldn't hold off any longer. Kissing Alain hard, he speared into him with sharp, deep thrusts. Alain liked a little force, and his cock thickened against his belly as Breeze grasped his waist and plowed into him, making their skin smack together. It wasn't enough. Breeze needed more of his body, more of a connection, just more. He pulled out, flipped Alain to his belly, and pulled his hips up. At first, Alain looked over his shoulder with surprise and maybe apprehension on his features, but then he nodded, and Breeze needed no further reassurance. He aligned their bodies and pressed inside, curling over Alain's back as he pumped savagely into him.

Alain buried his cries in the pillow, and Breeze felt his body tighten like a bowstring, quivering as he fought the desire to let loose and shoot. He wanted to come, but he wanted to make this wonderful for Alain too. He pulled Alain's back against his chest and drove into him with everything he had, sweat flying from his hair. Alain's hard cock bobbed with the force of Breeze's thrusts, and he choked in gulps of air as he tried to reach for the headboard to brace himself.

"I have you," Breeze panted next to his ear. "Won't let you fall."

"I know. I love you."

Goddesses, hearing those words was better than anything he'd experienced so far. Breeze tingled all over, his balls ready to knot up inside his body. He reached around Alain and gave his tortured nipple a sharp pinch and twist. Alain cried out, tensed, and shot a white stream to splatter against the dark wood of the headboard. When he stopped keening and shaking, he went slack in Breeze's arms, and with a few more pumps, Breeze emptied inside him as clusters of glowing white light flared behind his eyes.

They collapsed, still joined, and lay that way for many moments before Breeze rolled off Alain and onto his back. "Bloody Shades."

Alain made a noise of agreement as he flopped over on his back. Breeze had never seen him look more erotically beautiful, pale, trembling, hair disheveled, eyelids heavy, lips and nipples red against his white skin, come drying in his golden curls. Breeze reached over and brushed the tip of his pinky finger over one of Alain's abused nubs.

"Ow," Alain protested without much conviction. "I ought to show you how that feels."

Breeze continued toying with the flushed, swollen flesh. "You can do anything you want to me. I'm fucking yours, Alain. For as long as you'll have me. I'm sorry, but I like it. I like knowing they'll be sore tomorrow, and every time your shirt brushes against them, you'll think of me, maybe hurry home from the fields to get back to me and let me have another go at them." He stretched across Alain and pressed the tenderest kiss he could to that nipple.

Alain punched him playfully in the shoulder. "Foolish man. You'll be in the fields right beside me."

"Aye, I know it. Can't I pretend you only want me to service you in the bedchamber?"

Alain kissed him. "You can certainly do that too. You do it well."

"So do you," Breeze said. "We're good together."

Now that they weren't keeping warm by doing other things, they shivered. Alain lit the fires in both hearths, pulled out the chamber pot, relieved himself, and then squatted over it to let Breeze's seed out of his body. He wet a cloth from a pitcher and wiped himself down. Surprisingly, seeing it didn't dampen Breeze's fascination with him. He was no less alluring and perfect for functioning as all men did. Besides, wiping Breeze's ass and peeling the dead flesh from his wounds hadn't lessened Alain's passion for Breeze. What they felt for each other needed no illusion or artifice.

Breeze also relieved himself and washed, and then they cuddled together on the large bed. Their bed. Breeze didn't think he'd ever grow weary of that idea. He'd almost fallen asleep with his head on Alain's chest when he startled awake. "Should I go? Back to my room?"

"Not yet." Alain combed his fingers through Breeze's hair. "The children will sleep in tomorrow. You can stay, stay beside me tonight, as long as you don't mind waking before breakfast."

"I don't mind." He would sacrifice far more for a night by Alain's side. "I love you, Alain. I want to show you, prove it every day. All I want is to make you smile."

"You do," Alain said around a yawn. "And we have years and years. No more cutting, Breeze. Just growing. Sun and rain and flourishing and fruit. Finally, no more cutting."

"Aye, you strange, beautiful, perfect man. Growing." Breeze tried to imagine what Octavian might say, and if it came out sounding silly, Alain was almost asleep and probably wouldn't remember. "Give me your rain and light, and I'll grow. You've already made me better. I'll give you mine, and it'll be beautiful. It'll be beautiful, Alain, what we make together."

Alain rolled to his side and twined his limbs around Breeze like the vines in the jar he'd given him. "It already is, Breeze. The roots are strong, so the fruit, and the wine, will be wonderful."

Breeze nuzzled up and pressed his forehead against Alain's. They had several hours to enjoy sleeping in each other's arms. The foundations they'd laid were solid, and they were beautiful, and the wine and the roses they nurtured from what they'd sown would be sweet, deep, complex, and eternal.

AUGUST (GUS) LI is a creator of fantasy worlds. When not writing, he enjoys drawing, illustration, costuming and cosplay, and making things in general. He lives near Philadelphia with two cats and too many ball jointed dolls. He loves to travel and is trying to see as much of the world as possible. Other hobbies include reading (of course), tattoos, and playing video games.

For more info, visit Books by Eon and Gus:
http://www.booksbyeonandgus.com.

BLESSED EPOCH SERIES

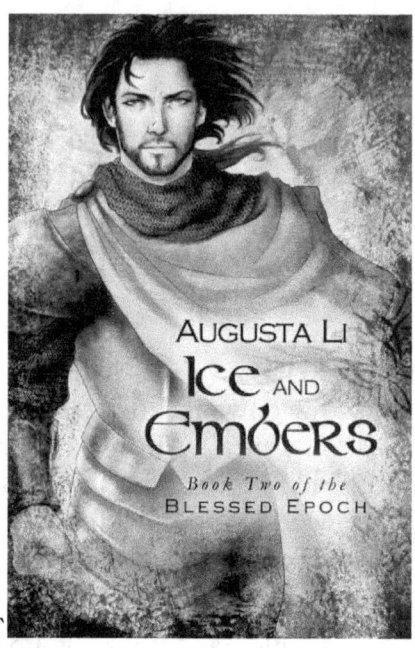

http://www.dreamspinnerpress.com

AUGUSTA LI

A
lesson
AND A
favor

http://www.dreamspinnerpress.com

Boots for the Gentleman

Augusta Li and Eon de Beaumont

http://www.dreamspinnerpress.com

A GRIMOIRE FOR THE BARON

AUGUSTA LI AND EON DE BEAUMONT

http://www.dreamspinnerpress.com

SNOWDROP

AUGUSTA LI

http://www.dreamspinnerpress.com

Coal TO DIAMONDS

AUGUSTA LI

http://www.dreamspinnerpress.com

AUGUSTA LI

ΠΕSΚΑΥΑ

http://www.dreamspinnerpress.com

ON
TINSEL
Wings

AUGUSTA LI

http://www.dreamspinnerpress.com